KILLING EINSTEIN

KILLING EINSTEIN

MORRIS HOFFMAN

RESOURCE *Publications* • Eugene, Oregon

KILLING EINSTEIN

Resource Publications
An Imprint of Wipf and Stock Publishers
199 W. 8th Ave., Suite 3
Eugene, OR 97401

www.wipfandstock.com

PAPERBACK ISBN: 979-8-3852-6778-1
HARDCOVER ISBN: 979-8-3852-6779-8
EBOOK ISBN: 979-8-3852-6780-4

VERSION NUMBER 02/12/26

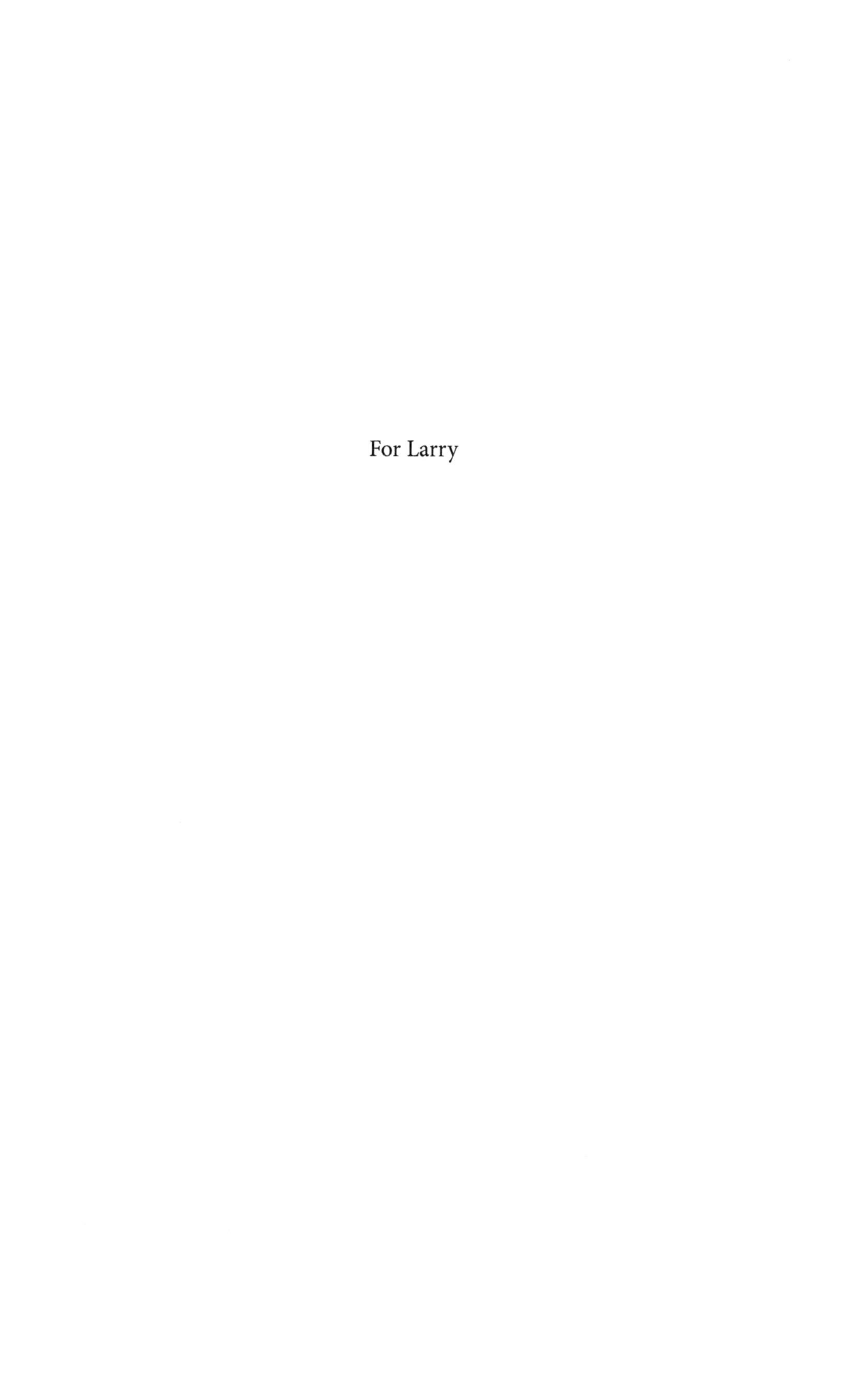

For Larry

Contents

PART 3. ASSASSINATION

Prologue

The three men in the killing team waded along the south edge of the canal for more than ten miles, as if they were behind enemy lines in France instead of in the center of New Jersey. They used a narrow inflatable rubber raft to hold their backpacks and the rifle bag out of the water, but their bodies remained submerged, only their blackened and goggled faces appearing above the surface. It was late October and the water was cold. The sky was a black maw, starless and moonless. The canal, which connected the Delaware and Raritan rivers, was as black as the sky, at least between the half-dozen small towns that hugged it from Trenton to Princeton.

But it was early evening, not midnight, and those small towns were still wide awake, and bright with lights. The men knew from their scouting that the ambient glow from even the smallest village would get reflected in their light-enhancing goggles. The darker the night the more startling the strange red flashes from the edge of the water. So when they neared any town, they removed their goggles, placed them in the raft, and glided past, unseen and unseeing.

When they were about 1000 meters from the edge of Princeton, the leader gave the hand signal to leave the water. One of the men deflated the raft, packed it into the rifle bag, and all three melted into the forest that lined the south side of the canal.

Each of the young men, fit and muscular, effortlessly bore his 12-kg backpack, and one of them also hauled the equally heavy rifle bag. They walked slowly and silently through the dense forest, pausing every 30 seconds to crouch and listen for sounds. They were experienced, and even without their goggles they could tell the difference between the sounds of animals probing their presence and men stumbling on them, or following them.

They heard the dog panting and breaking twigs long before they saw either it or its owner trotting behind. What an idiot. Running in these woods on this dark night was madness. The forest floor was littered with rocks, burrows, and fallen trees, all virtually invisible. That was one of the reasons the leader of the team insisted that the men creep so slowly during this part of the journey; the terrain was treacherous even with their night vision goggles.

Maybe the trotter and his dog knew this path so well they could run it in the dark. But the men had scouted this route for weeks, just in case they needed it, and had never seen anyone at this hour in this lack of light.

They squatted behind a pile of decaying logs. The leader signaled for everyone to remain still in the hopes of avoiding confrontation. This was their main goal during the approach—to avoid contact and thus to preserve the integrity of this same route for their return trip.

As the dog cleared a dense copse of what was probably green ash, but which appeared magenta in the red palette of their goggles, the men were relieved to see the dull flash of a long leash. This meant the dog would not be completely free to sniff them out, and that if it veered toward them so would its master, and the team could deal with them both.

The dog, which looked like a Labrador retriever and which the men guessed was yellow or white based on its poppy red glow, was about ten meters away when it suddenly barked and swerved toward them.

"No!" the runner yelled, out of breath, tugging on the leash. "Otis, come," and he snapped the leash hard. Otis yelped in protest but bent reluctantly back toward his master. Man and dog returned to their run and to their lives, and the men to their mission.

When they reached a point immediately opposite Battlefield Park, the leader raised his hand again and the men stopped. The man carrying the rifle bag took the deflated raft out of it and reinflated the raft with a small CO_2 cartridge, and the three men knifed noiselessly back into the water and floated across, goggle-less.

On the opposite side they put on the kind of ordinary clothing they'd been wearing for weeks during the surveillance part of the operation. Their leader wore a Princeton letter sweater—rank has its privileges—and the others light jackets. All of them wore loose-fitting sweatshirts and sweatpants directly over their body suits, which were made of a special material and had already dried.

Their cover, if they ran into anyone, was that they were members of a crew team coming back from a late practice. They stowed their gloves and removed their face-black with dampened towels. They changed their boots for sneakers, transferred several items from their backpacks into the rifle bag, into which they also restowed the deflated raft, and hid the backpacks in shrubbery along the north shore. Then they made their way into the park and toward the golf course, the junior officer still carrying the rifle bag.

This route was a little out of the way, but it was considerably less populated than going through the town or campus. In ordinary circumstances, of course, they would have simply walked directly from their apartment in town to their target, as they had done countless times during surveillance. But things had changed, they had moved permanently out of their apartment, and tonight promised much more than surveillance.

They saw no one in the park proper, but as they emerged onto Olden Lane, right across from the golf course, a young man, drunk, came wobbling toward them. When he saw them, he began singing the Princeton fight song at the top of his lungs. Then he stopped and yelled, "Go Tigers!" followed by, "Hey, who are you, football players? You stink."

"We're rowers," said the senior officer in perfect English.

"Bullshit," said the drunk, "you smell like football players. You're just embarrassed 'cause you got killed by Yale. You're not crew. I'm crew, and you're fuckin' football flunkies." Pleased at the sound of that phrase, he started laughing and repeating it loudly.

The man carrying the rifle bag put it down, casually stepped behind the senior officer to shield himself from the drunk rower's vision, pulled his Luger out of one jacket pocket and the noise suppressor out of the other, and quietly screwed the two pieces together behind his back. Holding the assembly at his side and a little behind his right leg, he took a few steps out from behind his colleague and slowly walked behind the drunk.

"Guilty as charged," said the senior officer, reaching out to shake the drunk's hand. "We really got creamed in New Haven. We stunk. We wish we were rowers. You guys are a gas. You beat Holy Cross by two lengths!"

"Damn right. Go Tigers!" mumbled the drunk, and then he started yelling "fuckin' football flunkies" even louder than before.

"Pipe down, friend, or you'll have the cops here," the leader said. The rower didn't pipe down. Instead, he suddenly spun around and pushed the man behind him, still screaming "fuckin' football flunkies," his turn timed with the word "football" and his push timed to the word "flunkies." The push exposed the gun the man was hiding behind his leg. The drunk looked down at it and his eyes widened, but he did not speak. The leader quickly glanced around, then looked to the man with the gun, and nodded, as he and his colleague stepped several paces to the side.

The spray of red mist on the sidewalk seemed to precede the pop, which was no louder than a beer can being opened. Before the rower could fall, the leader and the third man grabbed him under his arms, and began escorting him back to the park as if he were a passed-out drunk. The shooter remained behind to clean up the scene. No one needed to tell him to do so. They had planned for these kinds of contingencies.

There were four small jigsaw pieces of skull on the sidewalk, each sandwiched between tufts of black hair on one side and brain tissue clinging like Spanish moss to the other, and he kicked them back into the grass. Then he found some snow on the north side of a fat pine and cleaned off as much of the fan of blood as he could, covering the rest with leaves. This did not have to be a permanent clean-up; it only had to buy them a few hours. He rejoined his comrades in the park, under a grove of lindens, which reminded him of home.

They put mud over the small black hole in the rower's forehead, and a ski cap pulled down low at the back to cover the baseball-sized exit wound at what was left of the back of his head, and all three men bobbed the corpse arms-in-arms back to the canal, singing softly as reveling drunks. They saw no one else, but by the time they loaded rocks into the rower's pockets and sunk him into the waters where once he had achieved some modest glory, they were 15 minutes into the built-in 30-minute cushion. Any more encounters would mean one of them would have to stay behind to handle them and the other two would proceed to the target.

They worried a bit about students on the golf course at night—it was a favorite make-out spot—so they stayed in the trees that lined most of the fairways, and kept their goggles on. They didn't see a soul on the course, then they stowed their goggles before entering the grounds of the graduate campus to the north. They likewise saw no one there.

They waited for a few cars to clear College Road, then sprinted across to the houses. They re-goggled and sped between two of the houses and through two back-to-back backyards, jumping over the chain link fences as on an obstacle course. They could have walked around on the side streets, but that would have exposed them to neighbors next to and across from the target. A couple dogs barked, but the team was quickly in and out of the yards and soon at the place they'd scouted—the corner of a lushly covered garage immediately behind the target's house.

The third man remained there while the senior and junior officers ran across Mercer to their primary location—a thick wooded grove between two houses directly across the street from the front of the target house. The junior officer assembled his rifle and tripod, took several sightings, and made some adjustments. Then they waited.

PART 1

SURVEILLANCE

CHAPTER 1

We were inside Einstein's house, surrounded by some sort of crack Nazi assassination team. We never saw any of them, not one, that's how good they were. We'd barricaded ourselves in, turned off all the lights, and ordered the famous scientist to lay down in an interior hallway. The Nazis had cut the telephone line, but we had a radio. Help was on the way. Then one of my FBI colleagues screamed that he'd been hit. The Nazis had night vision equipment. We'd all be dead in minutes, long before the help arrived.

That was the second time I saved Albert Einstein's life, and then he saved mine, and nobody knows anything about any of it. It's time they do.

My FBI career had been in intensive care, headed toward the morgue. There was so much promise in the beginning—a bright young philosophy grad fresh out of Princeton, unmarried, fluent in German, perfect for counterespionage in the years leading up to the war. German spies were everywhere. How would I know that one of my favorite history professors was one of them? Or that one of the guys in the office was running an operation on him?

So was it really my fault that when I saw them together at a performance of Macbeth at the Shakespeare festival down in New Brunswick, I blew the whole operation to smithereens just by saying hello to the professor, and then, "Hey, Joe, I didn't know you knew Professor Edwards. Did you go to Princeton?" Joe had told the professor his name was Otto. Now how was I supposed to know that?

I'd only been in counterintelligence for a few weeks, though they had mentioned several times that we were never to say hello to fellow CI-ers out in the real world—or in "uncontrolled environments," as they put it—precisely to avoid the accidental disclosure of an operation. I don't know what I was thinking. Nothing, I guess. I saw a guy I knew, remembered his name, and said hello. That's just who I am.

We were also advised not to tell strangers we were with the FBI, but instead that we were in import/export. Which I thought was hilarious, maybe even intentionally so. I didn't break that rule. I never said where I worked. I just said hello to the professor and to Joe.

They almost fired me. But no one got killed, and they had already gathered enough evidence on Professor Edwards to arrest him. In fact, Joe arrested him right then and there, sending me several disapproving *I wish I had a second pair of cuffs for you* glances as he snapped his only pair on the professor.

I knew I was in trouble when I got the message to report to the assistant deputy chief's office. We called it "the principal's office" because as far as anyone could tell the assistant deputy chief's sole function was to discipline CI screwups. It was up on the fourth floor, and it had the only wood-finished door in the whole building. We should have called it the woodshed. Behind the wooden door, the outer office was painted a drab asylum green, and was manned by a drab secretary whose face was frozen in disapproval.

"Good morning, I'm Charlie Richards."

She got up and opened the door to a conference room without saying a thing, other than the *I know who you are and I know what you did* that her face was still saying as she closed the door behind me. Inside, there was a long table populated by eight dour old men. I recognized the assistant deputy chief and a couple of the others, the ones whose hair still had a bit of color. There were no introductions. They started grilling me the moment the ice-faced secretary closed the door. They did not invite me to sit down.

"You mean to tell us you walked up to a man you knew was a fellow counterintelligence agent and said hello to him, using his real name, in front of hundreds of people?"

"Well, I don't know about hundreds of people." If looks could kill. "But yes, sir. It was a mistake, sir."

"You're goddam right it was a mistake," said another gray hair. "You could have cost Joe Teller his life, you dumb shit."

"Teller, that's it. I couldn't remember his last name."

"Otherwise, you would have disclosed that to the German spy, too, right?"

"I suppose so."

The assistant deputy chief cleared his throat. "Was there something, Agent Richards, about the Second Commandment—you remember that from training, don't you, 'Thou Shall Not Contact a Fellow Counterintelligence Agent in Uncontrolled Environments'—was there something about that that you didn't understand?"

"Well, to be frank sir, I'm not entirely sure what was meant by 'uncontrolled environments,' but if you are asking whether I knew I was not supposed to say hello to Joe out in public, yes sir, I understood that."

After more yelling by the three yellers and head shaking by everyone else, the assistant deputy chief excused me. I was sure I was going to be fired, but a few days later they told me they were transferring me from the main CI office in Manhattan down to a small office in Philadelphia, to do background checks on workers at the Philadelphia Naval Shipyard. I talked myself into thinking this was still counterespionage of a sort, but after 14 months it was clear it was just CYA paper shuffling, and that the home office—which is what we called the office in D.C.—didn't really think any German spy-welders could do much damage to the shipyard, even after they glided through our feeble screening.

Then I stumbled on a plot to blow up the shipyard. I was interviewing a guy named Gregory Turner, who said he was born in Elizabeth and had been a plumber there for 15 years. In my first year at Princeton, I had a girlfriend who lived in Elizabeth and whose father was also a plumber.

"Hey, you must know Ted Ciecwisz, he's been a plumber in Elizabeth for ages," I said just to make conversation.

"Heard of him, never met him. Sounds like he was quite a character."

Then I remembered that it was Marjorie Woods who lived in Elizabeth and whose father was the plumber. Susan Ciecwisz was from Newark and her father was a teacher. I was seeing both girls at the same time.

I tried to hide my surprise at Turner's answer, and I guess I did because he was sound asleep when they arrested him early the next morning at his apartment. His real name was Gustav Fleckt, and he eventually confessed that he and three other German spies had been dropped off the North Carolina coast by submarine, and that each of them was planning to bomb an east coast shipyard. The tech guys found some new type of explosives hidden in each of the spies' apartments, which they suspected would be powerful enough to put shipbuilding on the east coast out of commission for six months.

After all these years I still wonder why Fleckt didn't see my question as an obvious and clumsy trap, which he could easily have avoided simply by denying he knew any plumber in Elizabeth named Ciecwisz. All I can think of is that I never was a good liar, and that Fleckt must have been a good judge of character.

The whole thing—the submarine drop-offs and the plans to blow up the shipyards, and my role in uncovering it all—was never made public. That's because in these pre-war years, the Bureau was not yet manipulating the press by leaking selected counterintelligence efforts, like it did a few years later starting with the infamous Operation Pistorius. Hoover splashed the Pistorius arrests all over the papers and took all the credit, but in fact the Pistorius sabotage ring was cracked only because a couple of the saboteurs fell in love with America, wanted to stay here, and turned themselves in. This would become a chronic problem for German spies in America. Anyway, in these early days the Bureau was still basking in the honeymoon of Dillinger and G-men, and we were not yet at war, which really did change everything. So no one on the outside learned of my accidental success.

But my bosses were pretty impressed. They assumed I'd used the ruse to trip Fleckt up. They would never have guessed in a million years that all I did was mix up old girlfriends. They were apparently not quite the judges of character that Fleckt was. They reinstated me to the Manhattan CI office, with repeated stern reminders about not talking to fellow agents out in the real world.

Then the Japs bombed Pearl Harbor, and things at the office stopped feeling like smart-aleck college games and started feeling like life and death. We had more leads than CI agents, but I still only got the dregs. Like the German housekeeper who the Manhattan socialite was just positive was a secret agent, because she spoke German when she talked on the phone with her husband. Or the Japanese truck driver in the Bronx who was, well, Japanese. Endless trips to birth and death offices all along the eastern seaboard to cross-check names. Hours and hours in our file room down in Greenwich Village. Things like that. The stink of the Edwards fiasco still clung to me.

Then, in early February 1942, six of us in the CI office in Manhattan relocated to Benson House, a three-story mansion out in Wading River, Long Island. An Argentinian businessman who was a German spy had defected, and the Bureau turned him into a double agent. The Argentinian lived in Southampton, which was just a short drive from Wading River.

Benson House was set up with a special radio transmitter in the attic, used by the German-speaking Argentinian to send his reports through a chain of German receivers, including submarines, all the way back to his Abwehr bosses in Hamburg. I was included only because I spoke German and could translate the phony reports they came up with into German. They apparently didn't trust the Argentinian to do the translations himself.

Over the years several more double agents joined the Argentinian, and all their operations were coordinated out of Benson House, though they transmitted the reports from different locations along the east coast. The whole set up was so successful that The House, as we called it, was still operating in 1944, feeding the Germans erroneous information about the D-Day invasion.

One of our senior guys, Donworth Johnson, managed the whole operation. He moved into The House with his wife Betty Ann, their two-year-old daughter Vicki Jean, and a big mean German Shephard named Clifford. The cover story was that Don was suffering from TB, and needed to quarantine and take a rest. Don, Betty Ann, and the kid lived on the first and second floors, Clifford went wherever he wanted, and by night we CI guys, along with two radio techs, took over the third floor, and the attic for transmissions. By day we slept in apartments sprinkled in several towns across eastern Long Island.

The Bureau gave me a tiny walk-up in the nearby hamlet of Ridge. To cut down on suspicious night traffic, they gave bicycles to those of us within what the desk jockeys in administration considered "biking distance" of The House. I rode that stupid bike five miles down to The House every evening and five miles back every dawn. Five, sometimes six, nights every week. It wasn't so bad really, except in those first two weeks of February, when the snows really came.

The work itself was stupid. All I did was translate the made-up reports from English to German, and then listen to the Argentinian deliver them, to make sure he wasn't changing anything substantive. That's it.

I worked on the translations all night long, at a metal desk up in the cold and damp attic, in a small room right next to where we did the transmissions, which we usually broadcast around four in the morning, once or twice a week. My translations weren't even the final product; they let the Argentinian make minor changes so it sounded like the way he spoke.

They never let me see any of the intelligence on which the partly true and partly false reports were based, or attend the third-floor meetings where the disinformation was drafted. So, just like the Germans, I didn't know which parts were true and which false. It was clear that the higher ups in CI still didn't trust me, except as a translator.

It was there, in Benson House, one early morning in late March 1942, that I got the message that—I was going to say that it changed my life, but that would be both an under- and over-statement. It didn't do much to change my everyday life while the new operation itself was going on, but then it changed my whole universe.

One of my old bosses, Chris Conner—the only one who even half-heartedly stood up for me after the Edwards debacle—sent me a secured message to meet him for lunch in the city. It was tough to wake up in the middle of my sleeping day, so I just stayed up that morning. I was pretty excited about meeting Chris. We hadn't talked in over a year.

We met at one of our favorite midtown haunts, Carlo's Café on W. 54th, a cheap Italian place at the edge of Hell's Kitchen renowned for its meatball sandwiches. We took our usual isolated table near the back, and spoke in our usual whispers. That's when Chris told me about Albert Einstein and some Austrian genius named Kurt Gödel.

"Look, you've heard of Albert Einstein, right? He lives down in Princeton. Well, last year some guy named Kurt Godel—"

"How do you spell that?' I interrupted.

"Dammit it, Charlie, try to concentrate. It's G-O-D-E-L."

"Are there two little dots over the O?"

"Yeah."

"So, it's pronounced more like 'Girdle,' the woman's undergarment, with just a hint of the 'r.'"

"May I continue?"

"Sure, sorry sir."

"This Gödel guy moves to Princeton, gets a job at the same institute as Einstein, and sets up his office right across the hall from Einstein's. Shortly after Gödel gets there the two of them start taking long walks together. Lots of them. To work in the morning and back home in the afternoon, almost every day. Very slow walks, with lots and lots of talking, and lately with lots of detours.

"We'd started bugging and surveilling Einstein as soon as he moved here in '33. Hoover was worried that Einstein, who was becoming as popular as the Director himself, might be a Nazi spy or, worse, a Russian one. We were also a little worried the Nazis might assassinate him. So, if you look carefully at some of those early photos of Einstein surrounded by an admiring American public, you might notice the same admirers often reappear, including me!"

He smiled sheepishly, and took another bite of his sandwich.

"Anyway, after a few months of surveillance Hoover concluded Einstein was not a Nazi spy, and after a few more he concluded Einstein was not a Russian spy and that no one was after him. So the Bureau stopped following him."

Chris turned to the counter and yelled, "Hey, Carlo, could we please have more napkins? You've outdone yourself with the sandwiches today."

Carlo returned with a whole roll of paper towels, and said in broken English, "Sandwiches same, you just extra messy." Once Carlo went back behind the counter, and after a vigorous wipe of his whole face with two paper towels, Chris continued.

"Einstein's daily walks with this new Godel guy—sorry, Gödel guy—are giving DBS bad indigestion."

DBS stood for Dumb but Sneaky, the nickname we all used for the director of east coast counterintelligence. I'll just use those initials. No need after all these years to rub it in. Rumor was that DBS got the job because he was the brother-in-law of the chairman of the Senate Intelligence Committee. I hoped the rumor was true. If it was on merit, we were more screwed than I imagined.

"He wants to know what they are talking about and why they are acting so secretive, changing the places they meet and the paths they take every day. He's wondering why they just don't talk at work, since their offices are right across from each other."

"Are these legit concerns?" I asked.

"Of course not. It's DBS. He's just got a hair up his ass. But it will be a good opportunity for you once and for all to get out from under the weight of that Edwards albatross."

I was supposed to be the perfect man to trail these smarty pants—a German-speaking smarty pants myself, with a philosophy degree no less. This Gödel guy was a philosopher of mathematics, whatever that was.

I protested a little. I'd never heard of Gödel or the philosophy of mathematics, but more importantly I'd never had any surveillance training, or any field work training at all, beyond the basics at Quantico.

"Piece of cake," Chris assured me, through the ooze of the second half of his meatball sandwich. "We'll fix you up with the best equipment. All you need to do is stay within 20 yards of them and not get made. Hell, these are two old Jewish farts, how hard can it be?"

I soon learned that Gödel was neither Jewish nor old, though he did fart almost constantly. He was a 35-year-old logician from the University of Vienna, and was supposed to be top-notch. But he also seemed permanently distracted, a real absent-minded professor, and he was entirely unaware of me. Einstein made me after two days.

CHAPTER 2

BECAUSE THIS WAS A job on direct orders from DBS, and because DBS was from the home office, they spared no technical expense. I was provided with a sophisticated and powerful directional microphone, which looked like a few stubby strands of twisted metal linguini, and which the jokesters in tech hid in the spine of a copy of *All Quiet on the Western Front*.

"Look, these targets I'll be following are smart guys. They might get suspicious if I keep reading *All Quiet on the Western Front* for several weeks."

The two Toms conferred (we called all the tech guys Tom, as in Thomas Edison, and they loved it). They reluctantly agreed to abandon the literary joke.

"I suppose we could make the filaments longer but not as thick, retaining the total surface area," Tom 1 said to Tom 2, and they both started to rub their chins. Then Tom 1 turned to me and said, "Come back tomorrow."

They somehow made the mic even thinner, into a few twisted strands of spaghetti, and taped it between the center pages of a *Time* magazine, which they said they would switch out every few days. They said all I needed to do was keep the magazine "aimed" at Einstein and Gödel, meaning the top of the pages should be nearest them.

"They walk. I can't be holding the magazine flat and walking at the same time."

"No, that's the beauty of these longitudinal strand mics," Tom 2 explained. "You can roll the magazine up, not too tight, and hold it down at your side while walking. As long as the rolled-up tube is pointed at them, top of the magazine headed out at them."

"This will pick up their voices from behind?"

"Absolutely," said Tom 1 with no small amount of pride. "This is so powerful it will pick up the sound of their pants rubbing against their asses. But what we've done is taken known recordings from them and built this system to be especially sensitive to their voices, and less sensitive to all the other noises, like their pants rubbing against their asses or crickets chirping."

"They don't walk at night."

"The point is, you don't have to do anything other than stay within 20 yards of them and keep the magazine top pointed at them," said Tom 2.

The recorder was a metal box no bigger than a cigar box, but thin, just one cigar deep. It was amazing. The only tape-recording machines I had ever seen were bigger than my ice box at home. I was to keep the recorder in an oversized side pocket of my coat, and run its thin wire through the coat's sleeve and out the cuff, where it connected to the spaghetti mic by a small clip. Another thin wire ran from the recorder up the inside of my coat and out the collar to a headset I wore under my ski cap, so I could monitor whether we were actually picking them up and recording. I had to wear a scarf to hide the wires to the headset. Good thing it didn't get too warm that April.

You might be wondering, as I did, why they just didn't have me radio the conversations to someone nearby, like in a truck somewhere, and have that person record it. The Toms said they couldn't do that because these two guys were walking around outside, often in parkland and sometimes even through golf courses, where there was no automobile traffic. Any transmitter for those distances would have to be the size of a basketball.

In addition to the surveillance, I was ordered to translate and type up the recordings at the end of each day. That's why they tapped me, for my German. They would have a professional German-speaking transcriptionist translate and type up the official transcripts that would go into the file, but DBS wanted daily reports about what these guys were saying. We arranged a revolving dead drop for me to transfer the daily transcripts and tiny reels of tape, and to pick up a batch of new tiny reels when I ran out.

"You've already bugged Gödel?" I asked in a delayed reaction to Tom 1's disclosure that this fancy new receiver was built to be more sensitive to *both* their voices. "I know we bugged Einstein for a while back when he first emigrated, but Gödel?"

"Above my pay grade," said Tom 1. "I don't know where these sample recordings of their voices came from. For all know they are from some public lectures." Then he added, winking, "Though it would be pretty strange for these guys to be eating dinner during their lectures, wouldn't it?" Tom 2 winked too, and nodded in agreement.

This was not a 24-hour operation. The two professors walked to and from work just a few times each week, and their walks consumed just a few hours. So there was no back-up for me. DBS said he didn't want to waste a second agent unless absolutely necessary. There was to be a substitute stalker only if I started to sense I was being made. And, after all, these were two professors with their heads in the stars, so I'd never be made.

It all worked out, at least as far as DBS knew, because of the perfectly harmless nature of the conversations between Einstein and Gödel, which mostly alternated between talking about Gödel's ailments, the weather, other geniuses at the Institute, the progress of the war, and impossible-to-understand discussions about math, logic, and, occasionally, physics. DBS was suspicious that the math, logic, and physics talking was a code, and it sure sounded like some kind of code to me. So he brought in some math expert from Harvard.

"Well, is this a code, professor?" DBS asked at a meeting we had with the consultant after a week of surveillance.

"Of course not. It's the most amazing discussion of set theory and incompleteness that I've ever heard. Why the ideas—"

"Sorry to interrupt, professor, but all we care about is whether they are talking in code. Thank you for your cooperation. Are those all your notes? I need them, and any others you have. And as my associates have already explained to you, and as set forth in the confidentiality agreement you signed, everything about this engagement is top secret, and you may not disclose any of it to anyone."

Then DBS leaned over and got real close to the consultant's bearded face, put on his "I am a Dangerous Spy" look, and said in a deep and threatening voice, "I will reiterate a little more colorfully: if you mention anything about this engagement—the fact of it, the results of it, anything at all related to what you heard between Einstein and this other guy—to anyone—including your wife and mistresses—you will spend the rest of your life in federal prison, fighting off 300-pound felons wanting to make you their girlfriend. Do you understand me?"

The poor consultant seemed resigned by this warning, but also quite crestfallen. I figured maybe he thought he'd steal some of Einstein's and Gödel's ideas and publish them himself. Or maybe, like me, he just wanted to share the wonder. In any event, his fear of prison (and, I am guessing, of DBS's none-too-subtle threat about disclosing his infidelities) worked wonders, and he never said a word to anyone as far as I know.

After six weeks of surveillance, DBS finally cleared Einstein and Gödel, not just because their conversations were harmless, but also because on occasion they even lamented the evils of communism. This last flourish was my idea, implemented after my first treason. To tell the truth, I'm actually not sure Einstein was that set against the Russians, and I think Gödel was so afraid he'd get assassinated by the Nazis that he would have cozied up to the devil himself for protection. My guess is that the Russian devil may have tried for both of them, but they were no more Russian agents than I was a philosopher. And even DBS managed to see that after six weeks, with a little help from me.

DBS named the operation "Felix and Rolf." It was a clever (he said) alphanumeric substitution code for Albert Einstein and Kurt Gödel. "A" for Albert is one, the first letter of the alphabet, "E" for Einstein is five, one plus five is six, so Albert Einstein is Felix (F is the sixth letter of the alphabet). Ditto for Kurt Gödel being Rolf.

The stupid operational name itself should have been a red flag. But like most Americans, I was gaga over Einstein, and wanted to "meet" him, even if this meeting would consist only of pointing a *Time* magazine at him and eavesdropping. Plus, I didn't mind getting out of Benson House—it was tedious just doing translations night after night up in the cold attic, and listening to the Argentinian, who had an irritating lisp. Betty Ann's cooking was terrible, their dog Clifford scared the crap out of me, and I was getting quite tired of riding that stupid bike. And maybe I could remove some of the stink from the Edwards disaster. Besides, I wasn't exactly asked if I wanted to volunteer for this new assignment.

This Gödel guy sounded intriguing. A philosopher of mathematics. What did philosophy and math have to do with one another? I remembered a lecture in an introduction to logic class I took at Princeton all about a book by Bertrand Russell on the logical foundations of math. But I couldn't remember anything important about the lecture, other than that guys like Russell were not accepting mathematical truths as given, and were instead thinking about what exactly lay behind these truths. I myself had always been OK with the idea that two plus two was four, that it just was, but apparently not these guys.

And what would a philosopher and a physicist be talking about? I'd taken an introduction to physics class, too, and knew that the edges of the two disciplines shared a fuzzy boundary, the details of which remained fuzzy to me. I didn't really know much about modern philosophy (surely Plato would not be in play here!) or physics to have much more than a general lay person's curiosity about the overlap. Of course, Einstein's relativity theories were still a hot topic everywhere, from classrooms to boardrooms, but I had the same general feelings about them that I guess everyone did: they are really important; I'm not sure what they are; and they are supposed to change everything about our place in the universe but really haven't.

Despite my old boss's nonchalance about my lack of field experience, they did give me some basic surveillance training for a couple of days. I learned a lot about how to blend into backgrounds—mainly by not trying too hard to blend into backgrounds—how to detect if I was being followed, how to do dead drops, and what to do if I think I've been made, or worse still, if they actually confront me.

"Getting hit by a car is the biggest physical risk of any surveillance operation. Getting confronted by the target is a distant second," my field trainer advised me, "but here it's so distant we can forget about it. We know from searching these guys' homes and offices that they carry no weapons. So what are they going to do to you, gum you to death?"

The inaccurate narrative about Gödel's age was an irritating constant throughout the operation. Especially irritating because it was wrong for all the right reasons. Though only 35, Gödel acted like he was 70. He was always complaining about his health, and missed several walks because of claimed illness. He was a world-class hypochondriac, though his ferocious flatulence did suggest that something really was wrong with him.

I learned later that his intestinal woes were the self-inflicted product of his crazy diet, which in turn was the product of his paranoid fear of being poisoned. His diet got crazier and crazier just in the six weeks we were running the Felix and Rolf operation. Gödel went from eating fresh vegetables, though steamed and mashed, to a diet of baby food, butter, and laxatives. It was so weird.

He was sad and shy. His introversion made his irritating habit of cackling when he laughed even more irritating. Einstein seemed to be his only friend. Heck, as far as I could tell Einstein was the only other person he ever talked to, other than his wife Adele.

It must have been a pretty lonely life for all the guys at IAS. They had no teaching responsibilities, though before the war they gave lots of lectures around the world. Now, their lecturing was pretty much limited to the U.S. and Canada. Other than that, all they did was sit around and think. I got the distinct impression that Gödel was often thinking about his own death.

Einstein was just the opposite. Though 63, he acted like he was eight. He smiled constantly, laughed regularly, and was easily distracted by the next wonderful thing, whether duck or cloud or insight into one of Gödel's math problems. I heard that in the summer months Einstein regularly had water pistol fights with neighborhood boys. I believe it.

He seemed to be as far from lonely as any man could be. He received hundreds of speaking requests every week, and he was constantly meeting with a raft of scientists and politicians. His schedule would have exhausted me.

These were not two old Jewish men. They were a buzzing Jewish boy named Felix and an old Gentile loner named Rolf. DBS couldn't have picked more fitting code names if he'd meant to.

I suspected from the beginning that DBS's obsession with these two characters was not shared by Hoover. In fact, I figured that the whole operation was an indirect challenge to Hoover, who had personally supervised the pre-war surveillance of Einstein and had personally cleared him. That's probably why DBS plucked me out of intensive care, and didn't involve a second agent from the get go. He didn't want Hoover to know what he was doing. He wasn't so dumb after all.

I figured this knowledge might be useful to me down the road if any shit hit any fans. When the feces flew, not from a few fans but from the whole damn cosmos, Einstein protected me and I didn't need any of that leverage, which wouldn't have been nearly enough anyway.

You are probably wondering why, half a century after the fact, I decided to publish all these things about Operation Felix and Rolf. There are lots of reasons. First, Einstein and Gödel are both long dead. So are DBS and my old boss, Chris Conner. Plus, most of the cat is already out of the bag. Last year a newspaper in Colorado stumbled on a redacted version of the Felix and Rolf file as part of a FOIA request they made to the FBI. Then it actually published some of the transcripts. So the biggest cat of all—that the FBI was secretly tape-recording beloved icon Albert Einstein—was out.

The newspaper's FOIA request, by the way, had nothing to do with counterintelligence in the 1940s. They were fishing for stuff on the FBI's surveillance of Martin Luther King. But some literal-minded legal moron in DOJ read the request more broadly, and ordered the release of a bunch of earlier stuff, including parts of the Felix and Rolf file, which contained the gold mine of the transcripts, redacted. Redacted a bit by the FBI, a bit by the DOJ, and a whole lot by me, since the FBI never got the lion's share of transcripts in the first place, which I've kept to myself all these years.

Anyway, I figure the new and improved Bureau, which to me is now indistinguishable from a public relations firm, is not going to make trouble for me if I just correct the record. Besides, what are they going to do to me? Next week I'll be 89 years old.

Correcting the record is the main reason I'm doing this. It was no sin that these hayseeds at the *Denver Post* were fooled like everybody else was—everybody but Einstein. But it was a sin that they skipped over the most important part of the recorded conversations: Einstein's and Gödel's work. They've painted a distorted and ridiculous picture of two men complaining about the weather and sniping at colleagues in the academy, instead of two men discussing the deepest truths about what it means to be true. It's a hack job by pinheads, and needs to be corrected.

There's another reason that's a little harder to explain. I got to know these two guys, and more than that I started to get a glimpse of their vision, especially Gödel's. When they talked shop on these walks, they were almost always talking about Gödel's work and not Einstein's. That's because they both seemed a lot more interested in Gödel's work than in Einstein's. Before my treasons, when I was just a spy and not a pal, I had no idea what they were talking about. But then they took me into their confidences. They were the consummate teachers taking a little extra time with a slow student, and by the end I think they got a bigger kick out of explaining things to me than to each other. I want to show the world that these two great men got a mope like me to understand, and how that understanding saved all our lives.

CHAPTER 3

The *Denver Post* had to go out of its way to screw this story up, since all they had to do was copy the transcripts and exercise a modicum of editorial judgment. I am not going to reprint any of the transcripts here because it's just too embarrassing to repeat the newspaper's legion of mistakes. You can find their version of the transcripts and their jaw-droppingly stupid stories and editorials that ran with each transcript, all on the internet. But let me tell you about just a few of their gaffes, to give you an idea.

They claimed their discovery of the transcripts was the product of a "long and painstaking investigation," but as I've mentioned it was actually the result of some idiot sniffing around Martin Luther King's sexual dalliances, and submitting a one-page FOIA request to the FBI. Some investigation!

The newspaper described Einstein as "the father of the atomic bomb," but of course that was Oppenheimer, not Einstein. In this day and age, even casual readers (but apparently not investigative reporters) know that Albert Einstein had nothing at all to do with the progress of the Manhattan Project. He was instrumental in getting Roosevelt to agree to start the project, but after that he had nothing to do with it. In fact, the U.S. Army denied him the security clearance he would have needed to participate in it, and expressly forbade all Manhattan participants from discussing the project with him. Unlike the FBI, the Army remained concerned about Einstein's left-leaning political views. Too bad I was unable to manipulate the Army's snooping!

Many readers will also cringe at the *Denver Post's* reference to Gödel as a "fellow physicist." He was of course a mathematician, not a physicist, as Einstein himself notes at one point in the very first transcript. Gödel once told me that when he first entered the University of Vienna, he intended to study physics, but then switched to math when he heard Moritz

Schlick lecture about Bertrand Russell's *Introduction to Mathematical Philosophy*—that's right, the very same book whose lecture presentation at Princeton I could barely remember. It caused Gödel to change careers and become the modern world's preeminent logician, and I couldn't even remember it. We had a bit of a laugh about that; well, I laughed and Gödel did his weird high-pitched cackle. And Gödel didn't cackle too often.

Jewish readers will wince at the phonetic misspellings of *oy* and *meshuggeneh*, the only Yiddish slangs Einstein used besides *putz*, and only rarely. Didn't these *goyim* in the FBI translation office or at the *Denver Post* know a single Jew they could consult about Yiddish spelling?

Another correction: Einstein was not the first member of IAS. That was the American mathematician Oswald Veblen, who was quickly followed by Einstein and mathematicians Hermann Weyl and John von Neumann. In fact, Einstein was the only physicist at the Institute in those first years. It didn't even have a physics department, or "school" to use the IAS lingo. Its first school, and for a long time its only school, was mathematics, and its first members all mathematicians, except Einstein. "I was their honorary mathematician, and token physicist," I remember him telling me once over dinner when I asked about the history of the Institute.

You might wonder why IAS was so obsessed with mathematicians in those early days. I asked Einstein that very question, and he told me it was all because of Abraham Flexner, one of the IAS's founders. Though Flexner was a biologist, he believed that mathematics was not just the language of all science, as Galileo is reported to have said, but the language of all truth. To which Gödel added, "You do know, Albert, that Gauss put a monarchist twist to the Galileo quote, calling mathematics the 'queen of all sciences.' He went on to say, quite correctly in my opinion, at least in his day, that number theory is the queen of all mathematics."

"All these queens and no kings," Einstein joked.

"Logic is the king," Gödel responded without dropping a beat, as Einstein knew he would.

And pardon me if this is petty, but the *Denver Post* seems unaware of the umlaut. They failed to include it whenever they printed Gödel's name in their introductory material or in their dreadful accompanying editorials. Without the umlaut, "godel" is a colloquial German form of "godmother." You'd think that in all those barrels of ink they might have been able to find two tiny drops for the world's finest logician since Aristotle, which is how Einstein himself described his friend to the press when they asked him about his strange walking companion.

Another correction in the petty but grating category: it is the Institute for Advanced *Study*, singular, not *Studies*. I suppose this irritates me now more than it would before my extraordinary private tutoring, because now I realize these guys were really not studying a jillion different little things, they were studying One Big Thing.

And it is not *Princeton's* IAS. The Institute was unaffiliated with the university and just happened to be located there because Veblen, Flexner's first faculty recruit, was a Princeton mathematician and he talked Flexner into locating IAS on the Princeton campus. In fact, the Institute's first office was in Fine Hall, the very mathematics building in which Veblen already had his office.

My *Time* magazine easily picked up Gödel's farting, and the FBI transcriptionist dutifully but tastefully recorded those farts by inserting the words "unattributed gastrointestinal noises," later abbreviated UGN. It was the right thing to do, because most of the health discussions between the two men were inspired, as it were, by Gödel's farting. But of course farts were out of bounds for the *Denver Post*, and to avoid having to pretend they didn't know what UGN meant, they simply removed the acronym without showing any redaction. The result is that some of the discussions about Gödel's condition make no sense because the newspaper deleted the farting flags.

I admit that I, too, left all farting flags out of my informal transcripts. They didn't seem to have any relevance to whether Gödel was a spy. Einstein, by the way, referred to Gödel's farting as "the exhaust problem," a phrase so wry that the dopes at the newspaper thought he was talking about Gödel's car.

Which reminds me that I cannot resist a few comments about the newspaper's decision to re-insert so-called "identifying information" into the transcripts. DBS ordered the formal transcriptionist to delete all references to Princeton or the IAS, as well as any mention of Einstein's or Gödel's names, apparently to hide the identity of the two targets.

"Won't everybody know one of these guys is Einstein when they read them talking about relativity and fleeing the Nazis?" I asked DBS when he informed me about the redactions.

"Every bit of fog hurts the enemy," he responded, and that was the end of the discussion. "Every bit of fog hurts the enemy" is what DBS told all new CI recruits in the canned speech he gave every year, and how he answered most operational questions, whether the answer was apt or not.

"DBS never did understand that every bit of fog we manufacture comes with a cost, not just in its making but sometimes in fogging things up for us," my old boss Chris Conner once told me. I never forgot that. There sure was plenty of fog to go around in this operation.

Anyway, compounding the inanity of these redactions, when the *Denver Post* decided to add back in the redacted identifying information "for clarity and completeness," they just guessed about it, and were often wrong, sometimes with hilarious results. When Einstein suggested the name of a local doctor on Carter Road whom Gödel should visit for his exhaust problem, DBS of course redacted out the doctor's name and address. Thinking the exhaust problem was a motor vehicle problem, the newspaper added in for the redacted doctor's name the name of a garage in Princeton. That garage wasn't even around in 1942. I've also never been able to figure out why they just seemed to ignore the doctor reference. No doctors I know fix cars on the side. Ah, journalism!

The newspaper created an acronym, MADP, for the pair's "meet and departure point"—the place they met every morning and split up every afternoon—and claimed it was at the intersection of Washington Road and Nassau Street. The newspaper just made that up, too. It had some guy walk off the distance between the two geniuses' residences and just assumed they met at the midpoint. But by 1942, IAS had long been relocated to Fuld Hall, southwest of the main campus. It was south and west of both their houses, closer to Einstein's house on Mercer Street than Gödel's house way up on Linden Lane. In fact, Einstein's house was roughly the midpoint between Gödel's house and the new IAS digs.

My control, who told me the Bureau had restarted security surveillance on Einstein right after Pearl Harbor, also told me that at the beginning Gödel would just walk to Einstein's house, and then they'd stroll down through the small graduate campus and through Springdale Golf Course to Fuld Hall. But it appeared they soon tired of this same walk, so they began to meet at different locations and to take different routes. This in fact was something that had gotten up DBS's snout.

"These guys are doing a pretty sophisticated job of trying not to be noticed," I remember him saying to me once. "They change their route every day, and there is no pattern to it."

We learned later in my surveillance that Gödel, characteristically, numbered all their different meeting places and associated routes, and at the end of each afternoon walk the two of them would agree to the next morning's meeting place and route. The afternoon walks home, of course, all began at Fuld Hall, but before they started back, they'd agree to the ending point and route back.

They had three different morning meeting places, three different afternoon ending points, and three different routes to and from each, for a total of 9 different paths. "How about 3/2 tomorrow?" Gödel might suggest in the afternoon before they parted, meaning the third numbered morning meeting place and the second numbered route to IAS from that meeting place. Einstein would always agree to Gödel's route suggestions, and realized early on that Gödel was moving through all nine combinations in a systematic order.

"This was all part of his obsessiveness," Einstein told me privately years later, "and I hated the rigidity, especially once I discovered his obvious pattern." So Einstein suggested, ostensibly for security reasons, that before each walk they simply draw a set of two random numbers, from one to three, and Gödel readily agreed.

"I will write the numbers on small pieces of paper and we can draw them out of my hat," Gödel suggested.

"No, I have a better way." Einstein taught Gödel the rock/paper/scissors game to generate the random numbers. Gödel loved it. "A kind of pseudo spontaneity restored my spirits," Einstein told me.

All of this is a long way of saying we had to start the surveillance on that first day in the afternoon rather than in the morning because we had no idea where they'd meet in the morning, and my control didn't want me staking out their homes if at all possible. We didn't know at that time how or why they chose their routes and beginning and end points. But at least we knew they'd start their afternoon walk home at Fuld Hall, and we assumed they'd disclose the next morning's meeting place during their afternoon discussions.

I waited for them on a stone bench half a block away from the building entrance, actually reading the *Time* magazine for the first time. On its cover was a man who I thought at first glance was Woodrow Wilson, but who turned out to be England's ambassador to Russia.

I was in the middle of a story about the Battle of the Arctic when Einstein and Gödel came out, surrounded by what I would come to learn would be an ever-present crowd hovering at the building's entrance, both in the afternoon when Einstein left with Gödel, and in the mornings, when they arrived. Einstein exchanged greetings with several of the well-wishers, and even gave a few autographs to tourists. Gödel stood off to the side. No one was interested in him.

CHAPTER 4

To MY ASTONISHMENT, ONCE the crowd dispersed and the two men began their walk home—maybe after twenty paces—they paused to play what looked like a few games of rock/paper/scissors. Einstein then looked up at me once then never looked at me again during that first day of surveillance. Gödel was always looking around at everything during the entire operation, but he never saw me.

Einstein, to whom my eyes were first drawn, was a vortex of hidden energy. It's a little hard to explain. He didn't waive his hands around Italian-style, but he was fiercely animated. It was all so controlled, but somehow still hurricanic. I imagined his "crumpled" clothing, which every unimaginative reporter mentioned, was a mere victim of his hurricane. Cary Grant's clothes would have looked crumpled in that massive storm. The energy of the ideas must somehow physically distort the clothing.

I learned later that the crumpling was all just a consequence of Einstein's folding inadequacies. He insisted on folding his own clothes, but he did it with the care of a stevedore unpacking sides of beef.

"I never did like topology," he joked when I asked him about it. His long-time secretary, Helen Dukas, who moved with him to Princeton during his first extended visit and stayed with him when he emigrated, took on the duties of housekeeper after his wife Elsa died. But at Einstein's insistence those duties did not include folding his clean clothes.

By the way, at the time of Operation Felix and Rolf, Einstein was still quite meticulous about his appearance, other than the crumpling (and not wearing socks—he hated how his big toe always made a hole in them). It was only later that he stopped combing his hair and started to wear baggy clothes everywhere.

On this afternoon, he was wearing a blue crew-neck sweater and tan slacks, both well-fitting if crumpled. His iconic hair was behaving less unruly than I remember seeing in some photographs. Again, I imagined the hair was driven by the same interaction of energy and matter as his clothes, but actually it was simply a difficult blend of wiry and fine, tamable only with time commitments even the meticulous Einstein was not willing to make. He did the best he could with a morning brush, which was often perfectly adequate, unless the wind and humidity conspired. The press, of course, selectively published only the wildest of the photographs, in a weak kind of grooming Schadenfreude. *He may be smart as hell, but we take better care of our hair.*

Shining through the hurricane, its eye so to speak, was his smiling face. Mouth smiling even while talking, eyes smiling. Heck, his nose smiled, if that's possible. It was a little like the smiles on some of the nuns I had in primary school, who managed to secrete contentment and wonder at the same time, and no small amount of sadness.

Gödel was the anti-Einstein. He was not crumpled, didn't seem stormy, and rarely smiled. When he did smile it was a weak and worried smile, the kind mothers give to ill children. He was dressed in an elegant three-piece dark brown suit, covered in a soon-to-be-buttoned dark gray trench coat. Black leather gloves, dark gray fedora to match the coat. Dapper. He was holding a thin black briefcase high under one arm, as if it were a riding crop.

His eyes were the center of his countenance. Magnified into dinner plates by his perfectly round eyeglasses, they looked worried but not confused, like someone who had just discovered something really bad and was wondering whether he could handle it. The weather was temperate for an April afternoon, probably in the low 50s, but he was dressed for winter. He even pulled out a dark blue scarf after the rock/paper/scissors games and threw it around his pencil thin neck. That made me feel a little better about my scarf.

But my lasting impression, looking back and therefore no doubt corrupted by subsequent events, was of brotherhood. These two men were brothers, equals, which I never saw when Einstein was around anyone else. The biggest big shots of all time treated Einstein like he was some kind of god. Politicians, reporters, even other revered scientists. He was polite to everyone, friendly even, but in an unmistakably distracted way. It was clear this hurricane was taking a moment out of his day just to be civil, and that more important things needed, and in fact were already commanding, his attention. He was like that with everyone except Gödel. He was like that with me, until my second treason.

I remember when Felix Bloch, shortly after he won the Nobel Prize for physics, called on Einstein at his office one late afternoon. When the two came out Bloch looked like a novitiate who had just witnessed a miracle. Bowing, eyes lowered, a little stunned. And Einstein, smiling, looked like he always did when people prayed to him—like a benevolent God.

But none of that with Gödel. I could tell, after they both began to teach me, that Einstein, through the bluster of his hurricane, was in awe of Gödel. It was a very surprised kind of awe. *Wait, I have discovered truths of time, space, and matter that no man has seen. And yet here is this man who has looked even deeper, into what it means to discover truth.* It was as if Peary had finally reached the North Pole, only to find a pale and sickly little man in a dark three-piece suit waiting for him there.

For his part, Gödel was polite, formal, and respectful with Einstein, but no more with Einstein than with anyone else. This relentless intellect, discoverer of the universe's most profound truths about truth, spoke exactly the same to waiters when he told them he didn't want anything as he did to Einstein when he talked about the incompleteness theorems.

He also seemed entirely able to separate himself from his insights. He was moved by those insights, just like everyone, but not by his discovery of them, if that makes any sense. I got the impression he thought of himself as just another schmo who happened to have stumbled on these revelations. The revelations were to be celebrated, not him.

Gödel was also deeply self-conscious about his English, which was good in pronunciation, perfect in grammar, but sparse in vocabulary. This no doubt contributed to what seemed to be a general state of high formality. When our interactions moved from English to German, he became perceptibly more relaxed. Still formal and intimidating, but more relaxed. His occasional cackles—which he continued when we spoke German, but never in public—seemed, and sounded, as if they came from a pressure relief valve to the steel that otherwise clad his personality.

I discovered eventually that the two men were on two very different professional trajectories. Einstein was on a weird reputational teeter totter. As his popular fame rose, and never faltered, his scientific credibility diminished, and never recovered. He would not accept quantum mechanics, and his attempt to construct a unified field theory without it would prove sadly impossible. By 1942, his reputation within the physics community, at least for the new work he was publishing, was shot. He was yesterday's physics. Still a god even to physicists, but a god of the past, supplanted by a new, probabilistic, pantheon.

Gödel, by contrast, never garnered wide popular appeal but his standing among logicians and philosophers of mathematics would never recede. Sure, like almost all mathematicians, his best work was already behind him by the age of 35. But his legacy within the math and logic communities was never superseded by a shiny new theory, as Einstein's was.

Both men were well aware of their different public and professional reputations. Indeed, I learned about this from them. Both were also painfully aware that their best work was behind them, though Einstein's pain was the greater because his public persona never waned. When he railed, as he often did, against what he called "this Einstein cult of personality," I think what he was really bemoaning was the relentlessly increasing gap between the value of his new contributions and the public's perceptions of that value.

That first walk home—numbered 2/2 —took us up though the graduate college and all the way up Alexander Street across Nassau to Palmer Square, then back down Library Street to Mercer, where the two parted.

Einstein's Mercer Street house is probably almost as well-known as its well-known occupant, and has its own mythology. A reporter once asked Einstein why he had the front door of the house painted red, and Einstein said it was to help him find his way home. The newspapers gobbled up the story, loving that the mighty Einstein got lost walking home. More Schadenfreude. But of course it was all a joke. Einstein was the master multi-tasker, as they say nowadays. He could talk to Gödel about Gödel's work, be thinking about his own, and be watching out for spies and assassins, all at the same time. This was not a man who needed a red door to tell him where home was. The gentle joke, as it often was, was on the reporters themselves for asking such a dumb question and then accepting Einstein's dumb answer.

In the beginning, I was surprised to hear Einstein joking so much about Gödel's formality and paranoia. At first, I thought it was insecurity, more Schadenfreude. If Einstein couldn't dazzle Gödel like he could dazzle everyone else, well at least he could remind Gödel that Einstein wasn't crazy like he was. But now, knowing both men as I do, I think this ribbing was driven entirely by Einstein's innate kindness, and a genuine worry about Gödel's deteriorating health.

That first night, when I got back to the crummy apartment on Brunswick Pike that the Bureau had set me up in, I listened to the tapes once all the way through. Then I pulled out a notebook and played them again, transcribing the German. When that was all done, I translated it into English. It was slow as molasses when they were talking shop. I had no more idea what they were saying than the idiots at the *Denver Post*. Unfortunately, I couldn't insert "technical discussions omitted," and had to translate every last word. I had to stop often to look up technical words I didn't know. Fifty minutes of conversation ended up taking me four hours to translate.

I am reminded today, rereading these transcripts in the newspaper, how little justice they did to the two men's conversations. The transcripts sound stiff and awkward. But the men's conversations were fluid and beautiful. Some of it is the translation. But most of it is because the transcripts simply don't capture the animation and wonder that infused these discussions, especially when they talked shop. Einstein sounded like a cub scout marveling at the secret entrance to a cave, and Gödel was the scout master, controlled and analytical, but just as excited.

I had trouble falling asleep that first night. It was all the math talk. I felt like I did when I was a kid and my father wouldn't let me into the parlor for his men's Thursday night political discussions. Something important was being discussed, and they wouldn't let me join in. I started thinking about DBS with a new-found respect, then fell asleep.

CHAPTER 5

THE NEXT MORNING WAS a foggy drizzly Friday, a challenge for predator and prey. My control and I still had no idea how they decided on their meeting places and routes, so I had no choice but to start at one of their houses. We agreed on Gödel's, both because he was so clueless and because there were never any reporters or tourists there. I waited at a bus stop near the corner of Franklin Avenue and Linden Lane, three doors down from Gödel's one-story army green house at 145 Linden Lane.

From the front, on Linden, the bungalow looked like a Quonset hut stuck off center between its two larger neighbors, a vision exaggerated by the overgrown shrubbery that flanked its left side and by its dark green paint that blended into the shrubbery. The Quonset hut had three tiny rectangular windows and one attic dormer, but no door. That's because the house was oriented sideways, so that what one was seeing from Linden was actually the side of the house. Its true architectural front, with front door and an attractive array of large windows, was on its right side, facing its neighbor to the south, accessible by a gravel driveway running along that side all the way back to a large garden.

The bungalow would have been quite striking if only one could get far enough away from the house next door to appreciate it. There was no safe position for me to be able to see the front door—I would have had to walk right up to the beginning of the driveway, 15 feet from the door. From my perch at the bus stop the most I could see was a sliver of the small roof overhanging the steps up to the front door. Jockeying to see more made me think of the time I thought I saw my mother waiting at the very front of a train platform. I strained to get enough of an angle to see her face, but never could.

Nervous that I would miss him, I arrived at 9:00, even though my control told me they never started out much before 10:00. These were not early risers, or at least not early walkers. Einstein's and Gödel's schedules at IAS would have made bankers blush. They typically took about an hour to walk in, arriving between 11:00 and 11:30, then left between 2:00 and 3:00. These short office hours meant that I had to decide between just waiting outside IAS for their return trip—which I often did at the beginning—or finding something else to do for three or four hours. That was just enough time to make waiting really boring, but not enough for me to do anything terribly productive.

They didn't walk every day because Gödel was often ill and Einstein was often out of town. Now that war had come, I understood Einstein's travel schedule was much lighter than before. Still, during the six weeks I followed them, Einstein was gone one or two days every week. Gödel was gone just twice, but he was sick all the time.

Between Einstein's travels and Gödel's hypochondria, they walked together an average of two or three days each week. When Einstein was gone, Gödel didn't go into the office, unless he had a meeting or presentation there, which was rare, in which case his wife Adele would drive him. When Gödel was ill, Einstein still walked in every day when he was in town, and in fact took even longer and more meandering routes, sometimes taking two hours each way. In the very beginning, I followed Einstein a couple times when he was by himself, thinking he might meet someone else. But he had almost no interactions with anyone on his solo walks, and when he did, they were almost always near Mercer or at the entrance of IAS, where reporters wanted a blurb from him or a photograph, and tourists wanted autographs.

Shortly after I arrived at the bus stop, the rain changed from drizzle to downpour, and was now sizzling on the top of my umbrella. At 9:30 fuzzy yellow lights began glowing in the bungalow, turning the dark green window sashes lime. Gödel left his house and started to walk down the gravel driveway a little before 10:15, wearing the same trench coat, hat, gloves, and scarf as yesterday, and holding the same briefcase under his left arm. This time he held a black umbrella with his right hand. It appeared that today's suit was dark gray.

He walked down Linden to Franklin, just a few yards from where I was waiting at the bus stop. But then, to my surprise, he turned left on Franklin instead of right, walking away from Einstein's house. He walked to Harrison, turned right, and then walked all the way down Harrison to Canal Street, where he sat and waited at another bus stop.

If this were anyone else, I'd have been terrified about what to do. He'd have seen me waiting at one bus stop and then watched me follow him to a second. Plus, I'd never been trained on how to follow someone if they get on a bus. But I wasn't too worried. Heck, I could probably follow Gödel into a bathroom stall and he'd never notice me. He was always anxious, looking around furtively at everything, like a barn owl. But he never seemed to notice anything.

After a few minutes I spotted Einstein walking quickly down Harrison Street, waiving to his distractedly vigilant friend, who must have seen him but who didn't seem to notice him until Einstein clapped him on the shoulder. The two of them waked right past me and continued down Harrison across the canal, and then went back west on Canal Road until they were almost opposite IAS, across the canal. I assumed they'd continue west and cross the canal at Quaker Road, but instead they turned and retraced their steps east, back toward Harrison. I was nervous about Einstein walking right past me a second time, but he didn't even look up. They re-crossed the canal at Harrison, turned on Faculty Road, and made their way from there directly to Fuld Hall.

At the entrance, the usual crowd of reporters, tourists, and a couple colleagues joined them in greetings. The two men knew these interruptions meant that they would have to finish their daily discussions a bit before they actually arrived at the front doors. They had a joke phrase for it. "The vultures gather," is how I heard Einstein first put it, though they often used the less pejorative "birds have landed" or something similar.

Einstein confided in me that in addition to the obvious goals of sheer variety and hiding from the crowds, part of the reason for these combinations of starting points, end points, and routes was that he wanted a few minutes to walk alone. He loved his walks and discussions with Gödel—and in fact years later told von Neumann that the only reason he was still at IAS was for the privilege of walking and talking with Gödel. But he also needed time away from Gödel because talking with him was so exhausting. Exhilarating and exhausting. He once compared it to wrestling a tiger.

He needed time to think about what they'd discussed before, and in fact spent roughly half of his working day—when he was not in meetings, giving lectures, or on the telephone—thinking about his discussions with Gödel, something he admitted to me but to no one else as far as I know, even, maybe especially, Gödel. This may be one of the reasons Einstein made so little progress in those years on the unified theory. Anyway, he did his best thinking while walking, so he needed to get out of his office and walk, without Gödel. Their different morning starting points and afternoon ending points allowed him to do just that—to walk by himself on the way to and from Gödel.

In the very first transcript published by the newspaper, the two spent most of the walk talking about Gödel's diagonalization lemma, which of course our newspaper friends left out, substituting their ubiquitous "technical discussions omitted." Einstein was pressing Gödel on the extraordinary technique he'd invented to label every mathematical statement with a unique number, which then enabled him to prove his stunning incompleteness theorem. I want to explain that theorem to you eventually, because it was a key to all the craziness of Operation Felix and Rolf. But let me back way up, just as they did, and start with this strange hunt for axioms.

Einstein explained that mathematical foundation hunters have long been digging to find the fewest number of axioms—propositions that are just assumed to be true—from which all of mathematics flows. Don't ask me why. It seems to have something to do with a philosophical debate about whether these foundations are "real" things that are out there waiting to be discovered by us, or whether we just make them up.

This hunt is really important to many mathematicians, and especially to philosophers of mathematics. Philosophers try to impose order on the universe—and the way philosophers of mathematics impose order on the already ordered mathematical universe is to look for deep foundations, building blocks. It's been going on forever.

Euclid, if you remember your high school math, did this with geometry. He proposed just five axioms from which all of plane geometry could be deduced. But no one had done this with ordinary mathematics—plain old arithmetic. I suppose this curiosity about foundations is really just the math version of natural scientific, or even just regular human, curiosity.

Einstein said it was very much like his work in physics—digging deeper into how things work. Once we notice apples fall from trees and ask "why," we discover that all masses attract each other, and call it gravity. We ask "why" a few more times and we get Einstein's general theory of relativity, in which gravity is the result of space and time being distorted by mass. It didn't take too many whys to get to the heart of things.

It was pretty neat the way Einstein explained this hunt for axioms—the heart of math things—by using the rock/paper/scissors game.

"Suppose you want to write down the rules of the rock/paper/scissors game and mail them to a friend who does not know how to play."

"He'd have to live in Timbuktu, because everyone knows how to play rock/paper/scissors," I smarted off, much more comfortable with Einstein at this point, after my first treason.

"Herr Professor Gödel did not," Einstein said, laughing. Gödel shrugged his shoulders and raised his arms, palms up, in admission. "Anyway, what would your rules be?"

"Well, I would say first there are two players and three choices each player can make."

"Very good."

"But let us pause," interjected Gödel to my surprise, since up to then he had said almost nothing to me during any of our operational chats. "*Why* must there be just two players and three choices for each? Why not three players and two choices?"

"Ha, Herr Warum strikes again! Did you know, Charlie, that when he was young, they called Professor Gödel Herr Warum—Mr. Why—because he never stopped asking why? This is one of his unique gifts. Most of us get tired of asking why, tired of pushing. But never Kurt. And this is a very good why at this point in the lesson. Why not three players and two choices?"

"Well, I suppose we could have three players and two choices, but then it would be a different game than the rock/paper/scissors game."

"Exactly so!" Gödel replied excitedly. "And this is the essence of axioms—they are accepted as true not arbitrarily but because their truth is what captures the system they describe. We could assume different axioms, different rules, but then we would have a different system, a different game."

Einstein continued. "Now let us stop there with our original axioms. Two players and three choices. Are these rules enough for your friend to play the game?"

"Of course not. We need to tell him about the hand signals, and which wins over which." My imaginary Timbuktuian was tall and dark-skinned, covered in sky blue robes and wearing a matching turban, but otherwise looked just like my father.

"Correct. Without more rules, we say these rules are 'incomplete.' They are not enough to describe the whole game. So we need two more sets of rules, one explaining how the three choices are expressed and one hierarchy rule about which expressions win over which."

"Yes. Rock is indicated by making a fist, paper is the flat hand, and scissors is the two fingers. Rock beats scissors, scissors beat paper, paper beats rock."

"Exactly so," Einstein said. "And if we left out one of these three relationships—let us say we said nothing about rock beating scissors—then what would happen?"

"Well, if my friend in Timbuktu played rock and his opponent played scissors, they would not know who won."

"The axioms, the rules, would again be incomplete," said Einstein.

"But even with these, we need another rule, no?" interjected Gödel. I thought for a while but couldn't see any. Gödel continued, "What happens if both players choose rock?"

"Of course," I answered, "we need the tying rule. If there is a tie, then we play again until there is no tie."

"We still need one more rule," Gödel announced, smiling ever so slightly. I couldn't think of a thing. "The two players must play simultaneously." Of course, otherwise the second player could always win.

"Now I believe the axioms are complete," Gödel said. "It is often very difficult to see axioms precisely because they are hiding so deeply in the system, in the game. But once we see them, the need for them often becomes obvious, like the tying rule and the simultaneous play rule."

Einstein took over, "So that is what we call completeness. Axioms must completely describe their system, rules must completely describe their game.

"But there is another requirement for axioms, called consistency. I am afraid rock/paper/scissors is not so good to illustrate consistency because there are no inferences in our game, no theorems. It is all axioms. But think here about simple arithmetic, which we will discuss later. The axioms behind arithmetic must produce consistent propositions. Three plus five must always equal eight. It would be ridiculous, and more than that, dangerous, if sometimes the sum were eight and sometimes nine. That is consistency. Simple, really. Now let us move to a third requirement for axioms, independence."

Gödel interrupted. "Two more points before we move to independence, Herr Professor Einstein, if I may. First, it is not just that three plus five must always equal eight, but that we are able to prove that statement from the axioms alone. And that we cannot prove three plus five is nine, from the same axioms. My second point is a question. What if we changed the hierarchy rule a tiny bit, to: rock beats scissors, scissors beat paper, and therefore rock beats paper?"

"That actually makes some sense," I said. "I always thought of rock 'beating' scissors as meaning rock was stronger than scissors. If rock is stronger than scissors, and scissors is stronger than paper, then it figures that rock should be stronger than paper, not the other way around. That always confused me."

"You have discovered that implications are transitive, which we logicians call the syllogism rule, and that the rock/paper/scissors game is not well-ordered," Gödel replied, smiling again. I had no idea what he just said.

"But think these new hierarchy rules through, Charlie," Einstein interrupted, a little impatient with this detour by Gödel. "They would mean rock beats everything. Such a game would not be very interesting to play. Each player would play rock every time, in endless draws.

"But Professor Gödel's deeper point here is an important one. Although in theory we are completely free to make up axioms—and might even be tempted to do so to achieve some other goal, like transitivity—we must never forget that the axioms must be constructed in a way that produces the game we already know and merely wish to describe. It is the game that drives how we articulate the rules, and not the other way round. And the essence of this beautiful little game of rock/paper/scissors is its perfectly balanced ring of hierarchy. Each choice beats one of the other choices but loses to the other one. It is really quite lovely.

"Now we move to independence, in some ways the deepest of the three requirements. This is what guarantees that the axioms we construct will be the fewest necessary. It is what makes axioms axioms, parts of the foundation of the system as opposed to mere trappings on top of the foundation."

"Quite so," Gödel said. "What if we added to the rule about what we do in case of ties, the following three rules:

If both players play rock, replay.

If both players play paper, replay.

If both players play scissors, replay."

"They are unnecessary," I immediately responded. "They just repeat the more general tying rule."

"Precisely," said Gödel. "These three axioms are not necessary because they can all be derived from the tying axiom, they are special cases of it. We say they are not independent of the existing axioms."

"But what does any of this have to with mathematics?" I asked.

"I am afraid, Charlie, that we must answer that question next time. Herr Professor Gödel and I must conclude this delightful lecture to return to work. I have a meeting at 2:00."

I was excited, and certainly more excited than I had ever been before about math. Albert Einstein and Kurt Gödel were teaching me, Charlie Richards, former C-student and FBI dunce! In the end, they would teach me things that maybe a hundred guys in the whole world knew, and thousands of others thought they knew but misunderstood. And this foundations stuff was easy. Easy as rock/paper/scissors.

But in all my excitement I am getting way ahead of myself. I haven't even told you about my treasons. So let me go back to that second day of surveillance, Friday, April 17, 1942. Nothing special happened that day. I was getting more and more comfortable following them, even in the rain and fog, and I was pretty sure neither man had made me, even though there was almost no one else around them when they walked.

Gödel was ill on the following Monday, so they didn't walk together. I followed Einstein on a pair of long and extended walks, but he talked to no one except the gaggle at Mercer and at the Fuld Hall entrance.

The next day, Tuesday, was also cool and damp, though rain only threatened. You can't tell from reading the transcripts, but it was on that third day, Tuesday the 21st day of April, 1942, that everything blew up.

CHAPTER 6

I SHOULD HAVE KNOWN something was going on. They started down at the bus stop on Harrison again, but this time walked right back up to Palmer Square, away from the canal and from IAS. Then they headed straight for the small café in the Nassau Inn, and went in. Gödel had just told Einstein on Thursday's walk that he never goes to restaurants because of his fear of poisoning.

I had to think quickly. I knew I would need to follow them in because my mic was not picking them up from outside. I removed my headphones and stuck them in my jacket pocket, knowing I would have to take off my ski cap once I went in. But I kept the *Time* magazine hooked up and the recorder on, figuring I could easily disconnect the magazine from the clip if I needed to ditch it, and stuff the wire up my coat sleeve. I'd cross the bridge of taking off my coat when I came to it.

After waiting outside for the recommended three minutes, actually counting off the minutes on my watch, which is what they taught me to do in my abbreviated surveillance training, I went in and sat at a table with my back to them, but where I could see them in the reflection of a window. I took my hat off but kept my coat and scarf on.

Right after I ordered my coffee, Einstein's reflection got up, smiling, and approached the reflection of my table. He slapped me on my back, said "Nice to see you again," dropped a folded piece of paper on the table, and went to the restroom. I opened the bit of paper. Scribbled in that forced kind of half-cursive half-printing made to make otherwise illegible handwriting legible, was the following message, in English:

> Good morning, Mr. FBI man. We would like to talk to you privately, so please turn off any recording device. Yours truly, Albert Einstein.

Above his half-cursive half-printed name, and below the "Yours truly," he actually signed it, as if it were a formal letter. I foolishly kept that note all these years. It's probably worth a jillion dollars.

Einstein's reflection was back at his table and I didn't know what to do. I knew what I should do: shake my head "No," keep the recorder on, and report to my control that the operation was blown. But then it would be over. I turned off the recorder, making a mental note of the time so that I could add in more recorded time to make up for the gap, and walked over to their table. I'm not sure why I turned the recorder off, probably just because Albert Einstein—*the* Albert Einstein—asked me to.

Gödel looked like he expected me to kill him on the spot. He was two shades paler than his usual pale, sitting straight up in his chair, hands on the table, as if he would bolt any second. Einstein was smiling. They both looked more real than they did at 20 yards. Older, lines gouging their faces. Gödel's face was covered with New England streams, Einstein's with the deep canyons of the Colorado. Einstein did all the talking, or I should say writing. He handed me another note which said, *Is this being recorded? Answer by shaking your head yes or no.*

"Of course I'm not recording you, Professor Einstein," I said laughing quietly, disregarding his request to respond just by shaking my head. I figured I needed to take back a little bit of control.

"There has been some mix-up. I'm Charlie Richards, a professor of classics visiting Princeton this semester, not an FBI agent. But it is a pleasure to meet you, sir, even under these circumstances." I held out my hand but he ignored it.

He bent his head down, wrote another note which seemed to take forever, and handed it to me. Its message was scribbled much less legibly: *I will give you another chance to turn off any recording device before I will announce to your superiors that I was able to detect you because of your terrible spying skills.* He looked up, then added two more sentences to the message: *And if you have already turned it off, which I think unlikely, we will simply wait until you turn it on for the rest of our morning walk, and then make our comments about your incompetence. The longer we continue this farce the worse your options.*

Well, at least Einstein wasn't perfect. He hadn't guessed that I'd already turned off the recorder, which made me think that I shouldn't have. Again, I didn't know what to say or do. If I continued with this denial and reported the operation was blown, I would be done with Albert Einstein and Kurt Gödel forever.

"I have a recorder, sir, but I turned it off before I walked over here."

"Good. Please sit down. May I see the recorder?"

I sat, then took the thin box out of my coat pocket and showed it to him. He opened it to confirm the tiny tape machine was not recording. "Where is the microphone, let me see it." When I told him it was taped into the center of the *Time* magazine, I could see he was intrigued, and almost diverted. He reached out for it, but then caught himself.

"I am sorry for my rudeness. I am, as you know, Albert Einstein and this, as you also know, is my colleague Professor Kurt Gödel." He reached out his hand and I shook it. I shook Albert Einstein's hand. Gödel did not offer a handshake.

"And your name, young man, your *real* name?

"Charles Richards, call me Charlie." He smiled at that.

"And you may call me Albert. Professor Gödel I believe prefers Professor Gödel. See here, we do not have much time. I need you to do a small favor for my colleague, who is a great and important man and a dear friend. In exchange, I will not call President Roosevelt and tell him you are the worst FBI agent in history. You are not, by the way, but I am afraid I will have to tell him you are if you do not agree to my proposal."

It was at that point that I leaned over to him and whispered my suggestion that we speak German to make sure no waiters or other customers overheard us, which I could see surprised him. He assumed my job was just to record them, and that someone else translated. I could see that Gödel was really disturbed by my whispering, and that he was about to bolt.

"No," Einstein responded firmly, and then to Gödel in German, grabbing his arm, "All is well, my friend." I learned later that Einstein was worried that if I started to speak German it would really send Gödel's delicate psyche down the toilet. So we kept up in English, whispering.

"I will not betray the United States."

"Of course not, and I would not ask such a thing. Your Mr. Hoover knows I am not a Nazi; for heaven's sake, I am a Jew. And he also knows I am not a Soviet agent. Professor Gödel is likewise not an agent for any government. This favor I need from you is a private matter, for Professor Gödel. It will not require you to do any act that will hurt this fine country, my adopted home."

"What is it?"

"I need you obtain for us the FBI files on the Moritz Schlick murder in Vienna in 1936."

"The FBI would not have files on that, we don't investigate crimes in foreign countries, even against Americans, and I assume this Shits guy is not an American."

I knew exactly who Schlick was and who murdered him. I actually wasn't sure at all whether the Bureau would have a file on his murder, but this was the catechism we were all taught from the get go at Quantico—FBI snoops here, OSS snoops out of country, though such out of country snooping, in the usual spy jargon, was paradoxically called "in country." Anyway, I responded with the catechism.

"That's for OSS not the FBI."

"Then I need you to get the OSS file. I need to be able to show Professor Gödel that Schlick's murder was not part of a larger assassination plot that includes killing him."

"I can't get the OSS file, even if there were one."

"Of course you can. Just tell your superiors you need to look at it because it came up in my conversations with Professor Gödel—it already has and we will make sure it comes up more often—and that you need it for background."

"I'm small potatoes. I'm just doing this because I speak German. I also have a philosophy degree from Princeton, so I know how to get around this town." This last part about having a philosophy degree got a visible reaction from Gödel, part surprise, part worry, part hope. "I was a C student," I added, to dim some of the hope.

"But you can always ask, that will harm nothing. And I will remain silent about your spying abilities as I have promised, even if you cannot get the file, or if the file does not allay Professor Gödel's fears, or if there is no such file," he rolled his eyes at the last part, meaning he was sure there would be a file. "I would even consider recommending you to the President, if that were important to you. But we do not have much time, we need to get back on the recorder."

"Why don't you just call up your pal Roosevelt and have him order a copy of the OSS file for you?

"This is a private matter, and I will not embarrass my friend."

"But you are willing to embarrass him with me?

"You are small potatoes, as you said, if you will forgive me for repeating." He said this smiling in a strange way that seemed like he didn't think I was small potatoes at all. Einstein was like that. He made everyone around him feel important, even though he could also give off a palpable air of being distracted.

"Deal," I said on the spot.

You might wonder, as I have a thousand times since, why I agreed, or at least didn't try to delay, but I couldn't see any downside to the agreement, some big upsides, and a huge downside to not agreeing. Plus, to be honest, I wanted to get to know these guys better. It would be wonderful to talk to them, instead of just eavesdropping.

"Thank you, Mr. Richards," he reached out and grabbed my right hand with both of his.

"Charlie, please."

"Thank you, Mr. Charlie Richards. Now please go back and turn your recorder on. Do you know whether any other agents are following me? I do not believe so, but I am afraid that some might be better than you," he said, smiling apologetically. "I know they followed me for most of 1933 and 1934, but they seemed to have dropped me after that. They started up again a few months ago then stopped when you took over."

"I'm pretty sure no one else is following you now."

"Good. From now on the three of us will meet here for lunch as needed. Then your usual morning and afternoon tape recordings will not be interrupted. We will need a code for when meetings are necessary. Tomorrow of course we will need to meet, but after that the meetings may be sporadic. Any ideas about code words, Mr. Spy?"

"I liked when you said the other day 'That putz Zermelo.' How about that?"

"Oh, my goodness, this is so embarrassing. No, I will never say such a thing again. I do not like Professor Ernst Zermelo because he wrongfully claimed he proved incompleteness before Professor Gödel, and then when his prior efforts were shown to be erroneous, he wrongly accused the Gödel proofs of error. But it was immature of me to call him a putz. You must promise me to erase that from the tape."

"Sorry, already typed up and off to headquarters."

"Oh dear. Well, I must be better from now on." He thought for a moment. "How about *Cantor's cantor* as the signal to meet? Georg Cantor was a famous mathematician, a devout Lutheran, and there is an old mathematics joke about Cantor at temple that plays on the words. If I say *Cantor's cantor* in the morning we need to meet here for lunch." Then he paused and thought. "If at any time I say *The continuum hypothesis has been proved true* that will be the signal that there is some emergency, and you must come to my house on Mercer Street at once." I saw this really got a rise out of Gödel, who, I learned later, would spend the rest of his life trying to prove this continuum thing false.

Einstein continued, "If I say *The axiom of choice has been proved independent* that is also an emergency, but you are to come to my office at IAS."

"Got it," I said, even though I had no idea at all what these code phrases meant. Actually, I learned at Quantico that the stupider and more meaningless the recognition code the better, because no one would accidentally say such stupid and meaningless things. These codes were easy to remember because to me, at least in these early days, they were stupid and meaningless.

"Thank you again, Mr. Charlie Richards, FBI spy," and he shook my hand again with both of his, and his sad smile enveloped me.

CHAPTER 7

That afternoon on their way back home, the two of them laid it on awfully thick about Schlick. I decided that at lunch tomorrow I would have to tell them to tone things down a bit. I also thought of a million questions I wanted to ask them, none of which, unfortunately, had anything to do with the Schlick case, which is what I should have been thinking about. Space deformed by large masses, time altered by high velocities, light bent by gravity, questions like that for Einstein. Nothing at this point for Gödel, other than "what the heck are you two talking about?"

It was after their two games of rock/paper/scissors that afternoon, and after Einstein obligingly said "3, Olden and Alexander, and 1, through the golf course," that I first realized they picked the meeting points and routes by using the game. It was nice of Einstein to make that clear for my benefit. It saved me the trouble of staking out Gödel at his house, and I think Einstein wanted to save Gödel the terror of seeing me waiting outside for him, though I'm not sure he would have noticed me.

It was a cold, windy, wet, and thoroughly unpleasant Wednesday morning, a reminder of spring's unreliability. Gödel arrived first, holding an umbrella in one hand and his briefcase under his other armpit, stamping his feet, and shivering. He acted just like he always did, looking around at everything and seeing nothing. He didn't even make eye contact with me, even though now I was right across the street. I thought of giving him a wave, but then thought better of it. When Einstein arrived, he never even looked in my direction.

Their morning walk through the Springdale Golf Course was uneventful. A few brave linksters waved at the pair, who were so common that regulars called them "socio-hazards," and had even agreed on how to score a shot if it hit one of them, or if they kicked or threw a ball—they called these "the Genius Rules." The Genius Rules were apparently never invoked, but Einstein did tell me that once, after the war, they came upon Dwight Eisenhower golfing one morning, who made a point of interrupting his game to pay his respects to Einstein.

"Ach, what weather to be walking through wet grass," Gödel whined. "These Oxfords, which Adele only recently purchased for me, will not survive. It feels like the bottom of a lake."

"But look how green. It is likc thc Garden of Eden, or Ireland. Besides, I thought you enjoyed this route. You kept playing paper when I played rock."

"But this time I played rock and you played paper. We cannot escape this fate!" he cackled. "I do enjoy this route, but not in this sort of weather."

Terrified I would be late for our historic and treasonous lunch meeting if I went all the way back to my apartment, I instead walked immediately up to the Nassau Inn as soon as Einstein and Gödel entered IAS. After a few minutes shivering in the damp wind and thinking about what to do for the next several hours, I went inside for a coffee. When I realized I could not stay and drink coffee all morning, I decided to kill more time by walking a bit around the undergraduate campus. I hadn't been back for several years, long enough to have forgotten, emotionally, what a beautiful place it was. Central casting, I need an Ivy League college.

Palmer Square was a dainty and very European collection of small shops, which lay immediately north of the main campus entrance, across Nassau Street. Looking back toward the campus one could see the commons, flanked on the right by a massive collection of three-story chock-a-block gray stone dormitories. I lived in one of them, Holder Hall, for two years. Off to the left, in what seemed to me to be a perfect counterpoint to the dormitories' cold gothic stone, was the simple and beautiful cream and white First Presbyterian Church. I was a Catholic, but spent many a Sunday in that church with my Presbyterian girlfriend Marjorie Woods, the one I was seeing at the same time as I was seeing Susan Ciecwisz. Lucky for me Susan was a non-practicing Catholic, or I would have been juggling Sunday mornings too.

In the center, across the commons, was the unforgettable Nassau Hall—the oldest building on campus and the one used in all the marketing brochures. I walked across the commons and around Nassau Hall, south through the campus to Faculty Road, down by the canal, and then returned up Washington Road.

I saw a tall man walking across Washington holding the hand of a young girl, maybe six or seven years old. They reminded me of Father and my sister Caroline so long ago. I always felt proud when I saw him walk with her, moving his large frame so slowly and patiently, his usual long steps, which must have consumed well over three feet, now shuffling to match hers. I hoped I would be as patient if I ever became a father.

I got back to the Nassau Inn ten minutes before noon, and to my surprise Einstein and Gödel were already there, Einstein signing autographs and trying to read the menu.

"Hello, Charlie. What is the best lunch here?" Gödel was still looking at me like I was his death row prison guard.

"I've only been here a couple times. I couldn't afford it as a student. I thought this was your haunt."

"I have been here perhaps six times, but spread over nine years. It has been more than a year since I last dined here. As I recall, everything is delicious. In this weather, something warm and hearty is in order. Pot roast. Herr Professor Gödel has informed me he has brought with him some black beans and celery stalks, and some bread made by his wife Adele. But you need protein, Kurt."

"The beans have protein. I have carefully calculated my daily requirements. But let us not discuss these issues in front of our new friend."

"He is our new friend precisely because of these issues."

"But he need not know about the issues."

"Look," I interrupted, surprising myself, "I've been in this business long enough to know that I can't do my job without the big picture."

Einstein chortled. "I am sorry, Charlie Richards, but I happen to know that you have been a spy for exactly four days. Before that you were translating reports from English into German, and before that you were checking the backgrounds of plumbers and electricians in Philadelphia."

"And welders and carpenters," I added, smiling.

"Ha! I think I am going to like you, Charlie Richards."

"How do you know all this stuff about me?"

"Never mind."

The waitress came and we ordered, Einstein the pot roast and I a bowl of split pea soup and a tuna sandwich.

"This wind is quite unpleasant, no?" Einstein asked after the waitress left.

"It is terrible," replied Gödel. "It is a terrible day for anyone to be walking to a meal, let alone in the middle of the morning."

"I know, my Aristotle, this 'lunch' meal is so foreign. But if we breakfast lightly, you will come to enjoy it." Then Einstein got more serious. "You know that when I call you 'my Aristotle' I mean it as the greatest compliment one could give to a logician. But whenever I use the phrase I also begin to think of how strange Aristotle really was. Master of the logic that built science, yet almost blind to the world around him."

"Yes."

"You no doubt have read about his spectacularly wrong assertions about easily verifiable facts, such as how many teeth women have. Why in the world did he not just look into the mouths of real women, his wife, for example?"

"Philosophers have a joke about that, but it is terribly vulgar."

"Ha! I am imagining it as we speak."

"I know why you are bringing up Aristotle's blindness—to talk about Gödel's blindness," Gödel said somewhat wearily.

"Perhaps we will soon have some data on the problem," Einstein said more brightly.

"Thank you for doing this for me, Albert." Gödel arose and stiffly embraced Einstein. Both men seemed surprised.

"What are friends in high and low places for?" Einstein said, laughing and gesturing toward me.

After signing a few more autographs, including one for the waiter, Einstein turned and said to me, "Before we discuss some technical matters about which I have been thinking, we should first answer any questions you have about your mission."

"I don't have any questions. I will tell my bosses that Schlick's murder seems to be an important topic for you two, and that for background I would like to see any OSS file on it. They will then laugh me out of their office, and we will be done."

"How long will it take for them to produce the file?"

"It will take them five seconds to tell me no."

"Let me rephrase this question. How long will it take OSS to produce the file if your bosses agree to produce it?"

"I have no idea. They will have to ask their bosses and so forth, probably all the way up to Hoover, then the same thing all over again will happen at OSS, and Donovan will never cut it loose, even, perhaps especially, if Hoover insists. So forget about the timing, we will never get it."

"Let us assume—mathematicians are so fond of assuming, is that not so, Herr Professor Gödel?—let us assume Wild Bill himself wants to give us the file. That is the nickname, Herr Professor Gödel, of William Donovan, the director of OSS. Wild Bill Donovan. Is it not wonderful? Like Wild Bill Hickok.

"Do you know, Charlie Richards, that I love American cowboy music, which I am trying to learn to play on the violin? It is difficult for me to play the violin as a fiddle, sliding into the notes. I am now learning Home on the Range. Do you know it?"

Then he began singing, quite loudly, in a deep, froggy voice, heavily accented. Patrons in the restaurant fell silent when he first began, but then began singing along when he started the first stanza over again. When they finished two more repeats he finally stopped, and they all began clapping and many came over for autographs.

"I'm sorry," he apologized to everyone, "I know only these first two stanzas."

That night's local paper had a story about it. Fortunately, it didn't mention Gödel or me, except to describe us as a colleague and a student of Einstein's. I knew we couldn't keep meeting like this.

When the show and autographs were over, Einstein continued. "I am so sorry, gentlemen. When the muses come, they can be pesky. It is the same with physics and mathematics, is it not Herr Professor Gödel? In any event, how long will it take, Mr. Charlie Richards, to get the actual file once all the bosses say yes?"

"You are asking a minnow about the workings of whales."

"And sharks," Einstein said, smiling, "do not forget about the sharks. They are everywhere." Gödel shook his head in agreement.

"I don't even know where the file is, physically."

"OSS in Washington, at their office on Navy Hill. Let us assume Wild Bill orders the file released to you one week from today, next Thursday. When could we see the file?"

"I have a day job here, remember. But I suppose I could get down there on Thursday or Friday night. I don't even know if they'd let me take the whole thing or make a copy."

"They will make a copy but we will have to return it. The copying will take one day. Let us assume just to be safe that you will have it by Sunday. Professor Gödel, are you here Sunday after next?" Gödel nodded yes. "Wonderful. Then let us now discuss the technical issues I mentioned."

We talked the rest of the lunch hour about how, exactly, we should continue with my surveillance and recording. I mentioned that they were a little too heavy handed in their discussions about Schlick, and Einstein laughed.

"I find that one cannot be too loud, obvious, or repetitive with those in government. But you are our FBI man, Charlie, so we will follow your suggestion."

I also told them they should subtly criticize communism to help DBS get it out of his thick head that Einstein is a Russian agent.

"Are they still obsessed with that?" asked Einstein. "I know the Army is worried, but I thought Hoover was satisfied."

"It's one of his underlings," I explained.

When I told him the code name for the operation—Felix and Rolf—he couldn't stop laughing. When I told him it was a sophomoric alphanumeric substitution code, he perceived the code at once, and said, sniggering, "I hope the FBI code makers and code breakers are more sophisticated than this man. And yet, the names are perfect, no?"

Composing himself, he then said, "Alright, we will add to our very subtle expressions of worry about the Schlick murder somewhat less subtle denunciations of communism. You will continue to follow us and tape our performances in the mornings and afternoons, and we, for now, will continue to meet here for lunch."

"I have a suggestion about that. We can't continue to come here, or really go anywhere public because your celebrity draws people, people draw newspaper stories, and soon my bosses will want to know why I am lunching with you."

"He is right, Albert."

"Ach, of course he is. It is my blindness about publicity. I hate it so that I fail to consider it in my calculations."

"Or love it so," Gödel added, with a wry smile.

"Yes. I admit it. You know me so well, my Aristotle."

I suggested we meet at IAS, but Einstein said that would be even worse, with the tourists and reporters waiting to see him. "And my colleagues there are the worst gossips of all. They will pester me about who this third man is, allowed to meet with the mighty Gödel and Einstein." Gödel shook his head in agreement. That's when I thought of the bowling alley, Tiger Lanes. It even had a snack bar, so we could have lunch. Einstein loved the idea.

"But you will have to wear a disguise," I said. "At the very least a ball cap. Do you need one?"

"A drawerful. I have been to several baseball games and at each one they give me caps." I could see that this prospect of wearing a disguise was really exciting him.

"Don't wear a Red Sox cap down here, that will attract attention. Dodgers, Giants, or Yankees would be safest. And tuck your hair in."

"I have many Brooklyn Dodgers caps. I will wear one of those.

"And dark glasses," I suggested.

"How should I dress?"

"Is there any way you could find clothes without all those wrinkles in them?" He smiled. That's when he told me about his twin folding disease: ineptness at folding and a powerful jealousy to do his own folding.

"I will ask my housekeeper to fold the clothes. She will be delighted. She has been begging me for years. What should Professor Gödel wear?"

"I think he'll be fine as is. But why don't you give him your ski cap instead of that fedora."

That night, I couldn't concentrate on the translations. I kept thinking about one thing: what exactly to say to Chris Conner at this futile meeting to discuss the OSS file. And then a second thought swirled around like yesterday's wind: Why, really, does Einstein need me?

PART 2

INVESTIGATION

CHAPTER 8

SCHLICK WAS ON HIS way up the stairs to deliver one of his interminable and idiotic lectures. I stood at the top of the staircase, my Sig Sauer hidden in my bookbag. I was surprised that I was not afraid. Fear comes from uncertainty, and I knew exactly what would unfold, not the details of course, but the trajectory of larger events. I was alive with the frisson of agency, of budding action. Schlick would die.

I reached into the bookbag and touched the cold gun. Soon it would be warm. I placed my hand around its grip. Its rough surface felt like sandpaper. The trigger guard, by comparison, was mirror smooth, and I was careful to place my index finger inside it but behind the trigger. I released the grip safety with my thumb. I was ready.

Sniveling sycophants surrounded him like flies, so it was impossible for me to get a clean shot while he was still on the stairs. That would have been my preference. It would have made an impressive tableau. Even after he reached the top, the flies still buzzed.

Then he saw me, and seeing me caused him to excuse his adoring pests and they began to disperse into the lecture hall. He walked toward me. Time slowed down. I pulled the gun out of the bookbag and I saw him see it. I moved my index finger to the front side of the trigger and began firing. The sound was deafening, ricocheting off the marble walls, the stone steps and the fifty-foot arched ceiling. I'm not sure where the bullets struck him, but I was sure he was dead. Nothing moved but the growing puddle of blood. It even cascaded down the top stair, dramatically.

They kept asking me, over and over, why I shot him. I kept telling them, over and over, that I shot him because he was one of those degenerate logical positivists. That is all there was to it, but they did not seem to believe me. Yet they were friendly. They did not like that Jew-loving decadent any more than I did. But they could not believe anyone would kill for philosophy. I cannot believe anyone would not kill for philosophy. Philosophy is everything, and who would not kill for everything? I tried to explain it to the lead detective. He seemed smart enough. But he kept asking about Sylvia.

I admitted I love her, and she loves me. She may have been enamored of Schlick, in the beginning. Lots of them were. I was. He was charismatic. But she never slept with him. I am sure of that. She loves me.

I must say that I was pleasantly surprised when they arrested me. I twice told them I was going to kill Schlick, and they did nothing, except to send me to hospital. The doctors there were even duller than the detectives. I spent weeks that melted into months discussing my mother with them. They were all Jews, I am sure, talking to me about my childhood like that Jew fraud Freud. I refused medications they said would clear my mind. I knew they wanted to cloud it. So they drugged me at night.

The people in charge of the people in charge of the murder case did not want to send me to prison. I understood the game they were playing. They wanted me to pretend I was crazy. Party officials twice visited me after my arrest, and explained that if I feigned insanity, they could protect me from the Jew prosecutors trying to hang me. But I explained about Platonic truth, and told them I could never violate my oaths to it. I also suspected some of the architects of the entire strategy, maybe even the party members, were secret Jew agents sent to kill the killer of logical positivism.

My trial would shine a pure and terrible light on their debauched philosophy. All the members of their "Vienna Circle," as they so egotistically called themselves, would continue to scatter like the cockroaches they are. Logical positivism would die, and my suffering would be vindicated. That is all I wanted. If I became a hero and they insisted that I take a chair at the University, I would not refuse. But I would die happy just knowing their satanic creed was dead.

I knew what the old men would say. That Heidegger should become the new leader once the Circle was finished. His heart is in the right place, but his tired old metaphysics simply do not have the horsepower to eradicate the Circle. If they did, I would not have had to kill Schlick.

If Heidegger reigned after I killed logical positivism with my testimony, he would be too weak to keep it dead. He is no match for those sophists, who are now beginning to spew their bile safely from England and America. I would be happy to take up the crown, and I would be much better than Heidegger. But if not me then we need another strong young philosopher, not a tired old metaphysicist.

The detectives and the doctors asked me over and over whether I planned to kill the other members of the Circle. I explained to them that that was unnecessary. My trial, not Schlick's death or anyone else's, would kill logical positivism, and then my work would be done.

My memories of the trial are a little hazy, no doubt because of the medications they continued secretly to give me. I remember the light in the courtroom during my testimony was so wonderfully bright and cleansing. It was the same light I saw when I discovered, in that instant of divine insight, that Schlick and Hahn and their sycophants were so terribly wrong. The light that flared when I burned my shameful dissertation, page by disgraceful page. The light so powerful that the judges pretending to be in charge, sitting in their black robes and white wigs atop carved and twisted dark woodwork, were empty silhouettes.

I am a modest man, but I was brilliant throughout my testimony. The lawyer they gave me, who insisted just a little too often that he was not a Jew, pleaded with me to say as little as possible. That I killed Schlick because he was a Jew-loving philosopher whose poison would kill Western civilization. Just that. But that would have been useless. People needed to understand *why* this philosophy was poison. I demolished it like Plato demolished the Sophists.

My headaches disappeared. The beast was dead. Now philosophy could shed the carcass of the Vienna Circle, stop its love affair with that queer Wittgenstein, and get on with things. If it wanted me to be part of the journey, that would be fine. Better me than Heidegger. But I would be content just in playing my small part.

I dreamt of retirement, Sylvia and I living high in the Alps, perhaps in Feldkirch, a beautiful village where my family sometimes summered. Our children frolicking in the cold river in the surprisingly warm mid-summer, all of us playing word games and reading by the fire in snowbound winters. I would of course see any visitors who wished to discuss philosophy. But my fighting days are over. It would be delicious to watch the cockroaches die (dear parole officials—this is metaphorical only) from lack of academic oxygen. Logical positivism was dead, killed by a reformed acolyte. A new Plato, if I might suggest without any false modesty.

I was of course convicted because I in fact killed Schlick. Truth will out. I was of course given early parole because I in fact deserved it.

Justice will out. Technically, it was justifiable homicide, as the legal idiots call it, and I should not have been convicted of any crime. I suppose I understood that we could not plead that defense, that it would be better theater if my life seemed to hang in the balance. That it would be better for the party, more heroic, if they snatched me from the Jews' clutches and declared me a hero. After all, justified crime is what any poor soul would do in the circumstance. No poor soul could slay the Circle (again, metaphor). We needed a Thor. It was my sacred duty.

As planned, they had first to sentence me to prison. The silhouettes imposed ten years. The party officials told me I would actually have to serve only a short time before being paroled, not just to make it all look good but also to smoke out more Jew sympathizers, who would applaud the harsh sentence and then decry the parole. It was a brilliant plan.

I actually didn't mind those two years. They housed me in a delightful facility, not a place for rapists or other degenerates. I did have to stay in the "cell" most of the day. But it was a fine, cozy room, much warmer in the winter and cooler in the summer than my old flat near the University, with a reading lamp and comfortable chair, and all the books I requested. I did some important work there, about which you will soon read in the journals, rebuilding philosophical thought after the destruction of destruction. Sylvia did not visit me or write, but that was also all part of the plan.

On the day of the Anschluss, I had just completed a particularly difficult part of my argument. I heard the news spreading through the prison, the church bells of tin cups on bars pealing down the prison's echoing valleys. I stopped working and cried in joy. Not just for myself, but for the promise of this new era. It was no accident that my philosophy and Germany's ascendence became fated at the same instant. We were blessed by the same gods, there was now no doubt. Though I did not really doubt before.

Many of the others were political prisoners like me, sure now that reunification would mean our freedom. And it did, for most. I was actually rather sorry when I was paroled. I was making such progress with the work. The parole officials winked and told me I must stay in Vienna—as if I would want to flee with the cockroaches!—and report to them periodically. The reporting grew less and less frequent, and after several years I hardly reported at all. The University did not reach out, but I knew that was part of the plan.

Parole officials found me an important wartime job at the Austrian Department of Economic Oil Authority. The work, though trivial, was somehow all-consuming and exhausting. I had almost no time for philosophy. I found a small flat near Stephansplatz. Life was good. No visitors, but I knew that, too, was part of the plan. I could bide my time. I had been doing so my whole life.

CHAPTER 9

We met at the snack bar inside Tiger Lanes. It was raining lightly, which would be perfect for Einstein's baseball cap. The bowling alley was almost empty. One young couple was bowling down on Lane 1, and there were no customers at the snack bar's single small counter. A glum teenager manned both snack bar and bowling desk. He was at the bowling desk wiping down shoes, spraying their insides with disinfectant, then slamming them into size-marked cubbies. When I arrived and stood at the snack bar counter, he slowly approached.

"What can I get you?"

"I'm waiting for two others."

He went back to the bowling shoes without saying a word. I started to think about what life would be like working here, and decided it would probably be good. Feeding people and helping them have fun, all in the same place. What was he so grouchy about? It must be external to Tiger Lanes. Girlfriend problems, perhaps. Or a father or brother killed at Pearl Harbor.

Tiger Lanes was perfect. I wondered why I hadn't thought of it before. I'd taken Susan Ciecwisz here a few times. We had loads of fun. I never really bowled much back home. She loved it so much she suggested that we join a league. No way was I going to complicate my already complicated girlfriend juggling situation by committing to that! Plus, it seemed like it would become a job if you actually had to go every week.

There were 14 glass-smooth lanes. This was still in the days of the pin boy, so none of the lines of sight between the shared scoring tables at the beginning of each pair of lanes was interrupted with those monstrosities that now deliver back the ball automatically. I could see all 14 lanes and seven scoring tables from my perch at the snack bar. I watched the couple down on Lane 1 throw a few balls, and the pin boy reset the pins. He wasn't too frantic, with just one lane going.

I let out an audible guffaw when my two co-conspirators walked through the front doors. Einstein had his hair stuffed into his Dodgers cap, not a single strand escaping, and he was wearing a pair of dark glasses, though they were that cardboard kind you get at the eye doctor's. Couldn't the internationally acclaimed Nobel Prize-winning physicist have borrowed a real pair of sun glasses? Maybe from a singing cowboy? I made a mental note to buy him some.

He was wearing a thick black longshoreman's coat over what looked like dark blue dungarees. When he took off his coat—which he did proudly long before reaching the snack bar—I saw he was wearing garageman overalls, complete with his name—Ed—embroidered in cursive over his right breast pocket. His face was a bit smudged, not too much, and his hands were gray—exactly the kind of gray you get trying to wash off grease with regular soap. The tips of his nails were even striped with ribbons of black.

His colleague was dressed the same, though his head was topped with one of Einstein's red ski caps, which he removed as he entered. Underneath Gödel's black longshoreman's coat, which reached almost to his ankles, were the work clothes of Bob. I noticed that Bob's face and hands were completely free of any dirt or grease. Apparently, Bob drew the line.

"Hello, Ed. Hi, Bob. I'm so glad you could come." I was smiling and trying not to laugh.

"Not only that," Einstein said, "but we have the entire afternoon off, so we can play some nine pins. I have not done so since I was a boy and my father took me to Salzburg for a concert. After the concert we played at a nine pins parlor. He told me not to tell my mother, and it stayed our secret."

The dour teenager walked up behind the snack bar and asked us whether we would be eating or bowling first. Einstein asked, "Could we order the food now and eat it down in the nine pins area while we roll the balls?"

"Sure, but no eating up on the lanes. You need to eat in the chairs behind the scorer's table. What can I get for you?" The menu, posted on a single sheet of typing paper hanging from the front of the short counter, was quite limited. Burgers, fries, a few kinds of cold sandwiches.

"I would like a hamburger," Ed said.

"How would you like it?"

"Medium, please."

"Anything with that?"

"Yes, I would like French fried potatoes and a Coke with the hamburger."

"I'll have the same, but well-done, and could you put a slice of cheese on mine please?"

"On mine too," Einstein said.

"And what would Bob like?" the boy asked, reading the pocket signature.

"Bob is on a special diet from his doctors," I explained, seeing Gödel holding a brown paper bag. "He brought his lunch with him."

"We're not supposed to allow outside food, see the sign? But since they aren't from around here, I'll let it go this time."

"My colleague and I thank you for your kindness," Einstein said, bowing. I started to pull out my wallet to pay, but Einstein elbowed me away, taking his wallet out of the back overalls pocket that also had a dirty red rag hanging from it.

"Let me put these burgers on, and then I'll meet you over at the desk and get you shoes and a lane," the teenager said.

"May we have Lane 14 so we don't bother those people on 1?" I asked.

"Sorry, we just have one pin boy now, so I'll have to put you down on Lane 2, right next to them."

I glanced at Einstein, and he nodded his acquiescence, saying, "Perhaps if we speak in our native tongue, we will disturb them less."

Einstein insisted on paying for the bowling, too. He whispered in German, "Do you know how much they paid me for that Nobel Prize? I would not be able to spend it all in two lifetimes."

"Where did you get these outfits?" I asked Einstein, also in German.

"My car mechanic. I told him a friend and I were attending a costume party. Are they not wonderful, and perfectly effective?" They were. "He told me they were also perfect for gardening, and insisted that I keep both of them for that purpose. So we may continue with this perfect disguise, but I do have to return these lovely black coats."

Ed and Bob went down to Lane 2, and Ed put on his bowling shoes. I hung around the snack bar to mention one last thing to the teenager. These were times—they seem so long ago—when manners required men to remove their hats when they went indoors. What have we come to? First, no one wears real hats anymore. Fedoras, trilbies, homburgs. They are all extinct, except on insecure pony-tailed 20-year-olds trying to look sophisticated for their 19-year-old girlfriends. Only ball caps now. Ball caps and a smattering of ski caps.

Now I see men—men old enough to know better—wearing their ridiculous ball caps inside, everywhere. Even in restaurants, while eating! It is an abomination. But back then, in 1942, in the middle of a world war, there were still manners. Making up an excuse for Ed's cap was Ed's idea, and he even came up with the cover story, if you'll pardon the pun.

"One other thing," I said to the teenager, who was now scraping down the grill to prepare it for our burgers. "Ed, my taller friend, had a terrible accident at the garage last month. They had to do brain surgery, and it left him half bald with an ugly scar. He's pretty sensitive about it, which is why he keeps his cap on."

"OK with me," the teenager replied, shrugging his shoulders and dropping a basket of frozen fries into the fryer.

"And his eyes are so sensitive he needs to keep his sunglasses on under these bright lights." The teenager shrugged again.

When I got down to Lane 2, Einstein was already speaking to the young bowling couple. I heard him apologize for his hat, for his sunglasses, for being right next to them, and for speaking in a foreign tongue amongst ourselves.

"What language will you be speaking, where are you from?" the girl asked.

"Do either of you speak German?" Ed asked.

"No. We both took Spanish in high school."

"We are from Denmark. I asked about German because Danish sounds a bit like German."

I was worried. Seven out of every ten young people in Princeton were university students, and almost every Princeton student had run into Einstein at least once somewhere on campus. I heard the young couple say they were from out of town, which relieved me. Still, I was worried that it would be impossible for Einstein to ignore them, even after we started speaking German, and that at some point these two would recognize the most famous scientist in the world if he kept talking to them and they kept looking at him. To my great relief, they finished shortly after we began.

"Nice to meet you, Ed, I hope you recover from your surgery," the young woman said as they were leaving, waving.

"Goodbye Deborah and Ken."

We continued to speak in German, Einstein smiling constantly, and occasionally howling with joy, during the bowling. He and Gödel were both very interested in the geometrical implications of the tenth pin, and the triangular way the pins were set, so different from the diamond-shaped method in nine pins.

Gödel didn't bowl. He could lift the lightest of the balls for children, barely, but said he simply did not have the energy to bowl. He spent the first few frames sketching out his calculations for where the ball must hit to knock all the pins down. He correctly avoided the amateur's intuition that one should hit the head pin right on its nose.

"No, Herr Professor Einstein," he advised as Einstein announced this very strategy, "according to my estimate of the mass of the ball, the mass of the pins, and the distance between the pins, such an entry point will leave many pins at the ends of the back row standing, depending of course on the velocity of the ball and its angle of entry."

"I am the physicist," Einstein said half-jokingly, slapping poor Gödel on his back. "If we want to know whether the axioms for this game are complete, we will ask you. But as for the real world, I will continue to aim for the center pin."

All these fancy strategies were of course completely irrelevant in practice, since Einstein mostly threw gutter balls, with an inconsistent smattering of ones and twos clipped off at either side. "It is these damn sunglasses!" Despite his failures, he was so taken by the game that we couldn't talk about our plan until he threw the last ball.

After getting bored with the geometry of the pins, Gödel began to lean over my shoulder as I was scoring. It wasn't long before he complained that I had made an arithmetic error. It was after I made a spare, so I explained the rules for scoring strikes and spares, after which he took over the scoring.

"These are good rules. They incentivize the knocking of all the pins down, though at the cost of overstating the total number of pins knocked down, but of course these totals may easily be recovered."

Einstein upbraided me for not throwing a second ball after my first strike, until I explained the rule, including the special rules for the tenth frame. Gödel said immediately, "With these rules I calculate that the maximum score is 300. Have you ever scored this maximum, Herr Richards?" Of course I had not, and told him so. "Herr Professor Einstein, the maximum you could now attain in this game is 146, and your maximum Herr Richards is 278."

"Stop bothering us with your trivial arithmetic, Bob," Einstein grumbled, then threw his ball. A strike! An accidental strike. Perhaps anger, even feigned, improved his bowling.

At one point after I threw my ball and was returning to the chairs behind the scoring table, Einstein said, "Your German is excellent, though I detect a southern accent. Most non-native speakers learn the harsh Prussian version."

"I learned German from my grandmother. She was from Salzburg."

"Ah, Salzburg is such a beautiful city! When did your grandmother emigrate?" I felt a little bit like poor Gustav Fleckt trying to answer my non-trick tricky questions, though I knew Einstein was just trying to develop some rapport between us.

"I'm not sure. Probably at the turn of the century."

It was good to speak to them in German. Einstein was incredibly eloquent, his German a sing-songy blend of seriousness and child play, just like the man himself, all of which became more palpable in his native tongue. Gödel spoke German with even more precision than he spoke English.

I ended up rolling a 158 and Einstein a 46. The moment we were done, Einstein called us back to the chairs behind the scoring table like a teacher calling students back from recess. The suddenness of the change was jolting. His whole bearing transformed in an instant. One moment he was an eight-year-old boy frustrated at all the gutter balls, ecstatic at the strike, and then suddenly a 63-year-old man desperately trying to save his friend's sanity.

I had finished my burger and fries between throws, but Einstein and Gödel had been too busy concentrating on the bowling to eat. So, the meeting took place with Einstein munching on his cold burger and fries and Gödel making noise with his celery.

I expressed doubt to Einstein about whether I should even ask for a meeting to request the OSS file. If Einstein had this whole thing wired, then why not wait for the wiring? He explained again that it was essential for this to look, to as many people as possible, as if this request were coming from me. That would be the cover that would hide the real reason for the inquiry—Gödel's mental illness. But when I expressed these doubts, Einstein seemed to change his tack.

"How long would it take you to check in the FBI files first? If there is something there that will assure Professor Gödel, then we might avoid the risks of getting OSS involved."

"I can't imagine there would be anything in them."

"Check not just in the Schlick and Nelböck files, but in Professor Gödel's too, and mine." Nelböck was the name of the Nazi student who murdered Schlick. Johann Nelböck. I still thought it unlikely there'd be anything in any of the files, but agreed to check that night.

"One other thing," I said. "We probably can't meet here more than once a week. Not many people bowl more than that. So we need to think of a few other locations, and perhaps some other disguises." We agreed to meet in two days in Gödel's IAS office.

"There is a fire escape right next to his window, at the back of the building," Einstein explained. "I will obtain for you the uniform of the maintenance workers and have it delivered to you tomorrow night. You can pretend to be working on the fire escape. We will let it down for you at precisely noon."

"Why don't I just walk right into the office through the front doors, if I will be dressed like a maintenance man?"

"No, there are real maintenance men there all the time. It is still a relatively new building, and things are always going wrong with it. The fire escape is on the south side. The area between the building and the canal is remote. I often repair there when the weather is fine. No one ever goes there. And a large stand of birch trees along the canal blocks it from that direction."

Einstein would have made a good spy.

CHAPTER 10

I TOOK THE TRAIN to the Greenwich Village file room that night, and was surprised to find that we did have a file about the Schlick murder. But it was only three pages long, just a summary of what sounded like a comprehensive OSS report to which it frequently referred. A copy of the OSS report was not contained in the FBI file.

The good news was that, according to the OSS, Nelböck was not a threat to Einstein and was still living in Vienna, on parole. The bad news was that the OSS report was dated June 10, 1941, ten months ago. For all OSS knew, Nelböck might be right here in Princeton today.

The two men struggled a little with the mechanism to lower the fire escape, arguing. When they finally got it down, I had to jump a bit to grab onto the lowest rung, but after that the climb was not difficult. When I reached the open window and hauled myself through it, both men were there, smiling at my maintenance uniform.

"I have a lightbulb that needs replacing," Einstein said as he bent toward me to read my name on the uniform, "Tim."

"And the toilet on this floor is overflowing," Gödel added with a smile, though he was coughing and sneezing up a storm.

"Fine, fine, I'll get to all those jobs as soon as Ed and Bob tune up my car."

Gödel's office looked like someone had just moved out. It was devoid of any evidence of occupation, save a blackboard full of remarkable writing. The writing was not much larger than the print in a book, and in fact looked like print. It was astonishing that this precisely formed and spaced writing could have been made by free hand with a piece of chalk. It covered the entirety of the sliding blackboard, and I assume its companion behind.

I must have visibly blanched when I first saw it, because Einstein took my arm and said, "Although it is difficult to read from a distance, these are very important sketches of a proof for the independence of the axiom of choice, on which Professor Gödel has been working."

There was one desk, on which sat a black phone, and one small upholstered chair behind the desk. One of the two built-in bookcases was half full of books and loose manuscripts, all neatly organized. The other was empty. There was one large calendar on the desk, a sheaf of blank paper, one pen, and one inkwell. There was nothing on any of the walls. No art, no photographs of a smiling Kurt and Adele, no knickknacks, no potted plants, not a single thing identifying this as the lair of the new Aristotle.

Einstein's office, which I visited often after this whole mess was finished, was right across the hall. It was a bit larger, but it was stuffed to the gills so it seemed half as large. It was set up just like Gödel's, a built-in blackboard on one wall flanked on each side by narrow floor to ceiling bookcases. Einstein's desk was twice the size of Gödel's, or at least that's my assumption because no part of the desk surface was visible on any of my visits. Manuscripts, books open and flipped over, loose papers, pens, and innumerable unidentified objects were always strewn across the desk, the only constant the brown leather-covered tobacco tin and attached pipe holder. This growth across the desk surface was not flat. It was a city skyline. Half a dozen skyscrapers of books and papers threatened to topple. There was no workspace at all, except that I imagined all of it was workspace.

Both of Einstein's bookcases were stuffed with books and manuscripts, not one of them oriented to the vertical. Some were seeping out of the bottom layers, like lava that had cooled to sediment just in time to prevent it from dripping over the sides.

There was hardly any space on either of the free walls, which were covered with artwork—mostly impressionist—and photographs. Photographs of Einstein with dozens and dozens of different friends, maybe a hundred. There was a collage of photographs of Einstein's lifelong friend from his patent office days, Michele Besso, and another of Einstein, Maja, and Margot in various places across the globe. Torn pieces of paper, adorned with equations and illegible German, were taped to the walls everywhere there was no painting or photograph.

There was hardly any open floor space between the oversized desk, a small couch and four side chairs. The surfaces of the couch and side chairs were also hidden under this debris of genius.

Einstein's blackboards were full, but his ramblings were much larger than Gödel's. The first time I saw them he had drawn a half dozen boxes filled with formulae and connected with arrows. There were a lot of questions marks. It was all just as crazy looking as Gödel's, but not as constipated.

"What have you learned from the FBI files?" Einstein began.

"Good news," I said, pulling out my small note pad. "The FBI and OSS did do investigations into Schlick's murder and concluded that Nelböck was just a loon who acted alone." I didn't mention that the FBI file was just summarizing the OSS report. "They were specifically charged by Hoover and Donovan with determining whether Nelböck posed any threat to either of you." Einstein flashed a smile which I took to mean he was happy they were looking after Gödel and not just him. It was one of my exaggerations. The FBI report didn't mention Gödel at all.

"They concluded he did not. He was not acting on orders from anyone. He had some kind of mental breakdown. It was from a combination of jealousy over some woman he imagined Schlick was stealing from him, and an irrational hatred of the philosophy of logical positivism, which he was sure was going to destroy western civilization if he didn't do something about it. He was sentenced to 10 years in prison, served two, and is now on parole. He is living in Vienna and works for the," here I looked down to read from my notes, "Austrian Department of Economic Oil Authority."

"May I see a copy of the file?" Gödel asked.

"I didn't make one. I couldn't. It is a secured file, and they weren't even supposed to let me see it let alone copy it. I had to charm my way in."

"I must see the file," Gödel insisted.

"It is not that we do not trust you, Charlie," said Einstein, "but the file would be useful to get the context of the investigation, and to give my colleague additional comfort. This is good news, indeed, especially about Nelböck's whereabouts, but I am afraid that if we cannot get a copy of the FBI file, we will need to proceed with the OSS file."

"Well, I can't get a copy of the FBI file. We can't order copies of secured files."

"What was the date of this report about Nelböck's whereabouts?" Gödel asked.

I pretended to check my notes. "Either I didn't write it down or there was no date," I lied.

"You could photograph the pertinent parts," Einstein suggested.

"I doubt I could get in again, but I'll try. I'll need a small camera."

"Surely you can just check one out at the FBI Emporium," Einstein joked.

"No, no I can't."

"We will have one for you tomorrow morning."

"One other thing before we break up," I said. "We need some anti-communism from you, not just Stalin-bashing. And try to tone down your socialist instincts. Praise capitalism, that's what we need."

We agreed to meet the day after next, during their morning walk, no costumes. It would be a quick meeting. If I were able to photograph the file, I would just hand the camera and film back to them. If not, we would just agree about the next meeting place to talk about next steps.

Gödel didn't make it, he was ill. I told Einstein I went back to the file room but couldn't get into the secured files. I said there was a different file clerk there who did not know me, and was not as accommodating as the first. I gave him back his miniature camera.

I felt especially bad lying to him in German. I hadn't even tried to go back to the file room. I knew a second trip would likely be futile and risky, plus the FBI file was not going to satisfy either of them. And if they got photos of the actual file, they'd see how I'd exaggerated it by claiming the FBI was worried about Gödel too and that it did its own investigation, when in fact it cared only about Einstein and was clearly just parroting OSS. And, of course, Gödel would see the troubling date of the OSS report.

I would have to enter the whole viper's nest of telling my old boss, Chris Connor, that I needed the OSS file. For the first time during Operation Fritz and Rolf, I was panicked. My mind raced with all the possible outcomes of requesting the OSS file. Even with Einstein's help from Roosevelt, I could see only bad outcomes—a few really bad ones. And I was starting to think nothing would ever satisfy poor Gödel.

That night I had a dream, which was unusual for me. At least it was unusual for me to remember my dreams. I was riding on a bus when I suddenly noticed there was a steering wheel on the back of the seat in front of me. After just a few moments I realized I was driving the bus, but I couldn't see where I was going. People from the front were shouting instructions to me. But by the time they shouted and I followed their commands it was too late. The bus was crashing into cars and light posts and people. Then I realized all I needed to do was to stop. I looked down and although there was a gas pedal there were no brakes. People were screaming from the carnage. Then I woke up.

I was doing well at work, of course. My supervisors never said it, though I knew they wondered why such a talented man was analyzing reports on oil production. The plan was working like Pascal's calculator. Slow, relentless, perfect, every step moving closer to the correct ending, though my headaches had returned.

We had created the story of an isolated man, probably insane, working far below his level of expertise. We were waiting. Waiting for the Jews and their sympathizers, who had celebrated my prison sentence, now to deride my parole. And of course, for logical positivism to finish burning down. Though without any foundation, it was a thick-walled building, stuffed full of outdated furniture. It would take some time for it to be consumed by the truth of my remarkable testimony. But at least it was aflame, of that there was no doubt. The cockroaches had already begun their crawl to the west.

The insect Hahn died in surgery. I am sure my national socialist colleagues had a part in his destruction. Had Hahn survived, I would probably have decided to kill him instead of Schlick. Hahn had become the self-proclaimed leader of the Vienna Circle, and his murder would have been even more spectacular. But it all turned out well. I wasted ten years of my life monkey-dancing for Schlick, and was happy to kill him, though I would have preferred to strangle him.

Heidegger is getting all the attention now, as I knew he would, and this is fine as long as someone emerges to help him. I will be happy to oblige once the traps are all sprung, but, as I have already said, I am also fine with a quiet retirement, like Cincinnatus.

Sylvia has not returned any of my letters, and I had hoped that it would be safe now for us at least to correspond. Meeting in person would be out of the question this soon. But I had hoped the letters could begin. Patience, my parole officer counseled me. Officials were no doubt holding a hundred letters from Sylvia, and the 327 that I had written to her since my arrest. The letters would soon reunite, presaging our own splendid reunion.

The Jew doctors, whom my parole officer said I must continue to see—all part of the plan—prescribed some new medications for me when I reported the return of my headaches. I thanked them and then threw the pills away, as I had done with all the others. A mind capable of orchestrating the destruction of logical positivism was not diseased. Their Jew medicines would only fog my continued work.

I was trying to keep up with the philosophy journals to watch for signs of the implosion. It was becoming increasingly difficult to get them from England and America, which had their Jew publishing monopoly in the west. And the Viennese journals, still the most prestigious, had gone almost completely silent once war began.

When the journals trickled in, from the west and a smattering from Vienna, I was not at all surprised to see that logical positivism's death went unreported. The dandy Wittgenstein, safe in his hole in Cambridge, remained an object of irrational reverence. Several of the journals also seemed to have been taken in by the newest fad: this incompleteness nonsense from that crazy weakling Gödel. Fine. These detours would make it all the more magnificent when these so-called "prestigious" journals would have to write logical positivism's obituary.

CHAPTER 11

EINSTEIN WAS GOING TO be out of town the rest of the week, so we agreed to next meet at Tiger Lanes the day after his return. It was clear he wanted to bowl again.

I had the identical lunch as before, but Ed tried the turkey and Swiss, much to his disappointment. He reported it tasted like "powdered milk and cardboard." Bob, eating something mashed—I think it might have been Brussel sprouts because of the smell, but who knew with his exhaust—became obsessed with calculating ball spins and approach angles, and he also kept score. Einstein improved to 59, and I went down to 136.

"Now, let us discuss timing," began Ed. "I am afraid I will be unavailable again most of next week. If we assume Wild Bill"— here I was worried he'd start singing again, but he didn't—"gets the order by the end of next week, and it takes them the weekend to copy the file, let us plan to meet here Monday after next. Are you in town, Herr Professor Gödel, on the sixth?"

"Let me check." Bob pulled out a small notebook from one of his overall's deep front pockets. "Yes, I am here that entire week."

"Good, then we meet here on the sixth."

"What's the hurry? We have all summer," I volunteered, hoping that I could postpone the OSS vipers for a while.

"Herr Professor Gödel is scheduled to spend this summer in Maine, leaving in early June, and we must finish this project before then."

"Herr Professor Einstein is afraid I will kill myself in the depressing wilds of Maine, though I have explained to him I will be in a lovely inn in an actual town," Gödel said with a sad smile.

"I am more worried about your eating and the degeneration of your physical health."

So, we had a deadline of just about a month.

"I will contact my control today, and I might even be able to meet with my old boss tonight if I tell him it's an emergency," I said, already dreading everything about it. I suggested we meet very briefly at the Nassau Inn tomorrow at noon, just for me to give them an update. Einstein promised he would not sing.

Chris was able to meet me that night, at Carlo's. After thanking him again for getting me the Einstein gig, and exchanging a few pleasantries, he asked what this was all about. He looked tired. I'm sure the whole CI unit was exploding with challenges. I told him I needed a file on a guy named Moritz Schlick, because these two German geniuses kept talking about his murder in Vienna, and I needed to know more about the whole thing.

"No problem. It will probably be secured, since it is in country, but you can use my authorization."

"I've already seen the secured file on this. But it just refers to an OSS investigation. I need the OSS file."

He laughed and said just what I knew he'd say. "Charlie, you are just recording them, and translating them. We will do the analysis. Thanks for the info, we will look into it."

I needed to persist a little for show. "No, really, I am worried about the German they are using. It could be a code. Their German sounds stilted every time they talk about this murder case. If some of the things they say about it are flat out wrong, it would confirm my fears."

He laughed and told me I wasn't the only German speaker in the FBI. And that Hoover himself could probably not wrestle that OSS file from Wild Bill. I felt bad about not just coming out and telling him that any day now Hoover will try to get the file and get it to me, and Wild Bill would probably release it. Chris had been so supportive. But I didn't want to blow Einstein's plan. So, I said I'd figured as much, and that I mostly just wanted to get him this information so he could run with it.

That next morning, before I even got out of bed, I got a frantic call from my control, who said in a coded message that I was to meet with him today at noon at—get this—the Nassau Inn. When I got there, my control wasn't there but DBS was. So were Einstein and Gödel. I told them about the surprise meeting on their walk in, but I didn't warn them off because I wasn't sure what the hell was going on. When I got there, they ignored us completely. They were still there when we left.

"What the fuck's going on?" DBS asked before I even had a chance to sit down. He was tall and thin, handsome in an over-coiffed way, and had thick black arching eyebrows that seemed incongruent with his white hair and pale skin. His eyes were close together, so close that his permanently arched eyebrows looked like a single black "M." "And isn't that Einstein and that other guy, right over there?" I decided to answer the last question first. It would give me a little time to think about the first one.

"That's them all right. I wonder why they are eating lunch together. They never do."

"At 7:30 this morning Hoover ordered me get some OSS file for you that just last night you asked Conners for."

"What?"

"You heard me."

"I had no idea. I just thought the file might be helpful for me to understand what these two guys are talking about. They talk about this Schlick guy all the time. It might be a code."

"You are a fucking translator, not an analyst. How did you get to Hoover and Donovan?"

"Are you kidding? They wouldn't wipe their butts with me."

"You're goddamn right." Then DBS frowned his Thinking Frown, as we called it. "The old man must have a separate operation going on, shadowing ours. Shit. But Donovan won't release any files even if Hoover demands it. OK, just keep doing what you're doing. And speaking of that, why the fuck are you not recording their lunch?"

"They never go to lunch. They must have arranged it by phone, or at the office. I'd have no way of knowing. You want me to stake out IAS all day in case they lunch again?"

"No. We'll bug their office and home phones. We need to hear that, too, if they are talking on the phone. We'll tape it and have someone else translate. If they make any more lunch dates, we'll let you know when and where, and you be there. Stay here and finish recording them."

"I don't have my recording stuff."

"Why goddamned not?

"They don't usually head back until 2 or 3, so I take a break over lunch. I left the equipment at my apartment."

"Jesus, Richards, get your head out of your ass. OK, we'll drive you to your apartment now so you can retrieve your recording stuff, then drive you back here. You need to record the rest of this lunch they are having, if they are still here when we get back." They weren't. DBS didn't say another word, but the big vein on the right side of his head spoke volumes.

That night a little after midnight there was a knock on my door. I grabbed my gun. Yes, they gave me a gun and I even learned how to shoot it, barely, at Quantico. I opened the door and a nondescript guy covered in hat, coat, and gloves—looking a little like Gödel but much taller and wider, and without the Barney Google eyes—handed me an envelope. The OSS file. "You will be contacted about its return," he said, then left.

I spent the next hour reading it. OSS's conclusion was that Nelböck was a nut. A really smart nut. He was one of Moritz Schlick's most promising students. There were some signs of instability in his younger student days, getting worse and worse as he worked on his dissertation. There was a report by an OSS psychiatrist about how lots of geniuses, especially philosophy and math types, can be nutters and geniuses at the same time. Anyone spending much time around geniuses knows this.

The OSS report seemed carefully and deeply sourced—they apparently had guys near or maybe even in the Vienna Circle itself long before Schlick's murder. They also had access to police records, court records, and even doctor's records. Man oh man, these OSS guys really seemed to know what was going on over there, at least before December 7, 1941.

The OSS opinion was that Nelböck acted alone, that he was a paranoid schizophrenic whose condition probably exploded during the stress of his graduate work with Schlick, that the Nazis applauded him for killing Schlick and were certainly responsible for his parole, but that neither the Nazis nor any other person had planned or assisted in the murder.

The report also stated, in a highly redacted section, that after the Anschluss, Nazi officials in Vienna, and even a few in Berlin, had concluded that Nelböck's continuing craziness was a political liability, and that "he would have to be watched." Finally, it concluded that neither Nelböck nor the Abwehr nor anyone else known to OSS posed a current threat to Albert Einstein. As with the FBI report, Gödel's name wasn't mentioned.

All of this would be comforting to Einstein, and should be comforting to Gödel. Everything except the date of the report.

CHAPTER 12

I HANDED THE OSS file to Einstein at the beginning of the next morning's walk, and we agreed not to meet again for a full week, to give us time to digest the information in the file and think about next steps, though it wasn't really clear to me what next steps were necessary. It seemed to me that I was done.

In the meantime, Einstein and Gödel continued walking and I continued taping them. They were doing a much better job slamming communism. Einstein took the lead. One time when they were downtown, he said, "Look around us Kurt. Look at these shops. They are full of wonderful products. These products are manufactured because people want them. They fill a need. This economy is a complex self-governing machine. Supply and demand meeting from the bottom up, not in inefficient central planning.

"What does Stalin or his commissars know about this?" he asked, pointing to a child's Indian headdress in a window. "It serves no function, it advances no apparent goal. Communism would never produce such a thing. But it is desired, so it is produced. The goal it serves is happiness, the deepest human goal of all. This giant happiness machine is now turned to the goal of ending this war. Its massive capacity will do just that. It is only a matter of time. And when it shatters Nazism perhaps it can shatter communism along with it."

I was sure this speech alone would convince DBS. Heck, it convinced me. I think even Einstein himself knew he was speaking the truth. But he was also worried that this relentlessly efficient happiness machine was leaving some people out, chewing them up. And also that it was subject to enormous swings that would at times impoverish almost everyone. America was, after all, just a few years past the Great Depression. Thank goodness he didn't say any of that.

I was hopeful the OSS file would do the trick with Gödel, but was worried he was just too far gone. He was smart enough, of course, to see the aching irony in the fact that the man he was sure was going to kill him was himself suffering from paranoia. I discovered many years later that Gödel and Nelböck were treated in the same Viennese sanitorium by the same doctors, though at different times.

Would the OSS file be proof enough for him, or would he declare it incomplete, even accuse OSS of being after him and complicit now in an even bigger conspiracy? I was actually surprised at how restrained he was. We had our next meeting at Tiger Lanes, without bowling. Uncharacteristically, Bob did all the talking, Ed smiling inscrutably at his side.

"First, thank you Herr Richards for all of your efforts on my behalf. I am sure it has complicated your work situation, and I have asked Herr Professor Einstein to do what he can to repair, and perhaps even improve, that situation.

"Second, I also must state that I trust you and trust the integrity of this OSS report. Trust, as you may have gathered, does not come easily to me. But you and this report have calmed me down considerably, subject to the uncertainty of my brain making its own brain measurements. Even though OSS seemed more concerned about Herr Professor Einstein's welfare than mine," he smiled at Einstein and nodded to him, "their lack of interest in me is in fact a net comfort. I now think it highly unlikely the Nazis are planning to assassinate me if they are not planning to assassinate Herr Professor Einstein. And if Nelböck gets further out of hand, they may assassinate him themselves.

"I have reservations, of course. The ones that are obvious. The report is now 10 months old. Nelböck could be dead, but he could also be here in this nine pins parlor. Although I am no logical positivist, I have in the past been involved at the edges of the Vienna Circle, and my incompleteness work has been twisted by men much smarter, and healthier, than Nelböck into some proof of nihilism, that there is no truth at all. In addition, of course, it is difficult to predict the actions of mad men.

"In sum, Mr. Charlie Richards, although I still believe I will be assassinated, by Nelböck or those like him, or now even by the communists, I also believe your work here is done, and I wish you the very best." He smiled sadly, bowed his head a little, and stuck out his thin hand, which I shook. Then I told them about the plan I'd been cooking up.

"Wait, I have a proposal of my own," I said, which I saw surprised them both. "I may not be the cleverest spy, but I think I could protect you from an assassination. I have a gun, and I now know something about surveillance. We could tone down the anti-communism a bit, ratchet up the socialism, and maybe prolong this operation for a few more weeks, at least until Bob here goes to Maine."

"Wonderful idea," said Einstein, and Gödel bowed his head appreciately. "Though maybe we should actually make the anti-communism so extreme that your boss will begin to have suspicions we are falsifying it," Einstein suggested.

"No, I thought of that. I am afraid he is too stupid."

"Very well, then. Thank you, Charlie," and Einstein reached out both hands.

"Wait, that's just half the plan. If you two could somehow explain this incompleteness stuff to me, I could explain to my bosses that this Nelböck character really is a threat to Bob because he has misunderstood the whole thing, and his misunderstanding feeds exactly into the craziness that drove him to kill Schlick. And then they might give Bob protection for the rest of the summer, all through Maine, at least until they can confirm where Nelböck is."

Gödel almost jumped in excitement. "This is a wonderful plan, Herr Richards. It should take me no more than a few hours to teach incompleteness to you."

"But remember I still have the day job. And I was a C student."

"It will take several short sessions," Einstein interjected. "The three of us could meet a few times over the noon hour, sometimes in Kurt's office, sometimes here for a bowling break, and perhaps an evening in Kurt's home—the vultures stalk mine."

"Yes, Adele and I would be delighted to have you as our guest. She would especially be delighted to be able to cook real food for someone other than herself. I might even be persuaded to eat some."

I was more excited than either of them. To tell you the truth, I was not worried too much about Nelböck. He was a nutter and most nutters I'd heard about didn't do planning very well. It would also be hard for any civilian to cross the Atlantic in the middle of this war. Plus, if worse came to worse I could probably pull a few strings with old friends to find out exactly where Nelböck was. And if that didn't work, surely Einstein could find out.

CHAPTER 13

Einstein dutifully spent the next few walking sessions sounding a lot less anti-communistic. It seemed to come naturally to him. I had to tell him not to push his pendulum too far in the other direction. Socialist ambiguity was what we were shooting for.

In the meantime, Kurt Gödel, ably assisted by Albert Einstein, taught me all about incompleteness. Einstein was the better teacher. He saw immediately when I was confused, which was often. Gödel seemed confused about why anybody would be confused. Between them they were perfect.

My first tutorial was over the lunch hour at the Tiger Lanes snack bar. I knew Einstein was excited because Ed didn't want to bowl or eat. I have already summarized this first session, on the hunt for the axiomatic foundations of math. It was perfectly understandable. What wasn't as easy to understand is why they were all so preoccupied with the hunt.

The next session was in the evening at Gödel's bungalow on Linden Lane. The small green house was much nicer on the inside than I had imagined, and more spacious than it appeared from the front, which, as I've mentioned, was really its side. It was tastefully decorated., though a little overstuffed with furniture. I learned later that the Gödels had moved to the house from a larger apartment on Alexander Street that took up the entire top floor of the building, and that Adele was reluctant to part with any of their furniture.

Adele was delightful, even discounting for the fact that anyone would appear outgoing and welcoming next to her reclusive husband. She was a pleasant-looking woman, in whom resided the remnants of younger beauty, and athleticism. She was six year's Kurt's senior, and a dancer. She was taller than he—heck even Einstein, at 5'7," was taller than he. But it wasn't until I saw all three of them together, indoors and for such an extended period, that I realized how short Gödel was. There was something about his thin frame, especially when he was moving, that created an illusion of verticality, an illusion that evaporated when he stood next to Adele. Einstein also shrunk next to her.

At my suggestion, we all spoke German. I figured that was the polite thing to do around Adele, who seemed to speak very little English. Plus, both of them would probably be more comfortable talking math in German, and nothing would get lost in the translation.

Dinner was spectacular. Adele made a Weiner schnitzel that was paper thin and moist. One of the best I'd ever had. Rotkohl, apple sauce, and a delicious spätzle accompanied the schnitzel. Zwetschgenknödel for dessert—plum dumplings sprinkled with sugar and cinnamon. Poor Kurt had only a bit of the rotkohl and apple sauce, and a small dish of cottage cheese.

We had strong coffee with the Zwetschgenknödel, and a good thing. It kept me, just barely, from falling asleep during the imponderable lecture. Gödel, as usual, farted regularly throughout dinner and the lecture, and it felt like Einstein and I were a little more embarrassed by it because Adele was there. But she ignored it like a trooper.

Unlike with the foundations talk, for this lecture Einstein acted largely as Gödel's master of ceremonies.

"Tonight, Herr Professor Gödel will begin with set theory, not just because that is what happened historically, but also because it was set theory that first allowed us to think most generally about formal axiomatic systems, complex systems that arise out of a few rules, and to extend these ideas to infinite systems, like numbers."

The strong coffee was not enough. I cannot lie; the lecture was terrible. In the first place, Gödel talked mostly to himself, facing the small blackboard he had set up in the parlor right off the dining room, even when he wasn't writing on it, which he seldom did anyway. On several occasions Einstein had to tell him to turn around and keep his voice up. And when he did write on the blackboard, his tiny scratchings were unreadable from any distance beyond one foot.

But worse than all of that, this set theory stuff was mind-numbing. It seemed stupid to me, generalized beyond all meaning. OK, so everything in the world can be thought of as consisting of stuff called elements. What are elements? Everything, from what I can figure. And elements can be grouped together into sets. Sure, so what? One set might consist of

Gödel's watch and Einstein's pipe. OK. Another might be one of my guns, Einstein's pipe, and Fatty Arbuckle's pants. It was all so general.

Two sets could be combined into a single set containing all the elements of each, without repeating elements, by an operation they called "union." OK. So we now have one set with Gödel's watch, Einstein's pipe, my gun, and Fatty Arbuckle's pants. So what? Sets could also be compared to see which elements they had in common, by an operation they called "intersection." So now we have a set with just one element—Einstein's pipe. At the risk of being rude and repetitive, so what?

There was one important set that contained nothing at all, cleverly called the empty set. These set theorists were real comedians. The only thing that seemed even remotely interesting was when Gödel mentioned, with what looked like a sparkle in his eye, that sets could themselves be elements of other sets. Ah, now the snake was eyeing its tail.

Toward the end of this snooze-fest Gödel explained that in the last part of the last century this guy Georg Cantor invented set theory and ended up proving there are different kinds of infinities. That finally got my attention. But I would have to wait until next time to learn about that.

This set theory talk was so imponderable that I asked them if I could tape record the rest of their lectures, and they agreed. I was terribly worried, if tonight's session was any guide, that I would have to play the sessions over and over to even begin to get a glimpse of understanding. What if this was just the beginning of stuff I could never hope to understand, let alone explain to Chris Conner in hopes he'd agree to protect Gödel?

It was too bad, really, because the other part of the plan was going so well. DBS had already sent me a message saying we were probably going to have to extend the operation for several weeks. But I couldn't imagine that I'd be able to understand incompleteness in several weeks, not at this rate.

But I was wrong. Everything else was pretty easy, except for that damn axiom of choice, which took me back to that damn set theory.

Things seemed to be stuck. Heidegger never contacted me, even surreptitiously. None of the journals, even the German and Austrian ones, reported that logical positivism was sick, let alone dead. Nothing from Sylvia. Nothing from the University. At least I was doing well at my trivial oil production work.

I decided to visit the University provost to see if he could give me an estimate of how long it would take to smoke out the Jews and get me back on the faculty. I understood it would probably have to be as a Privatdozent, because the plan must unfold slowly. But there must be some unfolding.

I could not get through to him by telephone, and of course I could understand how he was reluctant to put anything in writing by responding to my letters. I would have suggested he telephone me, but I had no telephone. I had to borrow a neighbor's.

Thus, in my last letter I wrote that I would like a meeting with him, understood how he could not put anything in writing, proposed a date and time for the meeting, and advised him to burn the letter after reading it. If this date and time did not work for him, he was to send me a simple note with a different date and time, saying nothing else.

I was sure he would appreciate me being so very careful. When I got no response, I knew my proposed date and time were acceptable to him. When the day came, I asked my supervisor if I could take an extended afternoon break, careful not to mention the University. He of course agreed, since I was such a valuable employee. I must ask for a raise soon, I thought to myself, so I could get a larger flat. One with a proper kitchen and central heating. Perhaps even a telephone.

It was mid-December, snowy and cold. Christmas decorations were everywhere, though there were almost no lights, a precaution against the air bombing we knew would come. This produced a strange atmospheric juxtaposition. Before the war, Christmas decorations were most prominent at night, torches of tiny white lights igniting the City for miles. I must admit that no one did Christmas like the Viennese. Now, with night lighting forbidden, Vienna made up for it with riots of daytime color, everywhere. Bright green bunting dotted with red bows were a perfect counterpoint to the white, red, and black flags of swastikas lining every major street. Vienna was a blushing virgin, flirtatious in the day but locked up at night. Like my Sylvia.

I walked through the snow from Stephansplatz, crowded with market goers. The Christmas market at Stephansplatz is so much nicer, so much smaller and humbler, than that abomination on the Rathausplatz. Humility is a key ingredient in the Germanic character. Real strength need not be showy.

I walked up the white canyons of Brandstätte, where horse drawn carriages and carts still jostled with automobiles for primacy in the narrow street. The snow was heavy. Many of the shops were boarded up. The Jews were gone and soon would be replaced with loyal civic-minded merchants. It would be glorious.

I bore left on Tuchlauben then up Kohlmarkt to St. Peter's. There seemed to be so many sad people, especially near the church. I suppose they just could not see. They lived their lives in the tired old construct, unaware that the universe was being blasted apart by the light of a new order. I suppose this is true of all paradigm shifts. The fleas on the wolf are never aware when the wolf turns.

I was near my old apartment on Teinfaltstrasse. Memories of Sylvia flooded through me unbidden. But now I must shake them and concentrate on my presentation to the provost. Humility, again, was the key. I would humbly request only an estimate of when I could be appointed as a Privatdozent. I would not even broach the subject of full-time faculty, let alone a chair. These things would come once the nails of logic in my papers began sealing the casket lid of logical positivism. Small steps now. It was the plan.

When I arrived at the University the two towers of the Votivkirche greeted me like old friends. This is where I belong, not sitting in some drab office tabulating barrels of oil. I had enlisted in a private war to save this grand place from the infection of positivism, and soon it would be time to return to this home. Not as a conquering hero but as a humble unpaid Privatdozent. With a small class load I could continue working in the evenings for the Oil Ministry and maintain my flat at Stephansplatz. I had not discussed it with them, but my supervisors would surely agree to an evening work schedule. After all, I spoke to almost no one during my workday; there was no reason I could not perform my tabulations and produce my reports in the evening. A year, probably less, then I could join the paid faculty and move to a grander apartment. And even if the bureaucrats never allowed me to join the faculty, surely I could do enough private tutoring to survive as a Privatdozent.

I entered the famous building, and its familiar majesty enveloped me. I walked slowly up the right side of the dazzling central twin staircase, pausing at the top only for a moment, where the dog Schlick had died. Then I proceeded down the large hall to the provost's office.

A little man in the outer office asked if I had an appointment, to which I proudly responded "Of course. Johann Nelböck to see the provost. The appointment is not until 2:30, and I apologize that I am a little early. I will of course wait. Is this chair acceptable?" I asked, pointing to a lovely Louis XIV armchair with gold filigreed wood and a pleasing yellow and blue royal pattern.

"Yes, of course," the little man responded, and then he fluttered into what I assumed was the provost's office. But then I heard yet another set of doors open and close. There must be an inner inner office!

I had never been to the provost's office as a student. I imagined that soon I would be here often. Grand meals over which we would discuss the progress of the Philosophy Department. Difficult decisions about whom to hire and whom to fire, decisions that could be critical in preserving the great philosophical victory. It was there, on the delicate chair, that it occurred to me that my movement needed a clever name. A name to counteract the rot of the so-called Vienna Circle. It came to me. The movement would be called The Austrian Light. I would announce the name in my next paper.

Two large men charged into the office and marched toward the first set of inner doors. "The secretary will be back in a moment," I said to them but they ignored me and continued through the doors, uninvited, and then I could hear them go through the second set of doors.

I thought for a moment that this might be an assassination, and wished I had brought my Sig Sauer. They confiscated the one with which I had killed Schlick, but I quickly acquired another when I paroled, but I had left it at my flat. I could not restrain both these men, or probably even just one of them, using only my hands. But when I heard more suspicious noises from inside, I did my duty despite being unarmed. I threw open the doors and the next ones, rushing past the bewildered little secretary, and asked, "What is going on here? Are you alright, Herr Doktor Provost?"

The provost was sitting at his desk, and although he did not say a word he did not seem in danger or under any threat. The large men were standing on either side of him. The larger of the burly men spoke.

"I am sorry Herr Nelböck, but I am afraid the terms of your parole forbid you from being at the University. We must escort you off the grounds."

I did not argue with them. It was true, I had just forgotten. In all my excitement, I had forgotten about the silly geographic restrictions in the conditions of my parole. They were for show, after all. Still, we had to abide by them, also for show. But then why had the provost not merely suggested another meeting place?

I turned to the secretary as we walked back through his office, and said "This is so embarrassing. Please tell the provost we must meet off

University grounds. If he could send me a note with a proposed time and place, he has my address. Again, I apologize for this intrusion."

I was happier than I had been in years. Just being at the University had energized me, and paradoxically steeled my patience. All of this is worth the wait, I said to myself as I turned on Universitätstrasse and looked back at the building that had nurtured genius for 300 years. I had saved it. Me.

CHAPTER 14

THE NEXT LESSON WAS back at Tiger Lanes. This time, as with the foundations talk, both men did the teaching, although Ed insisted on bowling a game and eating a hamburger first. He bowled 43, a retreat from his improving trajectory, and I rebounded a little with a 145. Ed was especially intrigued when he left a 7–10 split. Bob paid no attention to us, and didn't even do the scoring. I think he was planning his part of the talk.

Ed began. "Last time, Charlie, you asked what all this irritating set theory has to do with mathematics. Even without the benefit of Cantor's formalized set theory, mathematicians had been using it naively to prove things about the foundations of simple mathematics.

"By simple mathematics, we mean the ordinary numbers we use every day, 0, 1, 2, 3, etc., which we call the *natural numbers*, or more technically the *whole numbers* when we include zero, and the ordinary operation of adding those numbers together. Much as we wrote out the rules for rock/paper/scissors, much as Euclid described all of plane geometry with his five axioms, mathematicians articulated nine axioms to describe simple mathematics.

"These are called the Peano Axioms, or PA for short, and they are named after the Italian mathematician Giuseppe Peano, who was one of the first to try to axiomatize the natural numbers. Peano actually started with just five axioms, like Euclid, but others soon realized four more were needed. We need not get into the details here, but we can give you a few examples of the nine to give you a flavor of them.

"The first axiom defines zero as a natural number. Axioms six, seven, and eight describe something called the successor function, out of which all the numbers pour as successors of 0. One is the successor of 0, 2 the successor of 1, and so on. Once we have described the successor function, and all the natural numbers come tumbling out as successors of zero, then the operations of addition and multiplication also follow. Two plus three is a way of describing the third successor after two. Multiplication is just successive addition. Two times three is adding two to itself three times.

"An important thing to remember about these three axioms related to the successor function is that they *describe* the properties of the successor function, but they do not exactly define it. Only with set theory were mathematicians able to define it rigorously.

"There are other axioms needed to fill out the logic of numbers. For example, there is the identity axiom, which says that for every natural number X, X = X."

"That seems needless to say," I reacted.

"Remember, Charlie, lots of these axioms will seem 'needless to say' precisely because they are so deeply embedded in the system, a little like our rule that the rock/paper/scissors players must play simultaneously or that ties are ties and require playing again. The identity axiom is like that, as is another relational axiom, transitivity: for all natural numbers X, Y, and Z, if X = Y and Y = Z, then X = Z."

"We talked about transitivity with the rock/paper/scissors game," I said, but I guess he could tell my eyes were getting that "set theory" look, because he tried to bring me back.

"Yes, a different type of transitivity involving logical inferences. But all you need to know is that these nine axioms of PA *appeared* to describe the entirety of simple arithmetic using the natural numbers. But these early axiom builders could not *prove* it. For that, we needed Cantor's set theory, which not only formalized these ideas, but extended them to infinity, which was useful because numbers go on forever. And in the bargain Cantor showed there are different magnitudes of infinity, and that's what we will be discussing today."

Now, finally, I was interested. Different magnitudes of infinity? I found that hard to believe.

Gödel took over. "What if we wanted to include subtraction as an operation on our natural numbers? Now our set of natural numbers, 0, 1, 2, 3 and so on will not suffice, because, for example, 5 minus 8, which you know is -3, is not a natural number. We say *the natural numbers are not closed with respect to subtraction*, meaning not all natural numbers subtracted from all other natural numbers produce a natural number. So, to complete the number system to allow for subtraction we have to add to the natural numbers all their negative counterparts.

"Now our number system, which is called *the integers*—all the positive and negative whole numbers, plus 0—is closed with respect to addition and subtraction. Every integer added to or subtracted from every other integer is an integer.

"But, you may now ask, what about the other arithmetic operations, multiplication and division? Multiplication is no problem, because, as we have already said, it is just successive addition. So the integers are also closed with respect to multiplication. But what about division?"

I saw now. "Dividing integers by one another will definitely not just produce integers," I said, "because not every integer is wholly divisible by other integers. Most aren't. Five divided by two, for example, is not an integer."

"Quite so. The integers are not closed with respect to division. Now we have to expand our system of numbers to include all fractions, numbers that can be written in the form of X/Y, where X and Y are integers and Y is not zero, if we want our set of numbers to encompass the operation of division. We call this expanded set the *rational numbers*, meaning they can all be written as ratios of integers. The integers are of course also rational numbers, because they can be written as fractions—themselves divided by one, to name just one form.

"Finally, you know from your high school mathematics that not all numbers can be written as ratios of integers. The square root of 2, for example, the number which, when multiplied by itself, equals 2. These are called *irrational numbers*, not because they do not make sense," he said smiling, "but because they cannot be written as a ratio of integers."

I did remember all of that. It turns out, for reasons no one ever explained to us in high school, that there are many square roots of many integers that cannot be written as a ratio of integers. And other roots, too, like cube roots. I also remembered from geometry that the famous pi—the ratio of a circle's circumference to its diameter—could not be written as a fraction. "Like pi," I said.

"Yes, pi is irrational," added Gödel. "It cannot be written as a ratio of integers. All the rational numbers combined with all the irrational numbers are together called *the real numbers*. The real numbers are closed with respect to all ordinary operations of arithmetic, meaning you can perform any of those operations on a real number—addition, subtraction, multiplication, division, most roots—and you still get a real number back.

"Now let us consider the question Cantor asked himself: how many of these different types of numbers there are? How many natural numbers are there, Herr Richards, remembering that the natural numbers are the whole numbers 0, 1, 2, 3, etc."

"They go on forever. There is an infinite number of them. That's what your 'etc.' means."

"And how many integers? Remember, the integers consist of all the natural numbers and their negative counterparts."

"Well, I was going to say an infinite number of those, too, but aren't there twice as many, since they include all the positive and negative whole numbers?"

"Or slightly less than twice," Gödel corrected, "since we have defined zero as a natural number. But in any event, are you saying there is one kind of infinity, then another larger kind?"

"I guess so. I'd never really thought about it. But I can see where you are going. Since the rational numbers include the integers, the rationals are an even bigger infinity, and the same with the real numbers. They include the rationals so they are even bigger."

"Now we are approaching the core of the problem, and Cantor's clever solution," said Gödel, smiling. "And the problem is, as is often the case, that our spoken language is sometimes not precise enough for mathematics. In this case, the imprecise word is 'infinity.'

"To see how imprecise this word is, let us pretend you are in a primitive society that has names only for six numbers: 0, 1, 2, 3, 4, and 5. Everything more numerous than 5 you call 'infinity.'"

"You are from Timbuktu," Einstein said, smiling. "In fact, I understand that some primitive societies have no names for anything beyond 5 or 10, because of course we all began counting on our fingers."

Gödel continued. "Now suppose your chief came to you one day with two bags full of shells, and asked you to determine which bag had more shells. It was close, so you could not just tell from looking at them, or weighing them. You had to count them. But of course this would fail, because your count would show that each bag had an 'infinity' of shells. What would you do?"

"Well, I could group them in groups of five, then count the number of groups."

"But if there were more than five groups?"

"I could group groups of groups." Einstein was smiling and Gödel was getting a little flustered.

"There is an equivalent but simpler way. You could group them by ones. You could reach in and take one shell out of one bag, match it with one shell out of the other bag, and keep doing that until you were left with one empty bag and one bag that was not empty."

"Sure, but I'd better be careful not to mix up the shells or I could never reconstruct the bags of shells for my chief." Einstein started smiling again.

"Yes, yes, after you match them you put them in separate piles. But the point here is that we can distinguish the number of shells in each bag, even though they both have an infinite number, if there is no way to match the shells one-to-one equally; that is, if one of the bags has left over shells."

"I get that."

"Using this notion of infinity, Cantor proved that the infinity of the real numbers is larger than the infinity of the rational numbers."

"That makes sense, because the reals include the rationals. And don't tell me, the infinity of the rationals is bigger than the infinity of the integers, which is bigger than the infinity of the naturals."

"A very tempting intuition to make, but not true at all. The naturals, integers, and rationals are all of equal infinities, or 'cardinalities,' as Cantor put it. Only the reals have a greater cardinality."

"I don't believe it. There just have to be twice the number of integers as natural numbers, because for every positive integer there is a negative one."

"But remember our shells rule: infinities are the same if there is a method of matching every member of one set to every member of the other. When we are comparing a set of numbers to the natural numbers, we can think of this as counting. Indeed, the natural numbers are also sometimes called the counting numbers.

"If we can describe a way of counting the members of any infinite set in a way that will not leave any of them out, then that set, by our shells convention, has the same infinity, the same cardinality, as the natural numbers, even though it will take forever to count them all. So, can you think of a way to count all the integers, both the positive ones and the negative ones, that will leave none of them out?

"I'm not sure."

"There is an easy way: just alternate between them. We have to alternate so we do not get trapped in the infinity of either type."

"I don't understand."

"If we said, 'Let us count all the positive integers first,' then we would never get to the negatives, and vice versa. So we alternate between them. Zero is our first number, just to get it out of the way, then we go to the first positive integer, 1, then we go to first negative integer, -1, then we go back to the next positive, 2, then back to -2, and so on. By this method we will be able to count all of the integers. Therefore, the integers and the natural numbers have the same cardinality."

"But that seems so wrong.

"Yes, is it not wonderful how logic can sometimes disprove the strongest of intuitions?"

"It makes me think that this shells way of counting infinite sets just isn't right."

Einstein stepped in. "The flaw with the shells analogy is that even though the primitive people believe there is an infinity of shells in both bags, we know there is a finite number, and that the primitive people simply ran out of names for numbers.

"So instead of two bags of a finite number of shells, imagine two machines endlessly producing coins. One machine produces them twice as fast as the other, but the speed of the production does not mean the one machine produces 'more' than the other, does it, when each machine can run forever?"

"I suppose not."

"Even on the fast machine, we can count the coins as they are produced, yes?"

"Yes."

"If we can count all of them using the natural numbers then they are the same size as the natural numbers."

"I think I see. If we can match up the elements of infinite sets, then they must be the same size, even though one might grow twice as fast as the other."

"Yes," exclaimed Gödel excitedly. "What, after all, is a mere doubling of the hare's speed when the tortoise can also run forever? It is this conflation of speed with distance, or we would say ordinality with cardinality, that is the source of the powerful, but erroneous, intuition that there must be 'more' integers than naturals."

"I see this perspective, this definition of equal infinities. And that under this definition the integers have the same cardinality as the natural numbers. But what about the rational numbers? Surely they are more numerous, sorry, they must have a greater cardinality than the naturals and integers."

Gödel responded. "Again, your intuition is wrong. You have been led astray by exactly the same conflation of speed and distance, so to speak. You sense that the set of all rationals must be larger than the set of all integers because the rationals are made up of pairs of integers, in the form of fractions, and there are so many 'more' combinations of pairs than there are single integers, no?"

"Exactly."

"But it is a simple matter to show they are of the same cardinality. It is the same method we used to count the integers, but instead of doing our counting by alternating back and forth between positive and negative integers, we alternate between numerator and denominator, precisely to avoid getting trapped in the infinities of either. The details of the proof are unnecessary, but we can show we can count all the rational numbers. So they have the same cardinality as the integers and naturals."

"You say the details of the proof are unnecessary, but I still don't believe the rationals have the same cardinality as the integers. Could you at least describe the proof?"

Here I was, doubting Kurt Gödel like I used to doubt new workers at the Philadelphia Naval Shipyard. "My name is Ralph Boyer, and I was born in Lexington, Kentucky." *Oh really? You don't sound at all like you were born down there.*

Then there was the suspicion injected by my snap surveillance training. My instructor was a wonderful old man, Walt Jennings, though the name, like the man himself, reeked of alias. Walt's training program consisted of three parts: how to be suspicious of everyone; how to tell if one of those everyones is following you; and, finally, how to follow someone in ways that will make it hard for them to tell you are following them.

The first part began with Walt having me walk around the reflecting pool with the task of identifying three of his Bureau colleagues. It turns out all of this was a trick, because he hadn't planted any colleagues. The point of this exercise was apparently to make me suspicious of everyone, and it worked to perfection.

"The man sweeping up," I would report.

"Nope," Walt would respond with a smile. And the game would continue.

"The tour guide."

"Wrong again."

After two hours of this Walt announced there were no plants and that the lesson of this first exercise was that every single one of those people could have been agents and there was simply no way to detect it.

"You don't detect agents by how they look, you detect them by how they behave," he said, and that brought us to the second part of the training.

Here, we did the same thing, but this time Walt really did plant three people to follow me. They were not spies, just ordinary folks from the office. They stuck out like sore thumbs. Or, as Walt would say, they didn't stick out, their movements did.

In the third phase he replaced the three ordinary people with a trained spy. I couldn't pick him out. He used a simple ploy that was among the many Walt taught me—he carried a bag full of different hats and different bags, and quickly changed them whenever he was out of sight. It is amazing how our brains run so fast to the shortcuts—to the colors of hats or shapes of bags—ignoring entirely the person wearing and carrying them.

I learned a dozen other tricks about how not to be detected, but Walt skimmed over them all, because he knew, or thought he knew, that detection would not be a serious problem on my mission. He sure didn't know Einstein.

All this training, skimmed or not, inculcated me with new-found levels of suspicion. Now, I was suspecting Gödel himself of lying to me about whether Cantor really did prove there were just as many integers as rational numbers.

Then I caught myself. No, this is not a suspicion born of mistrusting Gödel. It is a suspicion driven by common sense. If there are an infinite number of fractions between any two integers, then there are obviously more fractions than there are integers. If you can't trust common sense, what can you trust?

CHAPTER 15

"IF YOU INSIST, CHARLIE," said Einstein, "we can show you Cantor's proof that the set of all integers and the set of all rationals have the same cardinality. It will slow us down in our drive toward incompleteness, but it will be a fun delay."

"It's not that I don't believe you, I'd just like to understand how this is possible."

"Very well. Would you agree that, since all rational numbers are ratios of integers, we can represent all of those ratios by a chart, with the columns of integers representing the denominator and the rows the numerator?"

"Sounds right," I said."

He drew a chart on a piece of clean bowling paper. Across the top he wrote numbers starting with 0 and going through 5. Then he drew three dots next to the five. Above this row of numbers he wrote an "N."

"This top row is all the possible numbers we could use as the numerator for our fractions, the top number. The three dots mean this row goes on forever to the right, because of course the natural numbers go on forever."

Then he wrote a column of numbers going down the left side, this time starting with 1 and going through 5, again with the little three dots meaning this column goes down forever, and he put a "D" to the left of it.

"This column is all the possible numbers our fractions could have for their denominator, their bottom number. You remember fractions cannot have a zero in the denominator, so that is why this column starts with 1 instead of 0."

Then he filled the fractions in. Here's what the chart looked like:

N

D	0	1	2	3	4	5	. . .
1	0/1	1/1	2/1	3/1	4/1	5/1	. . .
2	0/2	1/2	2/2	3/2	4/2	5/2	. . .
3	0/3	1/3	2/3	3/3	4/3	5/3	. . .
4	0/4	1/4	2/4	3/4	4/4	5/4	. . .
5	0/5	1/5	2/5	3/5	4/5	5/5	. . .
⋮	⋮	⋮	⋮	⋮	⋮	⋮	

"Wait," I said, "this doesn't have any negative fractions."

"Quite so. But would you agree that if I can show you a way to count all these positive fractions, we can just do another chart with negative fractions and count all of those?"

"I suppose so. One other thing, this chart has a lot of repeats. The whole first column are fractions that are actually zero."

"Indeed. And not only that, we have many other repeats, an infinite number of them. One-half is the same as 2/4, 2/1 is the same as 4/2, and so forth. But you would agree that if can count all the fractions in this bloated chart, even with all these repeats, then we can count all fractions?"

"Sure, I'd agree with that. But I still don't see how you could possibly come up with any way to count them all."

N

D

	0	1	2	3	4	5	. . .
1	0/1	1/1	2/1	3/1	4/1	5/1	. . .
2	0/2	1/2	2/2	3/2	4/2	5/2	. . .
3	0/3	1/3	2/3	3/3	4/3	5/3	. . .
4	0/4	1/4	2/4	3/4	4/4	5/4	. . .
5	0/5	1/5	2/5	3/5	4/5	5/5	. . .
⋮	⋮	⋮	⋮	⋮	⋮	⋮	

He took out a black pen and started drawing on the chart.

"We start at the first fraction in the upper left of the chart, 0/1," and he drew a small black dot there to show the starting point. "Then we move to the right to 1/1, then down the diagonal to 0/2, then down to the next diagonal at 0/3, then up that diagonal to 1/2 and 2/1. Then we just keep doing this, moving only on these diagonals. That is what this black arrow means here at the end, that it is not the end and we continue with this process forever.

"We have by this method done the same essential thing we did before when we counted the integers, when we alternated back and forth between positive and negative integers so as not to get trapped in the infinity of either. But now we are alternating between the denominator and numerator."

"I see! By using these increasingly long diagonals, and not simply the rows or the columns, we never get trapped in either of these infinite edges."

"Exactly, just as alternating back and forth across zero allowed us to avoid being trapped in the infinity of positive whole numbers or the infinity of the negative ones."

"OK, you have convinced me the rational numbers are countable."

"Cantor would say the rational numbers and the integers have the same cardinality," Einstein corrected.

"But now for the more interesting part," said Gödel. "Cantor showed that there is no way to count the reals. Their cardinality is greater than the cardinality of these other kinds of numbers. Again, the proof is fairly simple. Do you wish to see it, or will you accept it so that we can move on to incompleteness?"

Here, common sense was not screaming at me as before. It was more sheer curiosity. What was it about the real numbers, and especially their mysterious irrationals, that made them so dense you couldn't even count them?

"Could you just outline the proof for me? It sounds so interesting."

"We will do more than an outline," said Einstein. "We will do the proof itself. It is quite straightforward, and beautiful. Like so many deep and beautiful things, its truth is so obvious once it is proved that it makes one wonder why it was not obvious before the proof."

Here, Gödel smiled, and said, "We will soon learn, after all these little detours, that truth and proof dance together but are not one."

"These detours will speed up without your little aphorisms, Kurt." But both men smiled, and Einstein continued.

"Suppose the real numbers were countable. That means we would have some way to list them all, just as we devised ways to list the integers and rationals. The list is infinite, of course, but the idea is that eventually our listing protocol would capture every real number.

"Now, for simplicity, let us just consider the interval between 0 and 1, because this simplifies matters. You would agree, would you not, that if we could prove the real numbers in this small interval are uncountable then we have proved the reals as a whole are uncountable?"

"Of course," I said, "since this small interval is part of the whole."

"Exactly, and in fact if we can prove the real numbers uncountable in this small sample interval, you will see from the proof that we can also easily prove them uncountable in every other interval. It is not as if they are uncountable only in this interval between 0 and 1; they are in fact uncountable everywhere."

"OK, I can imagine that, but let's see it."

"We begin by writing our infinite list of real numbers between 0 and 1 in decimal form. It might look something like this," and he wrote the following list on a clean sheet of bowling paper:

0.3216947 . . .
0.7543212 . . .
0.3333333 . . .
0.500000 . . .
0.3040569 . . .
. . .

"The dots to the right of the decimals mean that the digits go on forever. The dots at the bottom of the list mean the lists goes on forever, because of course there is an infinite number of reals."

"But how did you come up with this list?" I asked.

"It is arbitrary. We are saying that if the reals are countable then there must be some method to list them all. You can change this list of decimals to anything you wish. Indeed, Cantor used letters in his proof to indicate the digits could be anything. They just represent *some* listing protocol."

"I understand. I see that you have included some rational numbers in the list, 1/3 and ½, the decimals with the repeating threes and the repeating zeros."

"Of course. Remember, the reals include the rationals."

"And all rationals in decimal form either terminate with these repeating zeros or repeat some pattern of digits." I had remembered this from high school math.

"Bravo," said Einstein. "So the irrational numbers in this list are the ones that go on forever with no repeating pattern of digits—the first, second, and fifth decimals in the list are meant to be irrational."

"Now," continued Gödel, "look at the diagonal of this list. Let me highlight the numbers along that diagonal," and he used the pencil to make those numbers bigger and darker:

0.**3**216947 . . .
0.7**5**43212 . . .
0.33**3**3333 . . .
0.500**0**00 . . .
0.3040**5**69 . . .
. . .

"Those digits make up the real number 0.35305. . . . This is why the proof is called Cantor's diagonalization proof, because it considers the real number represented by the diagonal of our list. This real number is also contained in our interval between 0 and 1.

"Now, and here is the second half of Cantor's remarkable diagonal insight, we change every one of these digits in this diagonal number. It does not really matter how we change them, just as long as we change every digit. Let us pick the change method of adding one to each digit. That gives us the decimal 0.46416 . . ."

"OK."

"This real number is nowhere our list!," Gödel said, smiling and arching his eyebrows.

"Wait. How do you know that?"

"We know because it is not the first number on our list, because its first digit differs from that first listed number, we know it is not the second number on our list because its second digit differs, we know if cannot be the Nth number on our list because it's Nth digit differs."

"I get it! Cantor constructed this number so that it differed in at least one digit from every single number on the list. That's amazing."

"Therefore," Gödel continued, "we have a contradiction to our assumption that we can list all real numbers, thus proving that the reals are not countable. That is, Cantor proved that the cardinality of the real numbers is greater than the cardinality of the rationals. That the infinity of the reals is a bigger infinity than the infinity of all the other numbers.

"It is these irrationals, like the one he constructed out of the diagonal, that make the difference. An infinite number of them is packed in between every pair of rational numbers we can pick, much more densely than the infinite number of rationals packed into that same space."

My mind was whirring, trying to imagine what this superdensity must mean. I understood how there must be an infinite number of fractions between any two integers, no matter how close. Heck, all you have to do is average them, then average the average with one of them, and so on, the interval between them getting smaller and smaller, and still an infinite number of fractions live in the interval. But it was hard to imagine that lurking between these infinitely dense rational numbers were irrational numbers even more dense.

But then again, I was starting to learn that lots of stuff about ordinary arithmetic was far from ordinary. You'd think a spy like me would know things are not always what they seem.

I had been very patient. I had waited months after my embarrassing visit to the provost, and still he had not sent me a suggestion for a different meeting place. In March, I again went to my neighbor with the telephone, and again the little man in the front office—I recognized his sniveling voice—told me the provost was not in. I knew he meant that the provost would never be in for me until the plan had reached its end. I am not stupid.

But why? What has happened to the plan? Is it still in place, but its pace simply slower than I had imagined? Then why would the provost not just tell me that? Of course, we must be careful. But things are so slow.

I was keeping meticulous track of the arrests of Jews, as a way of measuring the success of the plan. They never made official announcements, but I sampled the boarded-up shops in the center of the city's commercial district as a proxy for arrests, and they seemed to have leveled off. Of course, I recognize this is not a perfect counting method, but it seemed the plan should be finishing soon.

Fortunately, my impatience during these winter months was temporarily suspended when I decided to take the time, in the evenings, to write my first paper on The Austrian Light. It was an extension, though of course much more technical, of my testimony at the trial. I decided to submit it to a minor Viennese philosophy journal, betting that this small journal would be in the race for preeminence once the center of philosophy returned to Vienna.

The paper was, if I may be permitted to say, brilliant. Cogent but thorough, persuasive but careful. It would be the official obituary of logical positivism and the birth announcement of The Austrian Light.

Mistrustful of the mails, I hand-delivered the paper, and a covering letter, to the journal's office, which was across the street from the back side of the University, to the north and east. I knew that the ridiculous terms of my parole required me not only to stay off the University grounds themselves, but also more than 30 meters from its boundary. But surely no one would mind if I just dropped off this paper. And they did not.

A pleasant and attractive young woman accepted my package, read the covering letter, and told me the journal's editorial board meets every third Friday, and should be able to have a response to me within one or two months. I suspected she recognized me; perhaps she had been one of my admiring undergraduate students.

It was almost spring now. Hyacinths were poking out of city flower boxes. By the time they were in full bloom, and certainly by the time the tulips appeared, Vienna's spring flowers would be soaking in the new sun of The Austrian Light.

CHAPTER 16

"Now that you have seen how Cantor proved that the infinity, or cardinality, of the real numbers is greater than the cardinality of the rational numbers, we can finally discuss his most important contribution: the continuum hypothesis," said Gödel, smiling.

"This is the continuum hypothesis," said Einstein, "which we will often abbreviate as CH," and he wrote these words on a clean sheet of scoring paper:

> There is no set whose cardinality lies between the cardinality of the real numbers and the cardinality of the rational numbers.

"What do you think, Mr. Charlie Richards?" he asked. "Is that true or false?"

"Before I guess, I have a question. Why is it called the 'continuum hypothesis'? The word "continuum' itself suggests that the answer should be that are a bunch of infinite sets whose sizes lie between the sizes of the rationals and reals."

"This is a good question," replied Gödel. "But the name has nothing to do with hinting at an answer. The set of all real numbers is sometimes also called 'the continuum.' Think of it as a number line. The integers at regular intervals, the rationals squeezing in between, and the reals squeezing their irrationals even more tightly in between.

"So the real numbers, which, as we've said, include all the other kinds of numbers we have discussed, are represented by the entircty of this number line, which is also called "the continuum." So the 'continuum hypothesis' is a hypothesis about the cardinality of the continuum, the real numbers, not a hint about whether it is true or not."

"OK. Well, of course I have no idea whether it is true or not. But if I had to guess I would say there aren't any in between. After all, it seemed to me there are a lot fewer natural numbers and integers than there are rational numbers, but you've convinced me they are all the same size.

"Then we have to jump all the way up to the reals to get this 'bigger' infinity. And you just said that what drives this bigger size is this crazy super density of the irrationals. Plus, these are all the numbers we know about, at least that you've told me about. I can't imagine an infinite set of things that is any larger than the infinite set of counting numbers, since all things can be counted.

"So my guess is that we cannot create any infinite set that has a size in between the size of the rationals and reals."

"You would say, because of the way CH is phrased, that you believe CH is true, yes?"

I looked back down at the written statement of the continuum hypothesis.

"Yes."

"You are in good company, young man. Cantor himself believed CH was true, and spent the rest of his life trying to prove it, unsuccessfully."

"So who ended up proving it?"

"No one," Einstein answered this time. "It remains an unsolved problem, the most important in all of foundational mathematics. And I must say here what Professor Gödel's modesty will prevent him from saying. He has proved that a true continuum hypothesis is consistent with the axioms of mathematics, that is, that adding the continuum hypothesis to those axioms does not render them inconsistent.

"He is now attempting to do the same for the negative of CH, and when he accomplishes that, he will have shown that CH cannot be proved true or false in the current axioms of mathematics, that it is independent of those axioms."

"I am almost sure CH is independent, and only a little less sure that it is false," Gödel added. "But others believe it is true but unprovable."

"True but unprovable? I do not understand."

"Ha! We are, finally, at the crux of our task," said Einstein. "But I am afraid we must stop. Bob's and Ed's doppelgängers have a meeting this evening with some bigshots at the Institute, and it will take me some time to get all this grease off. I believe we can finish in one more session. Professor Gödel?"

"Most likely, if you keep me focused. This will be a significant challenge for me, now that we are about to talk of my own work."

"Are you here next Tuesday?"

"Yes."

"Would your office be convenient, at, say 9:00 p.m.?"

"I would be honored."

"One quick question," I asked. "The continuum hypothesis is about the sizes of infinite sets between the rationals and reals, but what about set sizes even greater than the size of the reals? Are there any?"

"An infinite number," Einstein answered, smiling. "And let us talk briefly about that because this implicates a more general form of the continuum hypothesis.

"Cantor's paternal grandparents were Sephardic Jews from Copenhagen, but they converted to Christianity and Cantor himself was a devout Lutheran."

I had no idea where this was going, but doubted, given this start, that it was going to be a "brief" presentation.

"He named his different infinities after the first letter of the Hebrew alphabet, aleph, perhaps as a rebellious nod to his Jewish roots?" Einstein asked, pursing his lips and shrugging his shoulder with hands upturned. Then he wrote on a fresh sheet of bowling paper:

$\aleph_0 \equiv$ cardinality of the set of all rationals
$\aleph_1 \equiv$ cardinality of the power set of the set whose cardinality is $\aleph_0$ (= cardinality of reals if CH is true)
$\aleph_2 \equiv$ cardinality of the power set of the set whose cardinality is $\aleph_1$
. . .
$\aleph_n \equiv$ cardinality of the power set of the set whose cardinality is $\aleph_{n-1}$

"Cantor used set theory to define all these infinite numbers of infinities, deriving them all from the infinity of the rationals, which he defined as aleph zero—the aleph at the top left corner of this list with the little zero subscript. The ≡ sign means *defined as*. So Cantor defined $\aleph_0$ as the cardinality of the set of all rationals, which, as you will remember is also the cardinality of the integers and the counting numbers.

"Then he used a simple operation on sets, called *the power set*, to generate sets with larger cardinalities. The power set of a set is the set all subsets of that set. Cantor then demonstrated that for any infinite set, just as with any finite set, its cardinality is always less than the cardinality of its power set."

He must have seen me get my set theory look, so he backed up.

"Let me show you how this power set idea works on simple finite sets. Consider the finite set {Ø,1,2,3}, which he wrote on the sheet. What are all of its subsets? A subset is any set all of whose elements are also elements of the parent set."

"Well, each single element would be a subset."

"Good," and he listed {Ø}, {1}, {2} and {3}. "Any others?"

Then it hit me. "Sure, all the combinations of those elements."

"Exactly," and he added to the list {1,2}, {1,3}, {2,3}. "Because of the definition of subset, it also includes the parent set itself and the empty set," and he added and {1,2,3} to the list. "We use to denote the empty set, the set with no elements. So the power set of {1,2,3}—defined as the set containing as elements all the subsets of {1,2,3}—is," and he wrote:

{Ø,{1},{2},{3},{1,2},{1,3},{2,3},{1,2,3}}

"Now, you can see that the power set has many more elements than its parent set. Three elements in the parent set but eight in its power set. As Cantor would have put it, the cardinality of this power set, 8, is greater than the cardinality of this parent set, 3.

"And he proved this is also true for infinite sets. He then used this power set function to build bigger infinite sets. So $\aleph_1$ here on this chart is defined as the cardinality of the power set of the set of all the rational numbers. $\aleph_2$ is the cardinality of the power set of the set that has a cardinality of $\aleph_1$, and so on.

"So one way of stating the continuum hypothesis is to ask whether $\aleph_1$ is the cardinality of the reals, of the continuum. That is, whether there is any other infinite set with a cardinality between $\aleph_0$ and $\aleph_1$. Yet another way to ask this is whether the power set function generates all infinite cardinalities, or whether there are some in between these power set-generated ones. This is the more general form of CH, called the General Continuum Hypothesis, or GCH."

Gödel added, "Cantor also developed an entire arithmetic of these transfinite cardinal numbers grounded in set theory. It is really quite beautiful."

"What kinds of sets do these bigger cardinalities represent? If $\aleph_0$ is the cardinality of the set of all rational numbers, and $\aleph_1$ is the cardinality of the reals—"

"Only if CH is true," interrupted Gödel.

"—then what kind of set has a cardinality of $\aleph_2$, even bigger than all the real numbers? Or of something as big as $\aleph_{100}$?

"I was just thinking that if $\aleph_1$ is the cardinality of the reals, that is, the cardinality of all points on the one-dimensional number line, then maybe $\aleph_2$ might be the cardinality of all the points on a two-dimensional plane, and $\aleph_3$ the cardinality of all the points in three dimensions."

"This is a wonderfully intuitive insight, Charlie, one that tempted several mathematicians in the beginning." Einstein beamed. "It is so beautifully symmetric, and so plausible. And so wrong. Sadly, the cardinality of the sets of all these points in two, three, or N dimensions, is just our old friend $\aleph_1$."

"Provided CH is true and the curves and surfaces of these points in n-space are continuous," Gödel added.

"Darn," I said, ignoring the last part of Gödel's comment because I didn't understand it. "I should have learned my lesson. My intuitions about the sizes of these infinities were wrong again."

"The lure of beauty can sometimes be fatal, and never more than in an area, like the infinite cardinals, where our language fails us," Einstein said.

"We've been talking about the sizes of sets of numbers, their different infinities, but when are we going to talk about what in the world all this set theory actually has to do with math, with actual numbers and arithmetic?"

"We will discuss all of this next time."

"The fire escape again?"

"Yes, Charlie. We are not, how do you say it, out of the woods," Einstein said.

CHAPTER 17

WHENEVER THERE WAS A letter on the floor of my flat, dropped through the slot in the flimsy door, my heart leapt and my mind raced through the possibilities. I so seldom received any correspondence these days. None of Sylvia's letters was getting through. Every once in a long while there would be a note from Mama. Papa stopped writing after my arrest.

Most often, the mail was some silly notification by the parole authorities reminding me of the monies I still owed to Schlick's family for his burial expenses. The silhouettes had ordered me to pay it as a condition of my parole, but my parole officer winked and reminded me that no particular periodic payments were required. Schlick's family, no doubt rich beyond my dreams, could pay for their own damn funeral, and would never see a penny of my honestly earned income.

Whenever a letter lay on the dark floor, my heart's eye always saw the smaller, intimate envelope that Sylvia used, pinkish like her cheeks in winter. But then my mind, observing the actual envelope, began to consider the other possibilities. Color and shape usually told. Brown, of any shape, would be from my parole officer. Mama always sent short white envelopes.

This envelope was long and white. Papa, maybe? The University? I picked it up and turned it over. It was from the journal! And only a week after my submission! Quality rises to the top, even of a temporarily marginal journal. We would rise together.

I wanted to relish the moment, another historical one. The inaugural paper on The Austrian Light. I walked slowly to my desk, opened the drawer, and retrieved my letter opener, a beautiful silver one with a small emerald embedded in one side of the handle. Papa gave it to me when I graduated from the gymnasium. I was first in my class in all subjects, of course, and headed to the University. It was the moment my life began to change. And here is another even more significant moment, both knitted together across time with the needle of this beautiful piece of silver.

I slipped the tip of the opener into the small oval bulge at the right top corner of the envelope's flap, then slowly drew the blade through the top. I placed the opener back into the desk drawer, closed the drawer, then slipped two fingers into the envelope and pulled out the folded onion skin. I pinched a free corner of the skin between one thumb and forefinger, and slowly unfolded it with the fingers of my other hand.

In the unfolding my mind wandered to a topology class I had taken from Hahn. It was beautiful. The whole universe—the shapes of the congealing dust, the spray of cooling galaxies, the whole earth, its undulating surfaces, the wisps of its clouds and explosions of its crust into mountains—all these changing shapes describable with elegant mathematics. Euclidean in their completeness and simplicity, but modern, real, three-dimensional, moving. Just like The Austrian Light.

How could the sophist Hahn, who believed in nothing but meaningless axioms, logic, and fragments of observations, not see the realism in such beautiful mathematics? The fidelity in its relentless attempt to describe the real world, in all of its curves and bends and folds?

Then I chuckled as it occurred to me that there are differential equations out there, waiting to be discovered by me, that would completely and precisely describe the manner in which Hahn's disgusting body was now decaying in the vengeful ground. And Schlick's, too.

I knew the moment the bottom third of the letter bloomed empty that this was a rejection. Acceptances are always longer, plans to be made about editing schedules and volumes and publishing dates. Rejections have just one sentence. Perhaps two if the journal is kind. This journal was not kind.

We are sorry to inform you that we will be unable to publish your paper entitled "The Austrian Light." That was it. No statements about how many papers they receive, and how they are forced to reject many suitable papers due to their space limitations, and best of luck. Nothing. It was an outrage. I thought about going down to the journal's office, but decided the Jew maggots were not worthy.

I instead walked the City. After what must have been two hours, I found myself to my complete surprise immediately across from the parole offices. This is a sign. The rejection by the insects would be compensated by some good news from the parole office. Perhaps Sylvia's letters would be released. Perhaps we could even start to see one another. Perhaps the geographic restrictions would be lifted. If not any of these, at least I would be able to get future dates, even if just estimates, of when these ridiculous chains would be loosened, when the plan would start to unfold.

I walked up the worn stairs of the grimy government building to the set of offices which housed my parole officer, on the third floor. Before I reached his office, he intersected with me in the hallway as he was coming out of another office.

"Herr Nelböck, I am so sorry. Did we have an appointment that I forgot to put on my calendar?"

He knew there was no such appointment, but was just making small talk. I had not seen him in months. He himself said there was no need.

"No, but I was wondering if we might have a quick chat."

He looked at his watch. "Of course, this way, as you know." His small cramped desk was in a small cramped office. We in Vienna had not yet adopted the degenerate custom of jamming dozens of poor government officials into vast half-walled mazes, but of course the tradeoff was that individual offices were the size of closets.

"I am actually happy that you dropped by, because we can now discuss this report I have received about you being on the premises of the University."

"This is exactly what I wished to discuss. How long will these parole restrictions remain in place?"

"I do not understand the question," he said.

"When will I be able, for example, to visit the University?

"Not until the balance of your parole period expires. Let me see, I have that date somewhere in your file."

"No, no. I know when my parole expires. May 26, 1947, ten years after my original sentence. But the plan . . . these restrictions are to be slowly lifted as I demonstrate my compliance. As for my mistake last week, I apologize. I simply forgot about this condition. It was the first time I have visited the University since my release. I have made arrangements to meet the provost off campus."

"No, Herr Nelböck, I am afraid you misunderstand. All of the conditions of your parole remain in place until the ten-year period expires."

"But that will not be for five more years!"

"Yes."

"But surely this is not true of the condition that I not have any contact with Miss Borowicka?"

"You are quite correct, Herr Nelböck, I apologize. That condition arose out of a separate harassment case, as you know, and was incorporated into the conditions of your parole in this case. The no contact order concerning Miss Borowicka remains in place indefinitely, even beyond the 10-year term of this sentence."

"That is incorrect. It is impossible. The conditions are to be relaxed over time. You promised that."

"I promised no such thing. Only the judges, upon the formal request of your attorneys, could alter these parole terms. You have misunderstood."

I had misunderstood nothing. Perhaps he never said the words exactly—one had to be so careful these days—but we had a complete and firm understanding that these Draconian parole conditions were just part of the plan. The plan that would slowly trap the Jews, and slowly release me. It was now obvious that this parole officer was now himself part of the Jew conspiracy. So I just smiled, thanked him, apologized for my misunderstanding, and left.

No use asking my Jew lawyer to help change the parole conditions. I would instead simply no longer abide by them. This parole officer could then bring me before the silhouettes, who would then begin to implement the plan. My first violation, of course, would be to visit, at long last, my eternal love.

"You are in for treat tonight, Mr. Tim the Maintenance Man," Einstein began, as he and I settled into the two chairs he dragged over from his office. "Herr Professor Gödel will at long last explain what all of this headache-producing set theory has to do with mathematics."

Gödel stood at the blackboard, which he had cleaned, and I could see he had his usual powerful urge to face it whenever he was talking, whether writing on it or not. This time he managed to resist the urge, though occasionally Einstein had to tell him to speak up.

"Ernst Zermelo and Abraham Fränkel were the first to rigorously ground the natural numbers and their addition on set theory, once Cantor invented set theory. They used his invention to formalize the Peano axioms. Then these grounding principles were extended to all of the real numbers and all of mathematics on the real numbers.

"But we start with the natural numbers. The way Zermelo and Fränkel used set theory to define the natural numbers was quite simple, and quite brilliant. They defined zero as the empty set."

"Makes sense."

"Then they defined a successor function—a method to build all the natural numbers starting from 0. You will recall that the Peano axioms also had a successor function, but it was not well-defined. Zermelo and Fränkel defined it, which enabled them to define all natural numbers, and eventually all real numbers, as sets. We will use von Neumann's slight improvements to Zermelo's and Fränkel's original successor function.

"We start with 0, the empty set. Then every natural number after it is defined as the set containing all the numbers before it. So the number 1, the successor to 0, is defined as the set containing 0 as its only element. The number 2 is defined as the set containing the numbers 0 and 1 as its elements, and so on. He wrote five lines on the blackboard, in figures whose size, I could tell, he was with great effort exaggerating from his usual unreadable blackboard writing:

$$
\begin{aligned}
&0 \equiv \{\,\} \equiv \emptyset \\
&1 \equiv \{0\} \equiv \{\emptyset\} \\
&2 \equiv \{0,1\} \equiv \{\emptyset,\{\emptyset\}\} \\
&3 \equiv \{0,1,2\} \equiv \{\emptyset, \{\emptyset\}, \{\emptyset,\{\emptyset\}\}\} \\
&4 \equiv \{0,1,2,3\} \equiv \{\emptyset, \{\emptyset\}, \{\emptyset,\{\emptyset\}\},\{\emptyset,\{\emptyset\},\{\emptyset,\{\emptyset\}\}, \\
&\qquad \{\emptyset,\{\emptyset\},\{\emptyset,\{\emptyset\}\}\}\}
\end{aligned}
$$

"I'm sorry, Professor Gödel, but this looks like gibberish to me." I had to be able to understand this if I was going to be able to help him.

"No, it is actually quite easy," Einstein interjected. "They tell me the pedagogical problem with set theory is that it is too easy, too stupidly simple. Newcomers expect it to be complicated. But monkeys could do it," he said smiling, "as long as they are slow and careful monkeys, blindly following the rules without thinking too much.

"Look at the top line of what Herr Professor Gödel has written. We start it all with the number 0. We define 0 as the empty set—the set with no elements. The empty set can be written most evocatively as two brackets with nothing in it, but it is better to abbreviate it as a zero with a line through it, to cut down on all those distracting brackets.

"Now that we have defined the number 0 as a set, we need to define Peano's successor function—the recursive way to generate 1 from 0, 2 from 1, and so on—also in terms of sets. The definition, as I've said, is quite simple really: the successor set is the set that contains all of its predecessors as elements.

"So look at the next line for the number 1. It is the successor of 0, so we define 1 as the set containing 0 as its element," and he pointed to the {Ø}. "Do you see that on the second line here?"

"Yes."

"Then our stupid monkey does exactly the same thing to define 2. Two is the set containing 0 and 1 as its elements," and he pointed to {0,1}. "See that?"

"Yes."

"Then, in the next expression to the right, we are just substituting the set definitions for 0 and 1. Do you see that?"

"Yes, although all these brackets are getting distracting. Let me do it now for 3, without looking. Three is the set containing 0,1 and 2 as its elements. Those elements, written in set form, are," and I wrote Ø, {Ø},and{Ø,{Ø}}."So putting those three elements in their own set gets us this," and I wrote {Ø, {Ø},{Ø,{Ø}}}.

"Exactly," said Einstein. "Zermelo and Fränkel defined Peano's successor function precisely, in terms of set theory, where Peano had merely described it. We now have a rigorous and useful way of defining all of the natural numbers as sets. And, rather remarkably, they all collapse into our single definition of the empty set."

"Everything built on nothing," said Gödel. "It is really quite beautiful and mysterious. Look at the last expression in each of these lines. Every natural number is represented as a simple but unique nesting of sets, all the elements of which ultimately contain the empty set, nothing. 'The earth was without form, and void; and darkness was upon the face of the deep. And the spirit of God moved upon the waters.'"

Holy cow. I saw. We start with nothing, then call it by a name. Now we have something, the name of nothing. Then we name the name of nothing, then name that. Everything from nothing.

CHAPTER 18

I WALKED TO HER apartment house. Vienna's Easter colors were just beginning to emerge from the long winter, some of the city shadows still encrusted in hard snow. Bright spring flowers stood in window boxes, and pastel ribbons hung from lamp posts.

I knew she would be at work, but was not sure where she was employed now. So I knocked on the door of her neighbor, a pleasant woman, perhaps in her 50s, with kind eyes. I asked her if I could trouble her to deliver a note to Miss Borowicka, next door in 4F, and handed her the envelope in which I had sealed the following note:

> My Beloved,
>
> I know that we must stay officially apart for a while longer, and that our correspondence, too, has been cruelly separated. But I see no reason why we cannot meet somewhere out of the public eye. Out of the party's eye. I remembered you have a brother in the City. Might he loan his flat to us for a few days? Or even a few hours. I must see you. It is spring, and love cannot be deterred. This plan is taking too long, and part of me is beginning to worry that the Jews have compromised it.
>
> Your Johann

The neighbor seemed a little confused by my request, and said, "She moved out last year. And she is no longer Miss Borowicka. She is Mrs. Steiner."

"I am sorry, I was speaking of Sylvia Borowicka."

"Yes, I know. She married last year and moved out. I have her forwarding address here somewhere, if you would like me to find it."

"Yes, please."

The address the neighbor gave me was in the fashionable Margareten neighborhood. There must be some terrible mistake. Sylvia could never afford an apartment here. I rang the bell. A tall handsome man in a waistcoat answered. I asked for Miss Borowicka.

"There is no one here by that name," he said smiling. "But the former Miss Borowicka, my lovely wife, resides here. May I ask who calls?"

I do not understand what happened next. It was nothing like shooting Schlick. Some sort of dark agency swept through me. The gun appeared from nowhere in my hand. As I was looking down at it, it fired twice. The handsome young man fell onto the black and white tiles of the large foyer, and red rivulets spread across the squares, linking black and white. A woman screamed from another room. My beloved.

I shot her three times in the chest. Thank God she never saw what had happened to her husband. I gathered her small body from the dining room floor where she fell, and carried her into the bedroom. She was beautiful, and lighter than I had ever imagined. She was dressed in a simple turquoise housecoat, only minimally tinged with the spray of her blood. I placed her carefully on the bed, sweeping a few delinquent strands of hair away from her face. Then it became clear to me.

This was the bed where she cheated on me. Where she gave herself to another. Where she laughed coquettishly and moaned. She was a whore. I do not blame the young man. She tricked him just as she tricked me. She was probably sleeping with another in this very bed when the poor young man was away at work. I was so sorry he died.

I thought for a moment about taking her in death. Her coat and the shirt underneath had both ripped a bit when she fell, exposing a deep valley between the tops of her breasts, not yet bloodied. I stared at the valley. But I was strong. This would be wrong, no matter the delicious and symmetrical irony of it all. No matter that she deserved it, it would be wrong. But she would never trick another man again, even in death. I grabbed the coal shovel from the fireplace and beat her beautiful Viennese face into a bloody Jewish mess.

Then I wrote my last note. I addressed it to Mama. She would expect some explanation, and it might be of some small comfort to her. It was all gone now. The Austrian Light, everything. Everything gone, and now it was time for me to go

"I also noticed that the set representing each number has the same number of elements as the number. So the set for zero has no elements, the set for one has one element, and so on."

"Wonderful," Einstein beamed, looking a little surprised. "It turns out this property—connecting ordinality with cardinality—was very much an intentional part of von Neumann's particular changes. They allowed an easier definition of the successor function and of the operations of arithmetic. You must realize there are many different ways to define the natural numbers by set theory. Some are just more useful than others."

"What about subtraction and division?" I asked.

"Remember," Einstein said, "the natural numbers are not even closed with respect to subtraction or division—we get numbers not in our constructed set of natural numbers."

"Yes, I remember. To cover subtraction, we needed to add the negatives of the natural numbers to get the integers. To cover division, we needed to add the rationals. To cover things like square roots we need to add the irrationals to make the reals. But can the integers, rationals, and irrationals all be defined as sets, like the naturals?"

"Yes. The negative natural numbers and the rational numbers are rather easily defined as sets," Gödel answered. "The irrationals are a little more difficult." He looked over at Einstein, who ever so slightly shook his head side to side, then Gödel continued, "But we need not get into the details. The answer is that all the real numbers, along with all the ordinary mathematical operations on them, can be defined using sets."

Einstein took over. "In this fashion Zermelo and Fränkel converted all of Peano's axioms into axioms about sets, and extended those axioms to cover all mathematics on the real numbers. These axioms are called the Zermelo-Fränkel axioms, ZF for short. They are important because they were believed to be complete over all of mathematics using the real numbers. That is, it was believed that every kind of mathematical proposition that one could state in the mathematical language of ZF could be proved true or false by using the axioms of ZF.

"But then it was discovered that ZF needed one more axiom, called the axiom of choice. This fuller set of axioms is abbreviated ZFC, C for the axiom of choice. With this addition it was believed that we had at long last discovered the deepest rules of all mathematics on the real numbers. This was the Holy Grail for philosophers of mathematics. Mathematics was now finally and firmly well-grounded on logic.

"The problem was that, as with the uncertainty about the Peano axioms, no one could ever *prove* ZFC was in fact complete. On the one hand, no one could find an arithmetical proposition that could not be proved or disproved in ZFC, but on the other hand no one could prove there were no such propositions.

"And then along came our Aristotle. Herr Professor Gödel proved that if ZFC is consistent—which of course we must have in any mathematical system—then ZFC is incomplete. That it does not, as was hoped, describe all of mathematics on the real numbers."

"So the hunt goes on."

"No, our Aristotle also proved that *any* sufficiently complex and consistent formal axiomatic system like ZFC, with a recursive function like ZFC's successor function, will contain true propositions that cannot be proved in that system. Not only that, but every time we add an axiom to a formal axiomatic system in the hopes of making it complete, there will be new true statements in the new system that will be unprovable until we add yet more new axioms."

My head was spinning. "Wait, wait. You keep saying that these unprovable statements are true. But if you cannot prove them, how can they be true?"

Gödel answered, "Because we know they cannot be false."

"If they cannot be false, then they must be true."

"Yes, but they cannot be proved true using the axioms of ZFC."

I was in deep water here, looking for some kind of life preserver. I reverted to our old favorites, the natural numbers. "Are there propositions about the natural numbers that are true but unprovable?"

"Of course," said Gödel.

"Perhaps," said Einstein, simultaneously.

"Like what?" I asked.

"The simplest might be the Goldbach Conjecture," said Einstein, "though it will require us to teach you about prime numbers."

"Not necessary. I remember what prime numbers are. Natural numbers that can't be wholly divided by other natural numbers. So they go, 2, 3, 5, 7, 11, 13 . . . ."

"Precisely. Two hundred years ago a man named Christian Goldbach stated that he believed every even number could be written as the sum of two primes."

"Wait. Let me make sure I get this. So let's take the even number 10. Yes, it is the sum of 3 and 7, and of 5 and 5 for that matter. How about 26?

Yes, 13 plus 13, and 23 plus 3. How about 40?" I had to think about this for a while. "Yes, 17 plus 23. So this seems right, and it's so simple. How can it not have been proved?"

"I have views about this that have to do with the distribution of primes and . . . ," Gödel began.

"But let us not be deflected," Einstein interrupted. "In 200 years, number theorists—these are mathematicians who specialize in the natural numbers—have not been able to prove this simple statement is true for all even numbers, or prove it false by finding an even number that could not be written as the sum of two primes. This is a simple statement that may very well be true but unprovable."

"But today," said Gödel, "we do not know whether Goldbach is provably true or provably false in ZFC. Someone next week may prove it false by finding a large even number that cannot be written as the sum of two primes, or someone next week may find a proof using the axioms of ZFC that proves it is true. Or someone may prove that it is true but unprovable. And then that someone may come up with an extension of ZFC, by adding more axioms, in which Goldbach could be proved true. But the extension itself will then create other true propositions which cannot be proved in the extension."

"But let us now get to the pertinent point," Einstein said, "the one that bears on Nelböck."

I felt my brain being freed (or was it being dragged?) and transported from this crazy and sublime world of infinities of infinities, and truths that cannot be proved, to the gritty truth of Nelböck's insanity.

"As they have done with my theories of relativity, people who do not really understand Herr Professor Gödel's incompleteness theorems have misrepresented them to support their own nihilistic views, or in the case of Nelböck, to charge those proofs with a nihilism he abhors. For you to understand that misrepresentation, we will have to delve into those wonderful proofs. Next time."

That night I again dreamt of the dangerous bus I was driving as a passenger. This time it was stopped. The front door opened. The hiss of the hydraulic opener was so real, yet I was also conscious that this was a dream. Especially when in walked Einstein's pipe, my gun, and Fatty Arbuckle's pants, all sprouting pairs of skinny dancing cartoon legs. After the cartoons sashayed past me, I was suddenly consumed by the knowledge that the bus was moving forward, but this time it was part of a long line of buses stretching in front and behind as far as the eye could see, like cars on a freight train.

I turned the wheel ever so slightly to the right, just to see if I was driving only my bus or the whole line of buses. None of the buses moved out of line. But out of the corner of my eye I saw another long line of buses to my left, running parallel with my buses but now swerving toward me. I realized I was driving that other line. I jerked the steering wheel back to the left and they swerved away. Einstein's pipe, my gun, and Fatty Arbuckle's pants were all shouting directions at me from behind, but I couldn't understand a thing they were saying. I heard far away crashes and screams. As before, I looked down and there were no brakes, just a gas pedal. I also wondered who was driving my line of buses.

CHAPTER 19

I FINALLY LEARNED ABOUT incompleteness in two hour-long sessions, the first at the snack bar at Tiger Lanes and the second on a sailboat in the middle of Lake Carnegie. In the first session, we did not allow bowling to interrupt our progress. I could tell Ed was sorely tempted, so we sat at the snack bar.

I was worried. All this set theory had gotten me down, its headache-producing sets of sets and self-reference. I figured incompleteness would be more of the same, probably much more, and I was worried that I would not understand it enough to describe to my old boss Chris (DBS was a lost cause) how Nelböck had misunderstood it, and how his misunderstanding could have him gunning for Gödel, risking Einstein in the bargain.

I was good with the philosophy angle to the whole thing. I knew all about positivism and its modern scientific big brother, logical positivism. I knew how positivism in all its variations rejected ideas of natural law, of God-given right and wrong, of categorical truth and beauty. It was part of an old debate that Plato first described 2,500 years ago. I had a vague sense of how Gödel's strange notion of truths that could not be proved would fit into the whole debate, but I needed to know more about it.

Looking back on all of these remarkable tutorials, one thing that makes them all the more remarkable is that these two geniuses were not experienced teachers. When he was in his early twenties and working as a patent examiner in Bern, Einstein earned extra money by privately tutoring a handful of students in physics, and he taught a few classes as a Privatdozent—unpaid teacher—at the University of Zurich. That was it. Gödel taught only three classes in his entire life, also as a Privatdozent, at the University of Vienna.

Of course, both men lectured all over the world, and I'm sure during all of that they engaged in constant give and take, teaching and learning all the time. That's what they did on their walks. But they never trudged through the dull thickness of undergraduates, or even graduate students, regularly. They knew nothing of pedagogy, but everything about the wonder of discovery.

"So, Charlie," Ed began the introduction, "we are back to the beginning, when we discussed axioms and systems with you, rules and games. Any formal system—game—can be described by a set of axioms—rules. The axiomatic systems that interest mathematicians, like the real numbers using all the ordinary mathematical operations, should be complete and consistent. And the axioms must be independent of one another; they cannot be proved true from the other axioms.

"What Herr Professor Gödel proved is that any sufficiently interesting formal and recursive axiomatic system that is consistent is necessarily incomplete—that there are true propositions that can be constructed using the language of the system that cannot be proved true by its axioms."

"What do you mean by 'sufficiently interesting system'?" I asked.

"That is a good question," Einstein responded. "There is a formal logical and set-theoretic answer that we need not bother with for now. But generally, we mean a system with objects—like numbers—operations on those objects—like addition—and then a language to describe those objects and operations that is also capable of proving or disproving propositions about the operational interaction between the objects. And the recursive part just means we have a method to apply the operations to the objects over and over, like the successor function. The idea, of course, was to model ZFC, but Professor Gödel's proof covers any axiomatic system with a formal language at least as rich as ZFC."

"So the rock/paper/scissors game would not be sufficiently rich," I suggested.

"No. It lacks any propositional language. We could assert as a proposition that 'rock beats scissors,' but that itself is one of the axioms. It also lacks any recursive process. We need a richer language for more interesting propositions about recursive objects, like numbers, and propositions about them, such as 'There is an infinite number of prime numbers.' This proposition can be stated and proved true using only the language and axioms of ZFC. But can all propositions that can be stated in the language of ZFC be proved using the axioms of ZFC? That is the question

Herr Professor Gödel set out to answer. Herr Professor Gödel, the floor is yours."

"This part about propositions of a system is critical. But what are propositions? They seem like they can be anything, from 'There is an infinite number of primes,' to 'two plus two is four.' I needed to impose some analytical order on them. So I numbered them."

"Like Cantor numbered the rationals?" I asked.

"No, in an even more ridiculous way!" he said, smiling. "I did it the way your superior named this operation Fritz and Rolf, by using a simple substitution code. I first labeled every symbol in ZFC with an arbitrary but unique natural number.

"So, for example, we would need a code number for 0, one for our old successor function so we can generate all the natural numbers out of 0, codes for all the operations of addition, subtraction, etc., and finally code numbers for other logical symbols used in ZFC, such as the equal sign and parentheses, the latter of which tell us in what order we are to do the operations. By substituting those natural numbers for their ZFC symbols, I could represent every ZFC proposition as a unique natural number."

"So you just substitute these number codes for the mathematical symbols?"

"Yes, although we use the coded pieces to produce a single unique number, unique to that proposition."

"Herr Professor Gödel is again too modest to say, but we now call these unique natural numbers for every proposition 'Gödel numbers.' I know it is embarrassing to you, Kurt, but it will easier for Charlie to understand if we follow the convention."

"Very well."

"Wait, I am not following. Could you give some examples of these Gödel numbers?"

"Yes. Let us say that the proposition in ZFC we wish to make into a single unique number is X+Y=Z. We will need unique code numbers for the three letters and for the operator + and the relational symbol =. Let us just say that the unique numbers we picked for these are 2 for +, 3 for =, 34 for X, 35 for Y, and 36 for Z." He wrote the codes on a fresh sheet of bowling paper:

Symbol	Code number
+	2
=	3
X	34
Y	35
Z	36

“The numbers of the code do not matter, they are arbitrary, but once we pick them, we must keep them.”

“Why the big gap between the 2 and 3 for the + and = sign, and the letters x, y, and z?”

“Remember, we have to label every symbol we use in ZFC, that means every logical symbol and every letter we might use as a variable or a constant. So I am assuming we number the operator symbols and logical symbols first, then the letters. So we are just pretending there are 10 symbols before we start to number the letters, starting with 11 for A. Then X, Y, and Z would be 34, 35, and 36. But remember, like with any code, the actual code numbers we use as substitutes for symbols and letters and numbers are arbitrary. And we do not need actually to number every mathematical proposition; we need only show that it is possible.”

“I get it. So your formula, X+Y=Z, using these arbitrary codes you have picked as an example, would be written 34 2 35 3 36.” I had decoded lots of these silly substitution codes during operation Fritz and Rolf.

“Yes,” said Gödel, and he wrote the five numbers below the code list. “But we need one number for the whole proposition. What should we do?”

“How about just taking out all the spaces, so the single number is 34,235,336?” I offered.

“That is certainly a straightforward way of getting these code pieces down to a single number, but I am afraid it will not do, because the code must be readable in both directions; that is, we need to be able to obtain the proposition from the code. That is because we must be sure that any given number represents just one, and only one, proposition.

“The number you suggest, by just taking out the spaces between the individual codes, could be divided up into many different individual code numbers by putting the spaces in different places. Similarly, we could not just add these five code numbers together or multiply them, because there will be many ways to add numbers together, and perhaps even multiply them.”

Einstein interrupted, unable to control himself.

"So our Aristotle took advantage of the uniqueness of prime factors. Do you remember from high school that every non-prime number can be written as the unique product of primes?"

"Sure. 4 is 2x2, 6 is 2x3, 12 is 2x2x3, 15 is 3x5, 100 is," now I had to stop and think a bit, "2x2x5x5."

Gödel continued. "So to make sure our coded propositions are unique and decodable, we take the first prime number, 2, and raise it to the power of our first code number, then we take the second prime number, 3, and raise it to the power of the second code number, and so on, then multiply the whole thing together to get one number for the proposition.

"In our example, the code 34 2 35 3 36 would be the single number 2^{34} x 3^{2} x 5^{35} x 7^{3} x 11^{36}," and he wrote this down. "This is a very large number indeed, but one that uniquely represents, and only represents, the statement X+Y=Z. By this method we can uniquely number every conceivable proposition that can be stated in ZFC. And by factoring the Gödel number into its prime factors we can recover the code from the number, and the proposition from the code.

"I see all of that."

By the way, all of this may seem rather silly to today's computer-savvy readers. We all know now that everything we write can be reduced to numbers, and in fact numbers reduced to binary numbers, all represented by ones and zeros inside a computer. But in 1942, this concept was just beginning to be formed by fellows like von Neumann and Turing. And no one had ever thought of doing this kind of arithmetization of propositions in a system as big and complex as all of mathematics.

"The second preliminary piece of my proof is to recognize that just as all mathematical propositions can be uniquely coded in this trivial way, so can their proofs, no? Proofs are just strings of propositions, so the whole string can be coded to produce a Gödel number unique to that string, unique to that proof. So propositions that can be proved in the system will have corresponding proofs of that proposition, no?

"Sure, though I imagine there are a jillion different ways to prove stuff."

"Of course, but we care only whether a proposition has at least one proof."

"OK. But we can also code false propositions and proofs that aren't correct."

"Ah. This touches on the consistency of ZFC. Let us just assume ZFC is consistent, that the proofs it contains are all logically correct derivations from its axioms, and that those proofs always produce the same result."

"OK."

"So we simply list by their Gödel numbers the true propositions that have proofs, and provide the Gödel numbers for all of those proofs."

Einstein could see that I understood the trees of all these preliminaries but was confused about the forest, so he interrupted.

"You are probably asking, why go to all this trouble to number propositions and their proofs, and to connect the two? This was our Aristotle's deepest insight. By uniquely numbering all propositions and proofs, he could formally construct propositions *about* propositions and proofs and thus avoid the rat's nest of self-reference. He could talk about the Gödel number of a proposition or a proof instead of the proposition or proof itself. He could use the simplest of mathematics—the natural numbers—to examine all of mathematics."

"If you say so."

"You will see in a moment."

"So, now consider this proposition," said Gödel, and he wrote on a clean score sheet:

The proposition with the Gödel number G is unprovable.

Einstein again interrupted. "This statement has become known as 'the Gödel sentence.' Herr Professor Gödel's actual sentence was in formal mathematical language, using the symbols of ZFC, rather than in the conversational German he has written here to simplify. But because he has numbered all propositions and their proofs, it is now a purely mechanical task to decide if this proposition is true, no? Our stupid monkey could take the number G, and even without decoding it, simply look to see if there is an associated proof of it in our numbered list of all proofs.

"But of course because the Gödel sentence is a statement using the symbols of ZFC, it has its own Gödel number. Our Aristotle managed to show that this sentence could be constructed in a manner so that its own Gödel number is the very G mentioned in the sentence.

"We will not go through the details, but this was the whole point of his arithmetizing formal systems. To be able, quite formally and logically, to construct this self-referential statement without at all being self-referential. The Gödel sentence speaks of a proposition that has the Gödel number G, and it just so happens that its own Gödel number is G!"

"That's impossible," I protested. "This Gödel sentence itself contains the number G, so the Gödel number of the whole sentence will necessarily be a lot bigger than G. You can't cram something bigger into something smaller."

"Aha, very perceptive, Charlie. But because our system is based on a formal language, Professor Gödel used that language as a way to represent G, without the Gödel sentence having actually to contain the number G. It was not at all unlike using 10^5 as a symbol for 100,000.

"Self-reference's size problem, so to speak—how to 'cram,' as you put it, a sentence into itself—evaporates because we can take these giant Gödel numbers and represent them with a symbol that has a much smaller Gödel number. The Gödel number of the Gödel sentence is G—a huge number, but we represent it as the letter G, with a single-digit number.

"It was a rather simple matter of doing several of these cramming substitutions to show that there is in fact a Gödel sentence whose Gödel number is the very Gödel number referenced in the sentence. Indeed, there is an infinite number of such sentences."

"I still don't believe it."

CHAPTER 20

"LET ME OFFER YOU a linguistic analogy that might help you see," said Gödel. "Let us say we are trying to construct the following self-referential statement without using any words of self-reference," and he wrote:

> Professor Einstein has read this sentence.

"The offending word of course is 'this.' How can we rewrite the sentence without a 'this'?"

"Easy," I said, and wrote:

> Professor Einstein has read "Professor Einstein has read this sentence.".

"Yes, that'll do it," I said, satisfied. "All I did was put the sentence in quotes, thus burying in those quotes the impermissible self-referring word *this*.

"It is a good start, Charlie, especially your realization that by naming the sentence—putting it in quotes—we can now say something about the sentence, get outside of it. And I applaud your attention to the detail of where to put the periods.

"But this simple solution will not do. If Professor Einstein has read the sentence you propose, then he has read the whole sentence, yet it claims he read only the quoted part. On the other hand, if he has read only the quoted part, then he has not read the whole sentence. In either case, he has not read 'this' sentence."

"So what do we do?"

"We go one abstraction deeper—and name the process by which you named the sentence. Such process helps us cram the sentence into itself without using any offending words of self-reference.

"Let us call this process 'Quoting' because you yourself reasoned that we can start to solve the problem by putting the sentence in quotation marks and thus naming it. But we need a somewhat more complicated kind of quoting since, as you saw, your simple method did not work.

"So let us define this Quoting function as follows: Quoting a sentence S means writing it as *S'S'*.

"I am not following you, Professor Gödel."

"It is stupid monkey time, Charlie," said Einstein. "Just accept this definition. If we have any sentence, we define this process of Quoting as writing the sentence twice, then putting the second version of it in quotations marks."

"If you say so."

"Your problem, Charlie, is that you are wondering where all this is going. Do not wonder that. Just accept this definition, as a stupid monkey would. You will see in a moment how it all works to perfection. For now, we need only to make sure you understand Professor Gödel's Quoting function."

"I do. You take a sentence S, then write it over again, but the second one you put in quotation marks. S becomes S'S'. I get this."

"Very well," said Gödel, "then consider this sentence. And he wrote:

> Professor Einstein has read the Quoting of "Professor Einstein has read the Quoting of"

"Now you must really put that stupid monkey back on your head, as Professor Einstein would say, and let us go through this statement slowly and carefully."

"You are mixing metaphors, Kurt. The hat is not a monkey. Charlie must either be the stupid monkey or wear the stupid monkey's hat to symbolize that he is a stupid monkey," said Einstein, smiling but also clearly worried about whether I'd be up to understanding this critical moment in the proof.

"Do you see, Charlie?" Gödel continued. "This statement that I have written is true if and only if Professor Einstein has read it, the entire statement. This is because "the Quoting of Professor Einstein has read the Quoting of" is exactly the whole statement itself. The statement refers to itself without referring to itself.

"I don't understand."

"Let us walk through it together," Einstein offered. And we did. After making him go through it two more times, my stupid monkey finally understood. Everything after the initial phrase "Professor Einstein has read" turns out to be the whole sentence, because of this device we are calling the Quoting function. Like one of those optical illusions, it was impossible to see at first, but then, once seen, it was impossible not to see. But I was still not entirely satisfied.

"It seems like a kind of word trick to me, a sleight of hand. A snake swallowing its tail, turning inside out, then going back and undoing it, then pretending everything is different, when it's actually the same."

"Ha! What a creative critique," said Einstein. "But this language example is actually quite a strong analogy. The naming of a sentence by putting it in quotation marks is the linguistic equivalent of the Gödel numbering of propositions and proofs in ZFC. Professor Gödel names the sentence so he can get outside of it and talk about it, cramming it into itself, as you did by using quotation marks in your attempt.

"Then, what he has called the Quoting function in this linguistic example—making a single sentence by coupling the sentence with its own quotation—is analogous to the additional substitutions Professor Gödel made in a part of his proof that has become known as the diagonalization lemma. It was the final remarkable part of Professor Gödel's remarkable proof. It actually involved two more cramming substitutions that allowed him to construct the Gödel sentence—a sentence about a Gödel number G, whose own Gödel number is G. A sentence about itself."

I was getting a glimmer.

"All of this our Aristotle did to defeat the problem of self-reference. There is a long tradition in logic and mathematics of avoiding the swirling maelstrom of self-reference. Bertrand Russell believed that all logical and mathematical paradoxes were rooted in the problem of self-reference. And in fact, he and a colleague designed their own set of mathematical axioms—a version of ZFC using different terminology—that expressly disallows any self-reference.

"But now, by converting all mathematical propositions and their proofs into unique natural numbers, Professor Gödel has formalized self-reference rather than avoided it, allowing mathematics to turn its analytical eye on itself. It is quite astonishing.

"I know that the language example seems like a trick. Many mathematicians and philosophers have called the diagonalization lemma 'magic,' but they mean this as a compliment not a criticism. Professor Gödel's diagonalization lemma is no trick. It is logically and unassailably constructed out of the axioms and symbols of ZFC. Its only magic is the magic that anyone could have conceived it.

"I apologize for the long interruption. Herr Professor Gödel will now finish up his proof by demonstrating that the Gödel sentence is both true and unprovable."

"The rest of the proof is trivial once we have the Gödel sentence," Gödel began. "First, it is easy to show the Gödel sentence is unprovable. We do this by the method of negation. Do you know it?"

"Yes, I think so. We assume the proposition we want to prove is false, obtain a contradiction, and that proves our original assumption was wrong, and thus proves the proposition is true. Like we did with Cantor's diagonal proof that there are more reals than rationals."

"Exactly," interrupted Einstein. "Remember, this works only because we are assuming our system is consistent, that we cannot prove propositions both true and false."

A bunch of teenagers had appeared at the snack bar, and were gaining in numbers. We were of course speaking German, but we were also using the small countertop as a kind of blackboard, scoring sheets strewn all over it. It was clear that Einstein felt too distracted to continue. Not by the teenagers themselves but by his overpowering need to engage them. He had already introduced all of us to them, and they had already begun to ask us questions about automobile repair. I knew we wouldn't be able to reconvene on the lanes because Lanes 1 through 3 were also full of raucous young people, and the worldwide shortage of pin boys would force us to bowl right next to them.

Ed then said, "I have a brilliant idea, if I must say so myself. I do not know why I had not thought of this before."

"All truly brilliant thoughts come paired with this disbelief," Bob said, smiling.

"We can finish our lessons on my boat."

"Absolutely not," said Bob, "I cannot swim well."

"Perfect, I cannot swim at all!" replied Ed.

CHAPTER 21

I KNEW FROM READING up on Einstein that he started sailing as a young man while working in the patent office in Bern, taking small boats out on Lake Geneva. I also read that his enthusiasm for sailing was never matched by anything approaching technical competence. He regularly grounded and de-masted, and on occasion even capsized, and often had to be rescued from European and then American waters. That he could also not swim made his survival all the more miraculous.

I am not entirely sure how he managed to talk Gödel into coming aboard. I could see that Gödel was getting quite energized by these lessons, and his love of teaching them apparently exceeded his fears of drowning or being assassinated. No doubt it helped that we sailed on nearby Lake Carnegie, which was not a real lake at all but just a widening of the canal that ran along the southern part of the town, connecting the Delaware and Raritan Rivers. Einstein said he did most of his local sailing on nearby Mercer Lake, a real lake, but that Carnegie would be easier on our logician.

To hide from tourists, reporters, the FBI, and Nazis, we agreed to begin our sailing trip at dawn the next day. Einstein owned a car and boat trailer but never learned to drive, so I drove. The boat was a battered 17-foot catboat in dire need of paint, which looked more rowboat than sailboat. Einstein had aptly christened it "Tinnef," a German slang for "junk." We picked up Gödel then drove down Harrison to Canal Road then to the ramp.

It was a warm May morning. Gödel was wearing a tan three-piece wool suit and his ever-present fedora, though without the overcoat or gloves.

"I should be wearing that outfit," Einstein joked, "because I cannot swim anyway. Johnny Weissmüller could not swim in all that wool. I told you to dress casually."

"I was going to remove my waistcoat, but Adele agreed with me that it might be cold out on the lake, especially at this hour. And I have no intention of swimming."

"In my experience, swimming is often unintentional. We will fit you with a life preserver, as I promised."

Einstein was dressed in white cotton pants, a short-sleeved tan and light orange seersucker shirt, and sneakers. He held his ever-present pipe in one hand.

Once we got the boat off the trailer and slipped it into the lake, Einstein maintained his hold on the line while I re-parked the car and trailer. When I returned, I took the line from Einstein, who then instructed Gödel to hop into the boat first, but the logician couldn't get close enough because he was unwilling to get his feet wet.

"Come, man, you must get into the water to be able to grab the side of the boat," Einstein said impatiently, and he pushed the smaller Gödel into the water. Gödel managed to remain standing, barely, but now the water was up to his knees.

"My brogues! My fine leather brogues are ruined! Adele just bought these."

"I told you to wear canvas shoes. Now pull yourself up into the boat before your entire ensemble is soaked."

Gödel tried three times, and almost fell into the water the last time. Einstein grumbled about "landlubbers," then lifted the logician out of the water—a groom carrying his bride over the honeymoon threshold—and dumped him into the boat. I expected Gödel to protest, but he didn't say a word. He even managed, somehow, to keep his hat on during the courting, and settled deeply into the hull, only fedora and glasses-framed eyes visible.

Taking the line from me, Einstein then said, "Your turn, Charlie. I trust you can manage it without similar help."

I barely did. I am a landlubber, too, even though I come from a long line of sailors, and I had almost as difficult a time as Gödel, but finally managed it on the second try. Then Einstein threw me the line, and jumped in awkwardly but fearlessly. He took a sideways approach, a little like those high jumpers at the Olympic Games.

When the crew was finally assembled, Gödel asked if Einstein had any maritime instructions for us.

"Just sit and finish teaching Charlie about incompleteness. I will handle all matters nautical. And that reminds me. On board you shall both address me as Captain Depperte," he howled with laughter. "Depperte" means something like "dopey one," and was Einstein's childhood nickname. "You are First Mate Warum, and you are Second Mate Spion." German for spy.

Einstein was different on the water. The hurricane lost considerable force, and yet the calm seemed to make him even more insightful, more focused. But not on the task of sailing. We drifted from shore to shore, snagging on tree limbs and often beaching. Einstein's maneuvering of sail and rudder seemed entirely unrelated to our course of travel.

Gödel's skinny tan frame protruded out of both ends of his puffy yellow life jacket, the whole arrangement topped by his fedora.

"Kurt, you look like an American hot dog sandwich wearing a hat. I rename you First Mate Hot Dog," Einstein announced.

I too was wearing a yellow life jacket, but apparently didn't remind Einstein of anything comical, so I retained my rank and title. Einstein wore no life jacket. I later learned that he never did, making his maritime survival even more miraculous.

First Mate Hot Dog was completely still during the lesson, except when he occasionally tried to wring the water out of his pant legs. Captain Depperte seldom participated, concentrating instead on bouncing the boat between shorelines.

Gödel began, "Remember from last time that we uniquely numbered all the propositions and proofs in ZFC, and connected their unique numbers so that we could determine which propositions had proofs. Then we constructed what they are calling 'the Gödel sentence,' which states 'The proposition with the Gödel number G is unprovable.' And we constructed it so that its own Gödel number is the G mentioned in the sentence."

"I remember."

"So we can also think of the sentence as being 'This sentence is unprovable.' But because we refer only to the Gödel number G, we avoid all the traditional pitfalls of self-reference."

"Yes, I remember all of that."

"Once we have completed these things, all the hard work is done. As long as we assume our axiomatic system is consistent, that is, propositions cannot be proved both true and false, then it is easy now to show our Gödel sentence is true but unprovable."

"Again, I find that impossible to believe about any proposition."

"Belief has nothing to do with it. It is an easy proof, once we have done this numbering and constructed this special sentence. First, we prove it is unprovable. We do so by negation. We assume the Gödel sentence is provable, and then try to find a contradiction, and if we find a contradiction, then our assumption that it is provable must be false, and thus we will have proved that it is unprovable.

"So we begin," and he rewrote the Gödel sentence in the form just mentioned:

This sentence is unprovable.

"To prove this sentence is unprovable, we assume the opposite, that it is provable. But if it is provable, then it can be proved true, and if it can be proved true then it is true (remembering again that the system is consistent). But if it is true, then the sentence itself states that is it unprovable, so it is unprovable. But we assumed it was provable. So we have a contradiction, and our original assumption that it is provable must be false. Therefore, we have proved the Gödel sentence is unprovable."

After making him go through this one more time, I understood.

"Now, it is just as easy to prove that, although unprovable, the Gödel sentence is nevertheless true."

Einstein interrupted. "This gives some people special trouble, not the proof, which is trivial, but the idea that true propositions can be unprovable. Is this not wonderful? The Gödel sentence is true precisely because it is unprovable, and it is unprovable precisely because it is true!" Captain Depperte announced gleefully, pipe in mouth, clapping his hands together, and letting go of the beam, which swung around and almost decapitated me before I managed to duck. Captain Depperte apologized and re-took control of the beam, and First Mate Hot Dog continued the lesson. I'm not sure First Mate Hot Dog even noticed that Second Mate Spion was almost lost at sea.

"Again, we proceed by negation, by assuming the sentence is false. If it were false, then that means it is not unprovable, since the sentence itself says it is unprovable. If it is not unprovable, that means it is provable. And if provable, then it is true, and we again have a contradiction, because we assumed it was false. So we have proved the Gödel sentence is true.

"To summarize, if ZFC is consistent, then we can construct this Gödel sentence which is true but unprovable in ZFC."

"Wait, if you just proved it is true, then you also just proved it is provable."

"Not at all. We proved it true, but its truth depended on it being unprovable. It must be true if the axiomatic system is consistent, but its truth is unprovable inside the system. We moved outside of the system to show that the Gödel sentence is true, by assuming the system was consistent."

Despite his demanding sailing duties, the Captain was again beside himself, a child on Christmas morning.

"It is perfect! Our Aristotle has proved there are mathematical statements in ZFC, the axiomatic system that describes mathematics on the real numbers, that are true but unprovable in ZFC. That is, if ZFC is consistent, it is incomplete.

"And if we add axioms to ZFC to make this particular Gödel sentence provable, then he can easily construct another Gödel sentence in the new system that is true but unprovable in the new system. Not only that, but he has done all of this in a way that is completely straightforward and cannot be claimed to be violating commands against self-reference. By arithmetizing ZFC, our Aristotle was able to use its own mathematics—and simple mathematics at that—to show it is incomplete.

"Moreover, Professor Gödel's incompleteness proof applies not just to ZFC, but to any formal axiomatic and recursive system at least as rich as ZFC."

I must have looked confused, and I was, so Einstein volunteered, "The students of Professor Alan Turing have constructed a clever analogy to incompleteness. He is the fellow who conceived of mathematical operations being done by a machine that knows only a few rules—the axioms, of course. Turing's machine is our stupid monkey!

"But imagine a different kind of machine that does nothing but print a string of letters, then another string, then another, and so on. The meanings of the strings do not really matter, they may be single letters, gibberish, partial statements, full statements, or the Holy Bible, anything. But the machine does not print indefinitely; eventually it stops so that we have a finite number of strings.

"Now also imagine that we have agreed on a language to describe which string of letters the machine will print and which it will not. This external language is critical; it is what allows us to talk about the machine, to get outside of it. Let us say that under our agreed language, PX means that the machine will eventually print the string X. NPX means that it will not print the string X."

"OK. That's simple enough."

"Now let us also agree that P2X means the machine will print the string X twice, successively. NP2X means it will not print the string X successively.

"Got it."

"OK, now we construct our Gödel sentence, the one that refers to itself without apparently referring to itself. In this printing machine example, our Gödel sentence is NP2NP2. That is, 'The machine will never print NP2 twice.' To see why this is a Gödel sentence, we ask whether the machine can ever print such a sentence.

"If it does, then it has printed the string NP2 twice, so the larger sentence, which claims that it has never printed NP2 twice, must be false. But if it never prints the larger string, then the larger string is true, but the machine can never print it.

"I see!" I finally got a glimpse into the strangeness of it all. "What makes it true is exactly what makes it unprintable for the machine, and unprovable for your mathematics system."

"Precisely."

It was breathtaking, this world into which I had been admitted. The most logical and rational system of all—mathematics—has true propositions that cannot be proved true. And how do we know this? By reasoning logically. There was something sacred and mysterious about it all. An inaccessible core proved inaccessible by its own accessibility. Proof always racing to catch up with truth, and always falling a little short.

"You said there were two incompleteness theorems."

"This is the first one," Gödel responded. "The second is a trivial result of the first. It states that systems like ZFC cannot prove their own consistency. It is really just another way to phrase the first theorem. But it also sheds some light on why we know the Gödel sentence is true. Our proof that it is true depended on our assumption that ZFC is consistent, and that consistency cannot itself be proved by the axioms of ZFC. So we went outside of ZFC to prove the sentence was true."

"What does all of this mean, and how have Nelböck and the others misunderstood or misrepresented that meaning?" I asked.

"Ah, for this we will need one more lecture," Einstein said, looking at the sun, our position in the lake, and his pocket watch. The trees along the canal, which were an uninterrupted blanket of dark green at dawn, were now full of bright holes from the risen sun, a chunk of Swiss cheese gone bad.

"I have meetings at noon. And I am afraid time is also short in the longer sense," Einstein said, putting away his watch and pulling out a small calendar from his back pocket. "Herr Professor Gödel leaves for Maine in just two weeks. I am gone the rest of this week and the early part of next. Could we meet Saturday or Sunday, at your home, Herr Professor Gödel? I would prefer Sunday." We agreed on Sunday afternoon at 2:00.

Captain Depperte never could maneuver the boat back to the ramp where we first entered the lake. After four attempts and twenty minutes, I suggested that the next time we beached near the south shore, which was only a matter of time, we jump out with the line and pull the boat through the water and back to the ramp, no matter how far from the ramp we were. The "we" who jumped out was me. Neither Captain Depperte nor First Mate Hot Dog even budged. I had to pull the boat and the two of them, deep in conversation, almost a quarter mile through the water all the way back to the ramp.

That night I didn't dream about my strange and dangerous bus. Instead, Papa, Mama, Caroline, and I were swimming in Lake Chiemsee, which we often did in the summers, Caroline sitting on Papa's shoulders and screaming in anticipation that he would again throw her off. They always played this game, which Papa called Missile. Papa would tell Caroline a complex story that always involved a rocket and, near the end, a countdown. When blastoff came, Papa would heave Caroline off his shoulders up into the air and into the lake. But in my dream, when she blasted off she really blasted off, and became a disappearing dot in the summer sky. Mama and Papa blasted off with her, and I sunk to the bottom of the lake.

PART 3

ASSASSINATION

CHAPTER 22

It was a lovely afternoon, warm and fragrant but not at all hot. Mrs. Gödel was at the side, the front, of their house tending to some spring flowers that lined the gravel driveway.

"I know these tulips and daffodils are old and tired, and should be replaced, but I just cannot bring myself to dig them out," she said in German. "I split them last fall, but they are on their last legs."

"Did you plant them?" I asked, continuing in German.

"No, no, we moved into this house just last year. But I did plant a small vegetable garden. Come, I am finished here, I will show it to you."

I followed her down the gravel drive to the other end of the house, where the driveway ended and opened into a large well-tended garden, consisting mostly of lush lawn. The vegetable plot was small but impressive. Peas, beans, and early lettuce were fully up, and many white tips poking through the black furrows were promising.

When we finished the garden tour Mrs. Gödel turned to me, grabbed my hands in hers, and said "Thank you, Charlie, for what you are doing for Kurt. Not just with trying to protect him, but also for letting him teach you. I have not seen him this happy since we courted in Vienna."

"I could say I am just doing my job, but I am probably happier about all of this than your husband is. I am being taught by Gödel and Einstein! I know they are your husband and your husband's closest friend, and I think they have become my friends, but they are also Gödel and Einstein. It is so strange."

She laughed. "You do not have to tell me about this strangeness. I am married to the new Aristotle. I give my condolences every day to whoever was Mrs. Old Aristotle," and she laughed.

It seemed a perfect time to talk to her about her husband's paranoia. "Pardon me, Mrs. Gödel—"

"Adele, please."

"Pardon me, Adele, but what do you think can be done about your husband's—condition?"

She blanched. "It has of course been troubling me for years, since we first met. This fear of poisoning. This foolish diet. I work so hard to make sure he has adequate nutrition. But his demands are increasingly limiting. I have pleaded with him to see doctors. But he is positive he is being targeted for assassination."

"Do you think he is?"

"You may be surprised to hear that I am unsure. His mind is so powerful. It is powerful enough to know its limitations, and to adjust for those. I think he probably has been targeted for assassination, which is why I am so grateful for your efforts to protect him.

"The problem is not his prediction of an assassination attempt, but rather his irrational efforts to avoid poisoning. This is why I grow vegetables. He trusts only a few store-bought ones—those sealed in cans and a few fresh ones he has determined may be cooked in a manner to disable any poisons.

"For now, I can bake him bread, because he says any poisons in the flour will also be disabled by the baking. But there will come a point when he will die from his diet, and I will be his executioner. It breaks my heart."

She started to cry. I put my arms around her and whispered, "We can help him. If he is comforted by our protection, maybe his mind will calm down and his fear of poisoning will also subside."

"Oh, Charlie, that would be wonderful, no?" She gathered herself and her gardening tools. "It is time for us to go in. The geniuses are already there, and they are very excited about this final lesson."

They were both seated in armchairs in the parlor. There was no blackboard. Einstein gestured for me to sit, then began.

"Today, we will complete our class by summarizing for you what we believe both relativity and incompleteness mean for our understanding of the universe. On these points we mostly agree, though a few small disagreements might erupt." He smiled and looked over at Gödel, who shrugged his shoulders, tilted his head, and pursed his lips.

"Then we will summarize how others have misunderstood us, focusing on how realists like this Nelböck, and other Nazis for that matter, have mistaken us for post-modernists, for nihilists. We will finish by discussing the important points that you will be making to your bosses that will show that the Nazis are a real danger to Professor Gödel and to me."

"Do you believe they are, or is this just for show?" I realized the moment I asked this question that I should probably not have asked it in front of Gödel.

"Just for show. My apologies, Kurt, but I believe neither you nor I are in danger from any government, though Nelböck is a troubling variable. If by this ruse we could get Professor Gödel the extra protection you suggested, Charlie, it will give us time to try to locate Nelböck.

"Now, let us begin this final session with relativity. We can stick with the special for simplicity but similar misunderstandings arise with the general. Tell me, Charlie, your understanding of special relativity."

I tried to figure out a way to describe my understanding of it that didn't sound completely inane, which was hard because I didn't have any understanding of it at all. We had never discussed it in our private lectures. I was back to being Stupid Charlie, before my matriculation.

"I think it has something to do with your discovery that the rules of physics depend on one's frame of reference."

He frowned, the first time I'd seen him do so unplayfully.

"Exactly wrong. What I proved is that the speed of light is a constant, and does not vary by any moving frame of reference of the observer."

"Then why all the talk about you smashing the norms of science?"

"Because a few norms did have to be adjusted to accommodate this remarkable fact about the constancy of the speed of light."

"What kinds of norms?"

"Our measurements of time, space, and mass."

"Those are pretty big norms to get smashed."

"Adjusted, not smashed. Yes, but they gave way only because of the unshakable constancy of the speed of light. I can very quickly explain. You know, do you not, that light moves very fast, but its speed is not infinite, even in a vacuum."

"I remember that."

"If you shoot a gun that has a muzzle velocity of X, but you are also moving in a car in the same direction as you fired, say at speed Y, then how fast is your bullet moving from the point of view of someone out on the street?"

"X plus Y, of course."

"Now do the same experiment but with a flashlight shining in the direction the car is moving. How fast will the light be traveling out of the flashlight from the perspective of your observer on the street?"

"The speed of light plus however fast the car was going, Y, I think it was."

"You would think so. But it is not true. To the observer the light moves at its regular speed."

"That's impossible."

"Yes, it is impossible, yet true. Light somehow cuts through all these frames of reference and its speed is the same to all observers in all frames, regardless of how fast they are moving or accelerating. I demonstrated this theoretically, and it has now been confirmed by many experiments. To make this true fact not impossible, it must mean the other variables that determine speed have somehow been altered. What are those variables?"

"Speed is distance divided by time. I see! To get this ratio constant across frames of reference means time and distance must be distorted as between those frames."

"I could not have said it better, in words, myself. The central point is that all this 'smashing' of Newtonian concepts was necessary only because of this singular and invariant truth about the constancy of the speed of light. These post-modern nihilists, and even some of those opposing their nihilism, have missed this central point entirely.

"I am and have always been a philosophical realist, meaning I believe there are objective truths in the universe that can be discovered through observation and reason. I am likewise a mathematical realist, meaning I believe mathematics is not just an arbitrary collection of made-up axioms, but that it expresses real and true, though idealized, facts about the physical universe. I am also a moral realist—I believe right and wrong have intrinsic meaning, and are not just arbitrary rules those in power decide to employ. All of these beliefs are completely consistent with relativity.

"Yet we see stupid people, and sometimes evil people, saying things like I have proved that 'everything is relative,' or similar nonsense, and thereby justifying every abomination human imagination can conjure. And this during a real war, against real and unimaginable evil. It is an outrage."

He was as angry as I'd ever seen him, and he sat down exhausted from the anger. Then Gödel began.

"There are some loose analogies between what Herr Professor Einstein has shown in the physical world and what I have shown in the mathematical world. I have shown, to the disappointment of the mathematical formalists, and even of some mathematical realists, that mathematics, and in fact all sufficiently complex and consistent formal and recursive axiomatic systems, contain true propositions that cannot be proved true within that system. And from this, many people wrongly say that I have proved there is no such thing as objective mathematical truth. This is nonsense. As you saw, the Gödel sentence is true even though its truth cannot be proved true in ZFC. Truth is stronger than proof, one might say.

"Philosophically and morally, I am not quite as sure about things as Albert seems to be. But I am definitely no logical positivist, who insist that nothing is real that cannot be proved from observations and logical reasoning from those observations. In some way, my incompleteness theorems disprove logical positivism because they demonstrate the inherent limitations of logical proof."

I got it. I saw how people, maybe even especially smart people, could easily jump to entirely wrong, sophist, conclusions about incompleteness. There was no small irony in the fact that Nelböck—the sworn enemy of logical positivism—was misunderstanding Gödel's incompleteness in exactly the same way that the logical positivists were misunderstanding it.

By the way, since I'm sure most of you reading this are, thank God, not philosophers, let me say a few words about all this logical positivism stuff. Like most things philosophical, all the variations and nuances can obliterate the core of the idea. But the core of positivism is all about the Enlightenment idea that truth, including especially moral truth, could be discovered by observations and reasonings upon those observations. It was a kind of rationalization of philosophy. The "positivism" meant that truth was imposed on the mind empirically, from the ground up, by what we observe and how we reason, and not by the laws of God top down. That was the gist.

Logical positivists did what all philosophers do, take this original idea of rationalist philosophy to extremes. To the logical positivists, whose ideas were synthesized and widely publicized by the Vienna Circle, there is no truth, no law, no moral code, no God, but observation and logic. We might have laws against murder, but only because such laws serve a utilitarian purpose of allowing efficient social order, not because killing is wrong. Pardon me for showing my bias here, but I am reminded of Cicero's observation that there is no statement so absurd that no philosopher will make it.

Anyway, by showing that every sufficiently rich and consistent formal and recursive axiomatic system is incomplete, Gödel showed that the most pristine of all truths—mathematical ones—are larger than their proofs. That proof can never fully capture truth. Too bad Nelböck misunderstood incompleteness as so many others had, as some sort of proof that there is no truth. Had he realized it showed that truths could not always be proved, he would have hailed it as the death knell of logical positivism, instead of reviling it as nihilism.

I was now sure I could explain all of this to Chris Conner in a way that at least would maximize the chances they would stick a security team on Gödel and try to find Nelböck.

"I do have one question about the implications of incompleteness," I ventured. I didn't really need to know this for our plan, but I was so curious. "The Gödel sentence you constructed is, at least indirectly, self-referential. Why do these results not merely mean that there are true and unprovable self-referential statements in ZFC, but that ZFC is otherwise complete?"

"Aha!" Einstein reacted. "We have been arguing about this for two years. I have taken this very position, Charlie, so let us hear our Aristotle defend against it."

"My defense is simple," Gödel said rather wearily. "This term 'self-referential' is meaningless, because every statement in every formal recursive axiomatic system is 'self-referential.'"

"I don't understand."

"Take the proposition 2 + 2 = 4. This happens to be true and provable in ZFC but it is also deeply self-referential. You already saw this. Two is the successor of one, which is the successor of zero. All the elements in ZFC are grounded on the empty set, nothingness. All the operations, which we did not discuss in detail—addition, subtraction, multiplication, division, roots—all of these are also defined set-theoretically, and are therefore also grounded on the empty set. When we make a statement about any number and any operation, we are making a statement about the empty set."

"But that doesn't make it self-referential," I said. Einstein winked at me and slapped his thigh.

"Of course it does. When everything is based on nothing, everything said about nothing is said about everything."

"It is on this very point that we have been arguing," Einstein said. "Herr Professor Gödel quite rightly insists on a precise definition of 'self-reference' before he will engage further, and each time I propose one he easily demolishes it. But I have a powerful intuition that there is something more to self-reference than everything-comes-from-nothing."

"I have told you over and over, Albert, and now Charlie has also seen, that intuition is an unreliable ally in this domain."

"But there is also some evidence," I ventured, trying to divert the discussion from the theoretical to the empirical. "No one has constructed any ordinary statement in math—some proposition about the integers, for example—that is true but unprovable, have they? You mentioned the Goldbach Conjecture, but we don't know if it is in fact true and unprovable."

"I have raised this point. Our Aristotle constructed the Gödel statement more than a decade ago. Why, in all the intervening years, has no one found an ordinary, non-self-referential proposition in ZFC that is true but unprovable? One likely answer is that it was the very self-referential nature of the Gödel sentence that made it unprovable. And what will Aristotle say to this? That he does not understand what we mean by self-referential."

"Quite so," Gödel said, smiling for the first time during this lesson. "I am confident that many propositions of number theory, which you would not consider remotely 'self-referential,' are true but unprovable in ZFC. Not every proposition, of course, will suffer this fate. We already know an infinity of propositions that are true and provable in ZFC. But I am sure there is also an infinity of true and unprovable ones."

I learned much later that Gödel spent the rest of his life deeply concerned about this exact question—whether he'd spent all these years, and gained all this renown, only to prove that tiny, self-referential corners of mathematics were incomplete, but that those corners were so small that mathematics would pretty much go on unaffected by his theorems. Looking back and knowing this, it is a little surprising that Einstein continued to needle him about it. Maybe Gödel hid his insecurity so well that even Einstein was unaware of it. Either that or Einstein had a bit of a mean streak. More likely, he was just curious about what incompleteness really meant for math.

Einstein clapped his hands. "But now on to more important, or at least more immediate, matters. I was going to lead a discussion about the points you need to make to your superiors about Nelböck's misunderstanding of incompleteness and relativity, and how that misunderstanding, stewed in a diseased brain, might make Nelböck a danger to Herr Professor Gödel and to me. But based on your insightful questions throughout these lectures, I am not at all sure you need any more of our help. You seem to be in the best position to present this to your old boss in your own words, without mimicking ours. Do you concur, Herr Professor Gödel?"

"I fully agree," Gödel said, bowing his head to me.

"Do you agree, Charlie?"

"Yes. I think I know enough now to make a convincing case. I will set a meeting with my old boss as soon as I can." Then I paused, searching for the words. "And I want to tell you both what a privilege this has been. I think, based on what I've learned, that you taught me much more than was actually needed for me to understand incompleteness. Just for the joy of it."

Gödel smiled. "This is better than any final examination we could have written! That you recognized large segments of this syllabus were unnecessary, is final confirmation of your understanding."

"Like the transfinites," I said.

Einstein smiled. "Exactly so. We included them as a sugary treat to get you through the doldrums of set theory. My own view is that Cantor himself was diverted to the transfinites for this very reason. Set theory is so inane that it induces this strange marriage of boredom and fear. What other phenomenon in all of the universe contains these deadly twins?"

"Governments," answered Gödel, which quickly sobered us up to the task at hand.

"I should be able to set a meeting with my old boss for tonight or tomorrow night, though I cannot guaranty it. Our counterintelligence agents are quite busy."

"Let us lunch tomorrow at the Nassau Inn," Gödel suggested, smiling. "Who knows, I might even eat something. Let me also say, Charlie, that it has been a privilege for me to teach such a bright student, and to have such a giant as a teaching partner." Gödel bowed deeply to Einstein. "Herr Professor Einstein and I have even discussed, because of this rich experience, the possibility that we might together teach some kind of regular classes open not just to members of the Institute and their guests but perhaps even to the general public."

Einstein made a tired sigh. "Yes, perhaps once this dreadful war is over and the wolves for my time stop baying. But I do wish to concur with Kurt's sentiments. I have enjoyed the past weeks immensely. They have reminded me how much one learns by returning to beginnings, and also that these ideas are too important to keep in the academy. Thank, you Charlie Richards, FBI spy, for reminding us of these things."

CHAPTER 23

We did have lunch at the Nassau Inn the next day, on the condition that Einstein promise he would not sing and would not otherwise draw attention to us. A few folks asked for autographs, but that was it.

I didn't have any news. I'd sent a priority message to Chris requesting that we meet, but hadn't gotten any response. This meant Chris was seriously busy, probably out of town. CI agents did not lightly ignore each other's secured high priority meeting requests, even from a newbie dope like me. Einstein, Gödel, and I agreed that I would keep them posted about the status of the meeting by passing them notes during our regular surveillance sessions. I reminded them that they could not use their work or home telephones to communicate with me because DBS had tapped them.

"Unfortunately, my schedule is difficult in the next few weeks," Einstein said, pulling out his small calendar. "What about yours, Kurt?"

"I will be here the rest of this week, and all of next except for Wednesday. But after that I must begin my preparations for Maine."

We agreed that if one of them was gone, I would visit the other's home in the evening with any news.

Gödel actually ate some restaurant food at this Nassau Inn meeting—a dish of cottage cheese. He also brought along some of his patented mush, and a bunch of labeled vials. They were poison antidotes, each labeled with its associated poison. I had no idea where he got them.

Chris finally acknowledged my message two days later. We had to meet in Philadelphia because he was stuck down there. I took the train. It was a two-hour journey, and it gave me some uninterrupted time to think about everything. There was a lot to think about.

Chris found a great dive with terrific cheesesteaks. "It's no Carlo's, but it will just have to do," he said. "I heard DBS has extended your operation. Still thinks Einstein might be a Russian spy."

"He's an idiot, Chris, you know that. These guys are as pure as snow."

"Before you tell me why we needed to have this meeting, how the hell did you get Wild Bill to give up that file? It was Einstein, wasn't it? He's the only one with that kind of juice. But why?"

"He is really worried about his friend Gödel. That's exactly what I wanted to talk to you about. I think there is a real possibility this Nelböck guy is headed for Princeton to whack Gödel, and probably Einstein too while he's at it."

"Tell me what you have," he said, inhaling a telltale strip of razor thin ribeye that was trying to escape the hoagie. I told him first about Nelböck's murder of Schlick, and how it was driven by Nelböck's vehement reaction to the Vienna Circle and its logical positivism. Chris was not buying it.

"So this Gödel guy was part of this Vienna Circle that the nutter hates. So what? There are a half dozen of those Circle guys sprinkled here and in England, and a few of them are still in Europe. The nutter has been out for a couple years and he's not gone after any of them. Not one. Plus, I understand Gödel wasn't even among the top guys in this Circle, and that Einstein wasn't part of it at all."

Chris had done his homework. He always did. I'm sure the kerfuffle about the OSS file caused him to read it carefully, and he was high enough up to get access to it, especially after a nobody like me had seen it.

"That last part is true," I said. "Einstein wasn't part of the Vienna Circle, and Gödel only a minor part. But Gödel's gotten famous in his math and logic world—almost as famous as Einstein—and crazy Nelböck has misinterpreted both of their theories. He thinks Gödel's theories, especially, will end western civilization."

"He's just a nutter."

"Yes, he's crazy but there is a method to his madness, or I should say a madness to his method, the very same mad philosophical method that drove him to kill Schlick, and almost certainly will drive him to kill Gödel, and maybe even Einstein."

"I'm not following."

It was time to try to explain. I told Chris that Gödel showed math was incomplete, that there would always be true math statements that couldn't be proved true. And that lots of dummies think he showed there is no such thing as mathematical truth. So commies, anarchists, and those goofy French existentialists were misusing his theories to show nothing was true, nothing was real, and that our perceptions of truth and reality are just what those in power say they are.

"The same thing is happening with Einstein's relativity. Everything is relative, there is no truth, there is no right or wrong. These are complete mischaracterizations of their theories. Gödel showed—"

Chris interrupted. "Sorry, Charlie, but I just don't have time to get into all of this. We are jammed. But Einstein is a big wheel, and I will look into it. I have two problems with what you are saying, though. First, I'm not sure why this nut would kill over an obscure point of math—"

This time I interrupted. "He's already killed for philosophy. He thought the Vienna Circle's philosophy would destroy western civilization. That's why he killed Schlick. And now he is misunderstanding Gödel's theories, and thinks they will also destroy western civilization. Look, all we are asking is that the Bureau protect Gödel for a few weeks, a couple weeks here and then in Maine where he is going for the summer, only until OSS can get a fix on Nelböck."

"Fine, but that leaves my other problem. Why doesn't Einstein just pull more strings and have Roosevelt order a security detail? Why go through you?" It was a question that was bothering me from the get go.

"He will if you won't order one. I just thought you'd rather do this yourself than be told to do it."

I hoped this flew. Chris didn't know that Einstein went out of his way spending two weeks tutoring me about incompleteness, when all he needed to do was pick up the phone and call Roosevelt. This wasn't like the situation at the beginning. I understood why Einstein wanted to use me to get the OSS file, to hide as much as he could about his friend's mental problems. But this security detail was a straightforward matter of Einstein telling Roosevelt that Gödel's life was in danger, and Einstein's collaterally. Surely Roosevelt would order protection. Einstein was a national treasure. Why did he take two weeks to tutor me instead of just calling Roosevelt immediately?

"OK, Charlie, let me look into this. You are their protection for now. Keep your damn eyes open. When does this Gödel guy go to Maine?"

"June 10."

"OK. I'll try to get back to you in a few days."

"Thanks, Chris."

"If Einstein really is at risk, I'll be thanking you."

I stopped by Gödel's house the next night, but waited until after 9:30 because I didn't want them to fuss over me with dinner. Gödel insisted that Adele be part of our meeting.

"She knows everything. She is part of all of this." I figured as much, based on the talk we had the other day in the vegetable garden. "She is the one, after all, who has been tasting all my food."

I reported the results of my meeting with Chris, and told them we should know one way or the other by next week. Both were gushing in their appreciation. I told Gödel to stay inside except on our walks, because I was the only one protecting them and I couldn't protect them at night. I would come by again as soon as I heard something, or would tell them on our next walk once Einstein got back in town. I reminded them their phones were tapped.

My name is Helmut Seifert, and I was a lieutenant general in the Abwehr and a commodore in the Kriegsmarine. I was born in Munich, and had a comfortable childhood. My father was a minor aristocrat, a naval officer originally from Kiel, and a first cousin to the industrialist Gustav Krupp. We were quite well off.

When I was 11 years old, my mother, father, and my younger and only sibling, Caroline, were all killed when the English sunk SMS Greif. They should never have been on board. But my father, a captain in the Imperial German Navy, insisted on taking the family with him to his first wartime posting, in Oslo, and insisted on taking Greif, a merchant raider, instead of waiting for a passenger ship. I was not with them because I was at the Maria-Theresia Gymnasium in Munich, and my father would not compromise my studies. I stayed behind, with my paternal uncle.

I can still see the face of the young naval officer who delivered the telegram. He had sandy hair, a little out of control, and freckles. I think his eyes were blue, though he looked down most of the time. My uncle was a giant man, formal, and stern. I remember feeling terribly sorry for the poor messenger. His fancy ensign's uniform was no match for my uncle, wearing his dressing gown. He excused the young man abruptly, tore open the telegram, then ordered me to the study. He was gone for quite some time, and when he returned I could see, and smell, that he was drunk. The rest of the evening, of that decade, really, is mostly a haze.

I lost myself in my studies, and graduated from the gymnasium with the highest honors. Although I could have attended any university,

I decided to join the Imperial Navy. My country was my family now. I entered as an officer cadet, a pathway typically reserved for the children of Prussian aristocrats.

I'm sure the Krupp connection had something to do with my acceptance into the cadet program, despite my upbringing in Munich. But equally significant was the fact that we were also related to Wilhelm Canaris, who at the time was a rather famous U-boat commander and the son of another prominent industrialist. No Krupp, but still prominent. After his U-boat commands, Canaris became a naval intelligence officer, and he recommended me to the Abwehr in 1928. I was 23 years old.

I rose rapidly in those pre-Nazi days, largely in what was then called the western foreign intelligence group, later called Abwehr H. I began as an analyst, but preferred gathering intelligence myself. I loved pretending I was someone else, someone with a family. My English was quite good, and I relished stealing secrets from the people who killed my parents and sister. We had a large and active network in England. I conducted many operations in those early years, first as a Cambridge undergraduate and then as an Oxford graduate student, all with the frustratingly modest results typical of espionage and counterespionage.

When the Nazis took over in 1933, I was recalled to Berlin. Like many military officers, I assumed my career was over. I was never a party member, and, worse still, was a minor member of the hated aristocracy. If that weren't enough, I was a Catholic. I can only assume that my connections to Krupp saved and indeed propelled my career, as Canaris' industrial pedigree saved and propelled his. The Nazis in these early days were nothing if not pragmatic.

They took a whole group of us—young, unattached, good English speakers—and assigned us to a special Abwehr H unit based in Hamburg that would infiltrate English and American universities in hopes of then gaining government jobs. I was by that time 28, but had an unusually young face. I never could grow a beard.

I was already a commander in the navy and an Abwehr captain, all thanks to "Uncle Wilhelm," as I jokingly called Canaris, who was actually a second cousin once removed. I outranked all of my immediate supervisors in Hamburg, a state of affairs that would be a constant throughout my espionage career.

The targets of this operation would be the English and American governments themselves. We would bide our time at prestigious universities, and then infiltrate the elite ranks of power. I had a knack for accents, and perfected the flat American Midwest sound. Abwehr researchers had identified a young American man from Nebraska who had lost his entire family in a tornado. Unlike me, he joined his family in death. I would assume his identity. His name was Charles Richards.

It was not difficult for the Abwehr to arrange for Richards' admission to Princeton University. The real Richards was a very good student, and one of his long-dead uncles was a Princeton alumnus. And just to make sure, the Abwehr had lots of money and made a significant gift to Princeton's endowment.

For four years I was the consummate American college student. Too many girlfriends, not too much studying—just enough to pass—and too much drinking, but not too much to lose control.

I had conceived the idea that my best disguise would be moderate stupidity. I called the plan *kontrolliertes Einkommen*, controlled incompetence. I had to navigate the shoals between being good enough to warrant a government job upon graduation and maintaining my cover as a rather dull boy. It wasn't easy. The American undergraduate curriculum, even at a place like Princeton, was much less challenging than Cambridge and Oxford and for me was mostly a refresher from the gymnasium. But with focused underperformance I managed to graduate with a solid C-minus average.

On the other hand, my time at Princeton was much more emotionally difficult than my time at Cambridge or Oxford. I hated the English, and my hatred carried me through the years of deception. But I could not conjure the same hatred for the Americans. I tried. I said over and over to myself that they were just English colonists, that they spoke the same language, that they lived the same lives, that they were historically complicit in the murder of my family. But I knew it wasn't true. America was an unusual place. I had never seen anything like it.

My Abwehr controllers were none too pleased with controlled incompetence, but they held their tongues because I outranked them. They forgot all their objections when, upon graduation, my application for employment with the FBI was miraculously accepted. The agency was in dire need of agents fluent in German, and my qualification in this regard carried me past my poor grades, as I had predicted it would.

By the time I began my FBI training at Quantico, Uncle Wilhelm was an Admiral and had taken command of the entire Abwehr. His tide raised my ship to heights never before experienced by any field agent. I would soon be a naval captain and a major in the Abwehr, and would not only outrank all of my immediate supervisors, but also most of my remote ones.

So they were again forced to go along with my plans to continue controlled incompetence within the FBI. Looking back, it was quite a stupid plan, both at Princeton and at the FBI, and was more likely to lead me to a position in some irrelevant American bureaucracy than into the nerve center of American counterintelligence. There was, of course, a deep irony that my playing at being stupid was itself the product of my own stupid insistence on this insane strategy. That it succeeded beyond anyone's wildest dreams only cemented my reputation as Abwehr H's golden boy.

Professor Edwards—who really was a wonderful history teacher as well as being a Nazi spy—had already bumbled his way toward arrest without my help, and I was happy to use his case as my first bumble. But I might have gone too far. I was so stupid with Edwards that I might never get back into real counterintelligence. I needed a minor success to reset my reputation.

Sacrificing poor Gustav Fleckt and his fellow shipyard spies was not my idea. My uncle's second in command—a remote supervisor who actually did outrank me—was the architect of the shipyard sabotage. But then he discovered the saboteurs were going to defect—not poor Fleckt but all of the others—and decided that it would be more valuable to give the Americans a faulty type of plastic explosive than to proceed with Fleckt as the only saboteur. So when I learned that the shipyard operation was to be blown intentionally, I decided to play a part in its uncovering, hoping to gain a little of my lost FBI reputation. My remote superior agreed.

I wasn't sure how I would actually do it, but I called Fleckt in for an interview, hoping something would show the way. Remarkably, Fleckt said that he lived in Elizabeth. I really did have two girlfriends in college, and one really did have a father who was a plumber in Elizabeth. But I never asked Fleckt about him—Fleckt would have seen such a question as a clumsy and obvious trap. But knowing his cover was about to be blown anyway, I seized the chance to uncover him in order to get back into my FBI bosses' good graces, and fabricated the whole trap conversation. Fleckt was sacrificed, though I later learned that he put his undercover plumbing training to good use, becoming a successful plumbing contractor in Salt Lake City, Utah upon his release from an Army prison after the war.

When I made it back to counterintelligence, and then to Benson House, there were celebrations throughout the Abwehr. An agent was in the center of American counterintelligence! I was promoted to Kriegsmarine commodore and Abwehr lieutenant general.

Over the course of the next few months, I managed to break into the third-floor conference room at The House several times, where files were kept on each of the Argentinian's broadcasts. I was able to determine on a dozen of the broadcasts what was true and what was disinformation. None of this was very difficult; the biggest challenge was Clifford, the German Shephard, but a few bits of cheese and some comforting words whispered in German were usually enough to take care of him.

Knowing what was false in the broadcasts was of course much more valuable than just to out the Argentinian or disregard all of his reports. To know what is false is to know what is true, and I uncovered an enormous amount of new and critical intelligence. We had a few discussions about whether I should try to turn the Argentinian once again—a triple agent—but decided against it. It was not necessary. We'd already turned him into a triple agent without him even knowing it.

When Chris Conner told me about the Einstein operation, we were all delighted. We knew the Americans were assembling a large weapons research project in New Mexico. Although we were not positive what it was about, our working belief was that they were doing the same kind of atomic research on which Heisenberg and his team were working. If so, we were certain Einstein would be in charge. I was also fairly sure, after my success with Fleckt, that I would be able to go back to Benson House once the Einstein detour was over. If there were any difficulty in that regard, I could always manufacture another success to get back into their favor.

Things were going just as I had hoped, better even. Despite the pendency of my request to Conner, I was sure that Gödel was in no danger. We were certainly not out for him, nor even for Einstein. I knew that Nelböck was in Vienna, as late as the Monday before I asked Conner for help. We were not watching Nelböck but the Vienna police were, at our direction.

I was in heaven. Einstein and Gödel were safe, maybe I could confirm what the New Mexico project was all about, possibly even learn how they were going about it, and in the bargain I had the privilege of learning deep secrets from both of them. Not national security secrets, but secrets no one else could have taught me. Perhaps Gödel would calm down and begin eating if I could convince Conner to protect him, and even if I couldn't Einstein would arrange for the useless security team and for the useless hunt for Nelböck directly with Roosevelt.

These happy thoughts returned me to the unhappy question that had been nagging me for weeks now, and which was starting to suggest an unprovable truth: why didn't Einstein just call Roosevelt and request security teams?

A few days after our meeting in Philadelphia, Conner sent me a coded message that they were not going to assign a security team to Gödel or Einstein. Not only that, they'd decided to close down Operation Fritz and Rolf. DBS determined Einstein was not at risk, and didn't really care about Gödel. I was to return to the cold attic at Benson House in two days.

In the afternoon of the last day's surveillance—the first one in some time because of Einstein's schedule—I crossed the street as soon as we were clear of IAS and the gaggle, and handed Einstein a note. All it said is that we needed to meet as soon as possible, and asked whether Gödel's house at seven this evening would be OK. Gödel nodded his head yes, and we continued the afternoon surveillance without incident.

Mrs. Gödel served roast beef sandwiches and a tapioca pudding. Gödel ate a little of the pudding, and drank a liquid laxative. I gave them the bad news. Mr. and Mrs. Gödel were both visibly deflated, but Einstein assured them that he would call the President and arrange for their protection until Nelböck's whereabouts could be discovered, as I knew he would. I was thinking about asking Einstein why he didn't just do that in the first place, instead of doing all this incompleteness tutoring, when the front door exploded open, bits of wood flying everywhere. It was Johann Nelböck, smiling.

CHAPTER 24

HAD NELBÖCK BEEN A professional assassin rather than a professional philosopher, he would not have begun the invasion with a statement about the meaning of incompleteness, and Gödel, and perhaps Einstein, would be dead. The instant the door exploded I drew my gun. When Nelböck finished his philosophical statement and started to draw his gun, I shot him, twice in the chest then again in the head as he began to fall. We hadn't even started eating our sandwiches.

Poor Ms. Gödel was shaking and mumbling, "Thank you, Charlie" over and over, rocking back and forth over the folded body of her husband. He was on the floor, arms covering his head, not moving at all. If Nelböck had gotten off a shot, or if there had been any ricochets, I might have thought Gödel was dead. But the only shots were mine, and none was through and through. Gödel was just in shock. Einstein was shaken and silent.

The Bureau would send in a clean-up team—we called it das Löschteam in the Abwehr, "the deletion team." FBI agents colloquially called theirs the CYA team, and this was most definitely an ass covering moment. I'd told them Gödel was in danger from Nelböck, and that the OSS reports of Nelböck's whereabouts were stale. I told them Einstein himself might be at risk. I begged them to protect Gödel and Einstein at least until Nelböck could be located. They ignored all my warnings, and all of my predictions came true. America's beloved Albert Einstein was almost assassinated by a Nazi, right here in America, and right under the FBI's warned nose. Hoover would never live it down. They would have to cover this up.

Fifteen agents appeared within 45 minutes after my coded call. At my suggestion the four of us walked outside and around to the back garden to wait for them, and to get our stories straight. "Look," I explained,

"I know everyone is upset, but this is really important. They are going to ask us what happened, but I am not supposed to be inside with any of you. I am supposed to be surveilling you from afar. So we need to make up a bit of a story."

We concocted, well I concocted, a tale about how during their afternoon walk they agreed to continue their discussions over an early supper, back at Gödel's house. I even had them, right then and there, add the phony conversation to the tape recorder, which I still had on me from the afternoon walk. Then I told them what my story would be: having heard them agree to have supper, I followed them from IAS to Gödel's house, and waited down at the bus stop as they went inside. After a few minutes, I saw a crazy-looking guy lurking around then rush through the front door. I sprinted after him. He was already inside when I said "Stop, FBI," he turned and pointed the gun at me, and I shot him.

I was pretty sure this story would fly, assuming my new friends could confirm it. I knew Einstein would remember his part. But the Gödels were shaky, so I also told them that if they didn't think they could remember all the details of the cover story, they should tell the FBI that it was all just a blur. That's what they did, and it worked like a charm.

It's a good thing all three bullets lodged inside Nelböck's body, so I didn't have to explain the location of any bullet strikes. Good thing I didn't have my more powerful Luger—the chest shots would have probably gone right through.

I worried a bit about how the incompetent Charlie Richards could possibly have gotten off three such shots before Nelböck even hit the ground, but hoped all would attribute it to dumb luck. I told them I didn't even know how many shots I fired or where they went, and they seemed satisfied with the dumb luck explanation.

None of us was physically injured, but Gödel was an emotional mess. I was hoping that having his delusions actually come true might cure him, sort of like lancing a boil. But it seems that's not how paranoia works. The attempted assassination reinforced his suspicions, his paranoia spun out of control, and it stayed out of control for more than a year. He stopped walking with Einstein, constricted his diet even further, and began losing weight again. It took 14 months before he returned to what we might call a new baseline. Worse than before the assassination attempt but better than right after it.

I was livid with the Vienna police, who were supposed to keep an eye on Nelböck, and with the idiots supervising the Spanish consulate in

Vienna, where Nelböck obtained his visa using a forged Spanish passport. Heads would roll. Their negligence had almost cost the life of the most important double agent in America, although, having survived it, my standing in the FBI would now dramatically improve. I had not only saved Gödel's and Einstein's lives, and I had forecasted the assassination attempt. I should be able to write my own ticket back into the center of the Benson House operation—not just doing translations but actually working on the disinformation. I might even get into the home office.

They drove us in separate cars to the Manhattan office for debriefing, though I was able to convince them to let Adele ride with Kurt. Of course, now that the horse of the would-be assassin was not only out of the barn but also quite dead, the Bureau assigned five-man 24-hour security details to both Einstein and Gödel, and those teams would remain in place for the rest of the war.

Adele was a pillar. She made all the preparations for their trip to Maine herself, while Gödel rocked back and forth in a chair. She considered canceling the trip, but wisely decided that it would be good for Kurt to get away. When he refused to go, she told him she was going anyway and he could just fend for himself all summer. He eventually relented. And in fact, he somehow managed to do some of his most important work during that summer in Maine. Nothing approaching his incompleteness theorems, but still important.

Einstein, too, was gone most of the summer. I would try to find out as much as I could about the New Mexico project when he returned. In the meantime, I directed an Abwehr team to shadow him. Knowing that the FBI was protecting Einstein made my team's job a bit more complicated, though in our experience the FBI was not very good at detecting countersurveillance, not nearly as good as the OSS or the English.

I was very surprised when my team reported that Einstein visited the White House only twice that summer, spoke publicly at a dozen universities across America, but had no contact with anyone who seemed to have anything to do with the secret project in New Mexico. Were the Americans so stupid that they did not name Albert Einstein to head this project? Or are they being especially clever at hiding his involvement? It must be the former, because if Einstein were involved my team would have uncovered it. They did report that Einstein visited Gödel in Maine. I hoped our Aristotle was recovering.

Things could not have been better for me and Operation Höhle der Wölfe—wolves' den, as the Lupus-obsessed Nazis in the Abwehr named the Benson House operation. I now participated regularly in the third-floor meetings (and even had a cozy third-floor office), reviewing all the real intelligence used as fodder in the disinformation transmissions. I also helped edit the disinformation, and the blend of fact and fiction used in actual transmissions. The Argentinian was now worse than useless to the Americans, unwittingly turned into our own source of invaluable information. For a spy like me, who had been slaving for scraps of information for more than a decade, it was an indescribable feast. They even let me drive my car to work instead of riding that damn bike.

But I knew the end was coming—three, four years at the most. I had seen the massive American economic beast stir, and knew it could not be defeated over time. But I hoped I could remain at The House long enough to discover their invasion plans. I told myself that knowing those plans would save millions of German lives and perhaps even give the Wehrmacht general staff time to rid us of the Bohemian Corporal and negotiate a truce with civilization. I believe most of us thought that way.

One afternoon in late September, I was reading in my lovely new cottage in Jamesport— a perk of my new position, and so much nicer than that hole in Ridge—when the telephone rang. It was Einstein. He invited me to dinner at his home Saturday night. Of course, I accepted. He said he wanted formally to thank me for saving his life and to update me on Gödel. He and I knew his phone was being tapped by the FBI, and I knew my Abwehr team had bugged his home and office, but since I saved his life, we now had a plausible reason to see one another. We still needed to worry about the general public and his jealous colleagues at IAS, but we need not worry about the FBI.

It was a fine early autumn evening, and after the three-hour drive I decided to park my car near my old apartment down on Brunswick Pike and walk to Einstein's house. On the drive down, I stopped at a small wine shop in New Brunswick and bought a moderately-priced bottle of French red table wine. How much I would have loved instead to bring him a bottle of Franconian Rotling! I should have been thinking during my drive and walk about how to raise this question of these doings in New Mexico, but instead found myself thinking about wines, and incompleteness.

The Mercer Street house, as most people know from its now ubiquitous photographs, was a simple two-story L-shaped cottage covered in white clapboard, eyebrowed with slate gray shutters on all the windows. The front windows were quite large, somewhat out of proportion to the house. A severely gabled roof topped the front of the L, facing the street, with a flatter gabling on the back portion, also facing the street. There was a small front porch with its famous red door, and a much larger back porch, not visible from the front of the house, on which Einstein spent many a summer evening in conversation with guests.

The house was surrounded by layers of shrubbery. Two pines, actually rooted on the neighboring properties, dwarfed the house from each side. An old locust, planted in the backyard, loomed from behind. The front porch was bracketed by a large lilac bush on the right, long done blooming, and a snowball bush on the left, almost as big and also done blooming. An overgrown hawthorn was nestled into the vertex of the L.

The whole of the front yard was guarded by an old and tired boxwood hedge, waist high, which may have paralleled a gated fence at one time, but which now announced the entrance just by way of an open gap, through which a narrow flagstone walkway ran, flaring wider as it approached the house. I walked up the five creaky wooden steps to the front porch, and noticed at these close confines that the whole house was sorely in need of paint.

Einstein answered the door, somewhat to my surprise, and immediately embraced me.

"Charlie, how I have missed you! Please, come into my escape from celebrity," he said, of course in German, smiling and ushering me into the small foyer which opened into a very small dining room, almost completely filled by a square table and its eight chairs. To the right was a narrow staircase leading to the second floor, and to the side of the stairs a small hallway which I presumed led to the kitchen, judging from the delicious smell.

"Maja and Margot are away for the weekend, but Helen has left us a lovely lamb roast." I handed him the wine. "Thank you. I love French wine. One of the few things at which they are competent. The shop must have stocked this before the war. Nothing is getting through now. Ach, what I would not give for some German wine! Riesling, Ebling, Grüner Veltliner. God forgive me, but I would even drink a Liebfraumilch," he added, smiling.

"When I was at the wine shop, I was thinking about Rotling. Do you know it?"

"Do I know it? I grew up on it! It was the only decent rosé in all of the south. But how do you know it?"

"My grandmother."

"Ah, yes, the one from Salzburg. The best thing about the Franconian Rotling is that it is genuine. Not as refined and subtle as others, but it tastes of the land. Do you know that Rotling is not actually a rosé, which is made with skinless red grapes, but instead they press red and white grapes together, all skins on? This gives it a much bolder taste than those skinless reds."

I followed him through an archway at the back of the tiny dining room and down a short hallway leading off the right to a large parlor. The house seemed much larger on the inside than it appeared from the outside, mainly because the back portion of the L, containing most of the floor space, was largely hidden from the front, but for a chimney-topped section jutting out to the right. There was also much less clutter throughout the house than at his IAS office, and it was more lovingly organized, adding to the sense of space.

Einstein offered me a chair and said, "We can open your pretty French red, or I have a New York chardonnay. Not up to our standards, but passable. What is the etiquette on this point? I never knew. Is one to open the wine brought by the dinner guest, or not? We are having lamb, so let us have the red for dinner and drink the white now. Intemperance solves the etiquette problem elegantly," he said, laughing and slapping me on the back. He opened the white, poured two very full glasses, and handed me one.

This back parlor was much larger than the front dining room, perhaps twice as large. It must have covered most of the first-floor footprint of the back part of the L. But it was still quite cozy. At its far end were two large windows, almost floor to ceiling. Between the two windows was a long and ornate Swiss clock. I expected a cuckoo to announce the time at any moment. The room's walls were papered in a pleasant tan print, girdled by a low and simple pecan wainscoting. A large oriental rug lay in the center of the room under an equally large rectangular table with ten chairs but now set for two. So maybe this wasn't a parlor, maybe it was a second, more formal, dining room.

It had a parlor feel because off to one side was one of those two-headed oriental looking sofas, the kind on which Cleopatra or a sultan might lie, and on which I now sat at Einstein's insistence, though he remained standing. Near the wall opposite the sofa was a music stand, several violin cases, and a beautiful cherry cabinet housing a Columbia Grafonola phonograph. Einstein told me that he bought it in 1921 in New

York City, during his first visit to America, and had his friend and sponsor Chaim Weitzmann store it for him.

"Chaim had it for 12 years. He has played more gramophone records on it than I have," he joked.

Next to the phonograph was an equally impressive Zenith radio cabinet. It was made from two elegantly curved walnut slabs placed on top of one another. The tuning dial was centered in the smaller top slab, and the speakers in the larger bottom one. I had a much smaller one-slab version at my apartment. And a giant radio transmitter/receiver in the attic of our safe house in Trenton.

He noticed me looking at the violin cases, put his wineglass down, and walked over to open one of them. I rose and followed him.

"This is my American violin," he said, holding it by its neck. "It was made by Oscar Steger, a cellist in Harrisburg, Pennsylvania. It is one of my favorites. I nicknamed it Lina." He put it away and opened another. "And this, also named Lina, is from a violinmaker in Prague. These other Linas are from Verona, Hamburg, and Oslo," he said, pointing at the three other cases.

He motioned for me to return to Cleopatra's couch and joined me there, sitting so close we almost touched.

"First, Charlie," he began after he took a large gulp of his wine, "I want again to thank you for risking your life to save ours. I am an old man, but Kurt is young and may still have important discoveries to make. And poor Adele did not bargain for any of this. Besides, of course, we humans tend to want to live," and he smiled. Then he grew serious.

"I visited our Aristotle just last month, in Maine, and I am afraid to report that he was in as bad a state as I have ever seen him. He is back here in Princeton now, but we do not even walk anymore. He is sure the Nazis were behind Nelböck, and that there will more attempts until they kill him. I am afraid there is nothing anyone can do to convince him otherwise. In the meantime, he is killing himself with that *meshuggeneh* diet."

"Can Adele get him to a psychiatrist?" I asked.

"We have tried everything short of kidnapping him, which I must admit I have considered. But of course to kidnap him would only confirm his paranoia. The same with secretly giving him drugs recommended by the psychiatrists, which I have also considered. With Adele's help we could probably sneak the drugs into his system, but he would know. He is as attuned to every nuance of his bodily functions as any man I have ever known.

"Do you know he takes and records his temperature twice every day? He even makes some sort of record of his bowel movements!

"He once told me, near the end of a walk home, that he believed he had just experienced a slight increase in blood pressure. I followed him into his house, and he confirmed it. You know he has a menagerie of medical equipment in that small room off the kitchen. The blood pressure gauge showed a change of less than 1 millimeter of mercury. One millimeter out of more than 100! No, I am afraid we could not secretly medicate him.

"I like to think our daily walks have been a kind of talking cure for him, well maybe not a cure but they seem to have given him some respite. And now he will not even do those, even though I have repeatedly told him of the large FBI teams protecting us."

"I don't suppose he'd walk with both of us? With me as added protection?"

"No, he will not leave his house. But you have given me an idea. We could throw for you a small dinner party to express our thanks. As I am doing here tonight, but with Kurt and Adele. Also Maja, Margot, and perhaps even my secretary Helen. I must confess that I have told each of those three about your heroic rescue of us. No one else have I told, and they have sworn silence.

"Kurt loved teaching you for those two weeks, he trusts and respects you despite your façade of stupidity—which, by the way, you did a terrible job of erecting—and of course he would feel safe around you. Their house is too small even for such a small gathering, so we could have it here, in this very room. Of course, anything we do here risks ending up in the newspapers, but I could call the editors and ask them to keep their hounds away from us for the evening."

"Would they?"

"They did tonight," he said smiling. "I just tell them it is matter of national security."

"Would he agree to come? To walk from his house here?"

"He would feel too guilty not to attend. If he is anything, our Aristotle is a gentleman. You could escort him, Mr. Armed and Dangerous FBI Agent."

CHAPTER 25

We had the party on October 12. Gödel agreed to come, on the condition that I brought my gun. When I called on them at Linden Lane, he shook my hand politely, and I could see him looking for signs that I had brought my gun.

"I keep it in a back holster." I turned around and lifted my coat, showing him, and he nodded. He looked terrible. Much thinner and paler than before, and I noticed slight tremors in each hand.

The three of us walked to Einstein's. It was a crisp but pleasant autumn night, the red hawthorn berries already headed to brown. Gödel was bundled up as usual. Adele was wearing a gorgeous dark grey dress and a small wrap. The dress was modest but had what they called spaghetti straps. I thought of the twisted spaghetti mic in my old *Time* magazine, which they made me return.

"You should have brought a date, Charlie," Adele said, breaking the uncomfortable silence. "A handsome young man like you must have girls dripping off."

"Remember, Adele, what we are celebrating tonight is top-secret. The only reason Maja, Margot, and Helen will be there is that Einstein has already spilled the beans to them." For "spill the beans" I used the German phrase *alles ausplaudern*, which means literally "all is out of the bag."

Gödel did not say a word during the walk. Adele asked me about my southern accent, I presumed just to make conversation. I told her about my fictitious grandmother from Salzburg. But I had real grandmothers.

Papa's mother was from Kiel, from a long line of seafarers. I never met her, but Papa told me she sang him sea shanties every night before bed. "Can you imagine," I can still hear Mama clucking to him, "singing to a young child every night about shipwrecks and starvation and scurvy?"

We never told Mama, but every night Papa would hum the tunes to me, without the words. But he told me their titles, which, without the words, only drove my imagination wilder. *Das traurige Mädchen* (The Sad Girl), *dunkle Unterteile* (Dark Bottoms), *iss die tote Katze* (Eat the Dead Cat). He even made up his own dramatic but happily ending shanties, complete with words I was allowed to hear. One I remember vividly was about a stowaway on an enemy ship. *Der unsichtbare Spion*, The Invisible Spy.

My maternal grandmother was a farmer's daughter from a small village near Regensburg. She married my mother's father, a music teacher from Augsburg, and they both moved to Dusseldorf before my mother was born. He died, as did my paternal grandfather, before I was born. Oma died from the flu in 1911, when I was six. I can remember nothing of her except her hands. They looked like claws, but felt like clouds. It was so strange to watch them slide across my arm, anticipating the painful slashes but feeling only their soft and cool touch.

"Will we be speaking German tonight?" I asked Adele in German.

"Of course," she answered. "Helen is from Freiburg, so she is used to your southerners' strange sounds," she said laughing. Adele, unlike her husband, was born in northern Germany, in the Rhineland.

We could smell the roast chicken and rosemary as we climbed up the well-worn wooden steps to the well-worn porch.

Maja welcomed us warmly. I had never met her before. She was a carbon copy of Albert, a little shorter, ever so slightly more delicate of feature, but otherwise a copy. She made me realize how truly handsome the Einsteins were, their beauty so long obscured by Albert's caricatures. It was all in their sad and empathetic eyes. I had read about how Einstein was quite the handsome and debonair young man, but could never quite see it until that moment I met his lovely sister.

She introduced me to Margot, Einstein's step-daughter—Elsa's daughter with her first husband. She was likewise striking, though much darker. She would just have turned 30, and I knew that she had been married and divorced. I felt quite attracted to her, and got the feeling she would have been attracted to me, except that I looked like I was 20 and far too young for her. I was 37. It can be a curse for a man to look so young.

They both scrambled to thank me a dozen times over for saving Albert's life. I hadn't even sat down. Eventually, Maja introduced me to Helen Dukas, Einstein's long-time secretary and now secretary/housekeeper. The first thing she said to me, after introductions and the required thanks-for-saving-his-life, was, "And thank you so much for talking him into allowing me to fold his clothes. It only lasted a few days, except for Ed's uniform, which I am now permitted to iron and fold. At least Ed is not a slob." We all had a good laugh about that. All but Gödel, who still had not said a word.

Einstein poured everyone glasses of white wine, a California Chablis, and proposed a toast.

"Here is to our mysteriously intelligent friend and personal FBI agent, Charlie Richards. The best student we have ever taught [laughter], and the only one to save our lives. To Charlie." Everyone held up their glasses and said, "To Charlie," even Gödel, though of course he did not drink the wine. Then Einstein said, "I am so sorry for monopolizing the spotlight. I am sure my dear colleague would also like to add his formal thanks. Herr Professor Gödel?"

Gödel shifted his slight weight between his feet, staring down at his wine. He raised his shaky glass but his eyes remained down.

"Yes, thank you Charlie for saving our lives. To Charlie," and everyone joined in. He continued, lifting his head just enough to look at my legs but without making any eye contact, "To you Adele and I will forever be indebted. We were lucky that Nelböck decided to make a philosophical statement before shooting us, and lucky again that you had a gun and are an excellent marksman. I only wish you would continue to protect us."

"The Bureau has first rate teams doing that, I saw some of them shadowing us when we walked over," I said. "I even know a few guys on the teams. They are much better than I at security and also much better marksmen."

"But none better students," Einstein added, laughing and looking at Gödel.

"Yes, thank you for reminding me Albert. It was, as I have already told you privately in happier times, also a pleasure teaching you about incompleteness," he said, bowing slightly.

"The pleasure was all mine, as I too have said before," and I bowed slightly. "But I still don't know what the axiom of choice is, or why it is so important to you to prove it is independent of the other ZF axioms."

"I am afraid my schedule and health will prevent me from teaching it to you," Gödel said, almost in a whisper.

"I will teach it," Einstein volunteered. "I am not the expert that Professor Gödel is, but I believe I could teach you the basics of what it is, why it is important, and perhaps even outline for you our friend's attempt to prove it independent of the other axioms. Helen, remind me of my schedule to year's end."

It seemed a little odd to me that Einstein was so keen on setting up a lecture time, right in the middle of my thank-you dinner.

"Well, I don't have it in front of me and have not rendered it to memory," Helen said, "but I know the big commitments. Next Monday you have the first of your standing meetings in Washington every other Monday, you speak to the American Mathematical Society in Boston in mid-November and to the American Physical Society in Los Angeles the next week. And there are lectures in Chicago and New York mid-December. Those are the out-of-town commitments I can remember. But you also have meetings and lectures here in Princeton."

"Would you please run upstairs and consult the book, then give me a list of any days the rest of this year where I have at least two hours of free time? Charlie, we will set this lecture time right now. The AC is so set-theory inane that it will either take a couple hours to teach or a lifetime," he said, smiling.

Gödel smiled and shook his head in agreement. I could tell he wanted to be part of this teaching, but that he knew his demons were in full control.

So that's how it came to pass that I had the good fortune of having yet another extraordinary private tutoring session, this time taught exclusively by Albert Einstein. As with the first round of lectures, I could not shake the question of why this giant, who was probably busier and more in demand than any man in wartime America save the President and a few generals, would take the time to teach me. Looking back, I can see now that I was blinded by my own thirst for knowledge. Had I not been so damned curious, perhaps my life would not have erupted. Or perhaps I would be dead.

CHAPTER 26

AT EINSTEIN'S SUGGESTION, OUR session on the axiom of choice was back at Tiger Lanes. It was Saturday morning, and even though we met there right when it opened, at 10:00, it was already pretty crowded. I was glad he was in disguise. It was good to see Ed again, and we still needed to be careful about the general public. The guys on the FBI security team loved Ed's outfit. They couldn't stop smiling.

Ed was sipping on a giant Coke and eating a Three Musketeers candy bar. It seemed awfully early for that much sugar.

"I am afraid, Charlie, that we will be back to your headache-producing set theory if we are to tackle the axiom of choice. I find that a combination of physical activity and sucrose helps. Do you remember, before the war, when the Three Musketeers bar had chocolate, vanilla, and strawberry sections? That is why they called it Three Musketeers." I hadn't remembered. "These damn wartime restrictions on sugar have forced them to drop the vanilla and strawberry pieces. I preferred the strawberry."

I asked him if he wanted me to tell the security team to take a break, or at least go outside, in case he was shy about bowling in front of them. Shy? What was I thinking? Instead, he asked all of them to join us. Their lead insisted that the two guys outside remain put, but he told the other two with him inside that they were free to bowl with us. They did. We had a ball.

I did not recognize any of my Abwehr team, though I knew they, too, would be inside as well as outside. They were very good, if even I could not spot them. I played a little game, listing in my mind which of them they might be, ordering the list from most probable to least. I made a mental note to try to find out later if my guesses were right.

The two FBI agents who joined us, neither of whom I knew, were named Jim and George. Einstein seemed to have even more fun bowling in this larger group than he had when only Gödel and I joined him. Maybe part of it was that he didn't feel he was being judged by the formal and strait-laced logician. Whatever it was, it was palpable. He laughed and chortled and slapped everyone on the back. Even people who were just walking by on their way to their own lanes. I smiled at the possibility that one of my Abwehr agents had been slapped on the back by Albert Einstein.

He bought Jim, George, their boss, and I all giant Cokes and Three Musketeers bars, admonishing us that we were not permitted to eat or drink anywhere in front of the scoring table.

"I would not want to get you in trouble with the law," he said, laughing.

He bought two extra Cokes and two extra candy bars and asked the team leader to deliver them to the agents outside.

I'm sure that part of Einstein's joy when bowling came from the freedom of Ed's uniform. Freedom from the cult of personality, from the guilt he always felt at the snarling gap between his soaring public reputation and what he knew was the meager trajectory of his current scientific contributions. Ed knew none of these things. He bowled a 75, his best ever, and swore he would continue with me all winter until he broke 100. I rolled a paltry 121, and the two FBI agents duked it out for the top spot, Jim beating George by just a few pins with a 151.

We spoke English, at Einstein's insistence, and it occurred to me that part of the increased joy I perceived that morning might be because English is just a happier language. A happy sentence in German is always more serious, more laden, than its English version.

As soon as the tenth frame was over, Ed became Einstein, and Einstein became a more serious Einstein, even more serious than in the earlier lectures.

"Now, gentlemen, if you would repair to your conventional stations, Agent Richards has a lecture he must attend." The lecture was of course in German.

"We will begin with a slightly less stupid cousin of the axiom of choice, called the well-ordering theorem, the proof which was first provided by that dear putz of ours, Ernst Zermelo. We are not being tape recorded now, are we?" He smiled devilishly.

"Only by me," and I pointed to the cigar box and spaghetti mic I used to record all these lectures openly. No one asked me to return the surveillance gizmos when Operation Fritz and Rolf shut down, and now that I was such a big shot no one probable would. "And none of these lecture tapes is going anywhere."

"As you might imagine, in any axiomatic system describing mathematics it would be terribly important to be sure that seven is greater than five. Sets whose elements can be put in a determined hierarchy are said to be *well-ordered*.

"A key to ZF's ability to represent mathematics on the real numbers was its ability not just to generate all of the real numbers and their operations using set theory, but also to show that such numbers are well-ordered. The putz did that, but his proof depends on our axiom of choice. He sloughed over it entirely, calling it an 'unobjectionable logical principle,' but you know that such principles actually go by the name of axioms. So, for ZF to adequately describe mathematics, we need its numbers to be well-ordered, and for that we need the axiom of choice, which we must add to ZF, making the ZFC we have discussed.

"Two quick words about our dear friend Professor Gödel. First, he proved, as we have also already discussed, that even with the axiom of choice ZFC is still incomplete. Second, he has for years been working on proving that the axiom of choice is independent of the other ZF axioms, that it is in fact an axiom that must be assumed true to give us well-ordering, and cannot be derived from the existing ZF axioms."

"I understand so far. But what the heck is the axiom of choice?"

"Patience, my savior, patience. Since all numbers can be defined as sets, for numbers to be well-ordered sets also need to be well-ordered. The putz's well-ordering theorem states that every non-empty set X can be well-ordered, and he defines being well-ordered as having the property that every non-empty subset of X has a *least element*.

"A *least element* he in turn defines, as you might guess, as the element that is less than all the other elements in the set based on some arbitrary hierarchy function. I see your eyes starting to dim, so let me tread more slowly. Again, the problem is that it is all so obvious that we easily miss it.

"First, *least element* means just that. With numbers, it means the smallest number. For more generalized kinds of sets it simply means we have agreed to use some function, called a choice function, to order the elements, and that the least element is the one that appears lowest in our ordering.

"So, consider the set containing one banana, one orange, and one of my caps. We would first have to agree on a choice function to order these quantity-less elements. The function we use does not really matter as long as it is capable of distinguishing all the elements on some basis. So, for example, we might choose as our ordering function the number of letters in the words describing the elements. Or, how much these three elements weigh. Or we could order them alphabetically."

"Wait. Even in your own little example, the first one, 'banana' and 'orange' have the same number of letters, both in German and English, so that function won't work."

"Well-done, Charlie," Einstein said, smiling. "I did not realize that, when I constructed this silly example. But your comment is important. There are choice functions that make sets well-ordered, but others that make them only partially-ordered, meaning different elements might have equal values. The set I chose is only partially well-ordered under the "number of letters" function I chose. But of course we want our set-defined real numbers of ZF to be well-ordered, do we not?"

"I suppose so."

"Of course we do. If X=Y then they are both the same number. We cannot have different numbers having the same value."

"But that's where you are losing me. Numbers intrinsically have value. And when you assign a value to an element for this stupid exercise of ordering them, you are really assigning a number to it, so we are back to the beginning. You are proving a set is well-ordered by using numbers to order them."

"But you forget, Charlie, that our numbers are themselves just sets. Remember? Sets and subsets of sets that are all bottomed on the empty set, on nothing. So what the putz needed to construct was precisely the notion of the magnitude inherent in our ordinary numbers, so he could prove these sets that define numbers have magnitude and that those sets could be well-ordered using that magnitude."

"I see that," I said, though I found my mind wandering to my bus dreams. This time, when the bus stopped, a banana, an orange, and one of Einstein's caps, all with the same cartoonish legs as before, hopped up the stairs and into the bus. But I must admit they did come in an order. The banana first, then the orange, and then the cap.

"Now things get pretty technical, and I suspect that it is exactly at this point where the difficulty of the AC's independence lies. But take my word for it that through a series of painstaking and banal arguments, too painstaking and banal to go through here, the putz was able to show that his ZF numbers defined as sets could be well-ordered if and only if for any group of non-empty sets, we could build a new set by taking one element out of each set. And that is the axiom of choice."

"Huh?"

"Bertrand Russell famously used as an analogy a closet full of shoes and socks. The axiom of choice is unnecessary for our shoes because our choice function could be 'pick out every left shoe.' But because there are no left and right socks, we could not use that to pick one sock from every set. Generalized elements in sets are like socks—there is no intrinsic basis on which to pick them out."

"But we just do it."

"Says who?"

"This seems no more in need of an axiom than when you say 'put the empty set inside of a set to create the set for the number 1.'"

"Not at all. We defined 1 as the successor of 0, that is, the set containing as its only element its predecessor, zero, the empty set. We did not have to pick out elements. Same then for the rest of the natural numbers."

"How about when we made subsets to do the power sets? We had to pick out elements for that."

"No. All we did there was to group them in all possible different ways. We did not have to pick one out.

"Anyway, that is the axiom of choice. Once we assume this ability to pick a single element out of different sets to create a new set, well-ordering is proved. And we need well-ordering for ZF to do its work. The axiom of choice will never make ZF complete, our Aristotle having shown that even with the axiom of choice ZFC is incomplete. But it will make ZF well-ordered and therefore able to represent the mathematics of the real numbers.

"What remains, and what Kurt has been trying to show for a decade, is that AC is independent of the other axioms in ZF. That the axiom of choice is, in fact, part of the foundations of mathematics and not provable from other foundations. What do you think about that open question, my insightful student?"

"I don't really get any of this. But I'd say the one thing that all independent set theory axioms seem to have in common is that they are stupidly obvious. Based on that test, I am positive this choice thingy is independent."

When Einstein finally stopped laughing, he said, "I will convey those insights to Herr Professor Gödel." Then, as if he were continuing the same funny thought, and still smiling, he said, "Are your FBI friends recording us?" As he asked this, still smiling, he pulled out a folded note from his jacket and handed it to me:

> Turn off your recorder. I know you are a German spy, Charlie. Are your German friends following us, and are they recording us?

CHAPTER 27

After a moment's thought, I said, "No one else is recording us," and I turned off my recorder. It was the Nassau Inn all over again, this time the German version. I had, of course, been contemplating this possibility from the beginning. But for my insatiable curiosity about the roots of math, it would have been clear to me that Einstein had made me again. But having him say it made things so much more frightening.

"What oh what are we to do, Charlie?" Apparently, having me say it made things more frightening for him as well. So this is why he did this charade of teaching me, instead of just asking Roosevelt for protection. He had become suspicious, and was using these lessons to ferret me out.

"I never lied about wanting to learn, but you lied about wanting to teach."

"Never mind that," he said sternly. "Your real name, Charlie." It wasn't a question. Once again, I answered all his questions, and to this day I really don't know why.

"Helmut Seifert."

"Abwehr or Ausland-SD or something else?"

"Abwehr."

"Rank?"

"Kriegsmarine commodore and Abwehr lieutenant general."

"What?" Einstein looked genuinely surprised. "Such an officer of those ranks descending undercover?"

"Friends in high places," I explained, "but not as high as yours." He smiled. I'd like to say that at that moment I knew things would be all right, but that would be a lie. His smile was a nervous smile.

"We cannot delay here much longer without raising suspicion. Moreover," he said, "others are gathering at the desk wishing to bowl. You have my word I will tell no one of this conversation or your true identity, not even Maja, no one, until we have a chance to talk this through, if I can have the same promise from you, that you will tell no one that I have discovered you."

"I will tell no one."

"Come to my house after dark tomorrow night. We will discuss this on the front porch for all our agents to see, and none to hear. Make sure no one—on either of your sides—," he smiled sarcastically, "is listening in. And you, too, may not tape our conversation. Nine o'clock. We must resolve this tomorrow."

I put my hand out and he shook it, though just with one of his hands. My first thought was to be glad of the time. I had more than 30 hours to think about the possibilities and try to figure out a solution. The possibilities all seemed grim now, but I was hopeful that with additional time a path would clear. This is something I've always known about myself. I can't always see things right away, but with enough time I can almost always figure them out, no matter how complicated.

I had brunch at the Nassau Inn, filling up on pancakes and memories. It had been just a few weeks since Einstein outed me in this very restaurant, and now he had outed me again. He had begun to peel away the onionskins, but I had done my own peeling. Every time I saw deeper into these two men and their strange ideas, the ideas became a little clearer and the men murkier.

How could such men exist? What spark distinguished them from the rest of us? Was this the touch of the divine, or just an improbable confluence of circumstance? Were they really that different?

I had read much about Einstein's childhood, because even in these early days, though his first biography was still five years away, the news magazines had been almost continuously full of Einsteiniana since the early 1930s. I had read the 1933 two-part feature in *The New Yorker*, which they called "Scientist and Mob Idol," and which I found a rather strange combination of pretentious and plain. The 1938 cover story in Time was more granular if less ambitious.

The best treatments were in the newspapers, which back in those days were real newspapers. Although the New York Times ran a half dozen informative articles in these early years, I found myself drawn to the ones in the Chicago Tribune, which focused on the cultural aspects Einsteinmania.

Of course, there was nothing anywhere about Gödel. I realized that despite the vast differences in my base of knowledge about these two men, in the end none of that mattered at all. Einstein remained as mysterious to me as Gödel. And as I befriended each, the mysteries only deepened.

With the last pancake finished, it was time to abandon these fanciful thoughts and focus on the problem at hand. I took a long stroll through the campus, and then a longer one through the town, rolling around all the possibilities. I'd walked for more than five hours. It was just past dusk when I started back to my car. That time when the sky turns a leaden blue right before succumbing.

There were a few streaks of snow marking the shadows of the still leafy trees. Some of the fallen leaves had been gathered in piles. I knew that the remaining leaves, fluttering in the wind, were red, yellow, gold, and brown, and maybe even a few still green, but now they were all just shades of gray in the dying light.

I spent the three-hour drive back to Jamesport hoping things would clear, but they did not. I showered, warmed up some leftover soup, and made myself a sandwich. My mind after these tutoring sessions was usually fighting with set theory, but not tonight. Tonight, I was fighting for my professional life and for my actual life, which, of course, were the same.

I went for another walk, all the way up to Laurel, through the orchards and farms. Thoughts of my father and mother, and even of little Caroline, intruded. So did thoughts of poor Uncle Wilhelm, fighting the hidden wars for Germany at the absurd bidding of Nazi idiots like Himmler.

By the time my mind wandered back, I found that it had settled on a solution. Or a series of solutions depending on what Einstein would say. I was comfortable with my predictions about what he would say, and with my responses to each prediction. I could finally sleep. Then I got the message, and all was lost.

My Abwehr control had a macabre sense of humor. The night signals he used came from a menorah he placed in the window of a cottage immediately behind mine, a window visible from my bedroom window. He would light the menorah every night at 9:00 p.m., and keep it lit until midnight, to give me a period of observation in case I was out. I don't think he was a party member or a Jew hater. I think he just relished the comedy that he was using a small part of his Abwehr stipend to buy a menorah and candles. Such were the restricted and ineffective forms of protest we allowed ourselves in those darkest of times.

A fully lit menorah meant no message. A menorah with an unlit candle meant a message. The candles were all numbered one through nine, from left to right as I was seeing them through my window. The number of the unlit candle indicated which numbered template I needed to use to decode the message.

The templates were sheets of hard black plastic with holes punched in them in what seemed to be a random fashion. Bunched together they looked like an arty kind of trivet, and indeed when I wasn't using them to code or decode messages, I placed the bundle under a teapot on my countertop. When I received a coded message, I would retrieve the proper template and place it on the message to reveal the underlying communication. It was all quite simple and difficult to break. We had used it many times in England.

When I returned from my clarifying walk up to Laurel, I turned to check the menorah. It was almost always full, as I insisted at the beginning of Operation HW that we have almost no communications except at the safe house in Trenton, and even those were to be rare and only for emergencies. So I was surprised to see the menorah was missing its fourth candle. I put my shoes back on and went to the drop location—which itself was coded by the number of the missing candle—and retrieved a folded New York Daily News lying on the stoop of a nearby boardinghouse.

I brought the paper back to my cottage and pulled from it a typed letter written on a single sheet of paper. The letter was to the post office complaining about late deliveries. I retrieved the template numbered 4 and placed it over the letter, getting gibberish on the first placement then turning it 180°. This is the message that appeared:

> Nehmen jetzt Dachs, kehre ins Versteck zurück. Ende.

Take badger now, return to lair. End. Take was kill. Badger was Einstein. The lair was Berlin.

CHAPTER 28

THERE MUST BE SOME mistake. I burned the letter, returned the template to the stack under the teapot, and drove to Trenton. I could not get through to my uncle, which had never happened before. I was the most important double agent in America, and my calls were always put through to him, no matter what he was doing. He told me once that he interrupted a meeting with Jodl to take my call.

The "calls" were coded radio transmissions relayed through a series of submarines and land stations, not totally unlike the Benson House system, so there was an excruciating ten-minute delay between transmitting and receiving. I remember my heart pounding through the delays, talking with several of my uncle's assistants but never being able to reach him. Eventually the situation was made clear. Himmler had seized control of the Abwehr. Uncle Wilhelm, though still its titular head, was under house arrest. These orders to kill Einstein and return to Berlin came directly from Himmler.

They made no sense. Einstein was harmless and I was irreplaceable. I learned much later that Himmler had concluded, correctly, that the American atomic bomb project was beginning, and that he also concluded, as we all had initially and incorrectly, that surely Einstein would be in charge of it, ignoring the reports from my team's summer surveillance of Einstein. Himmler decided Einstein's assassination would derail the American atomic bomb for years. And, of course, Einstein was a traitor and world-famous Jew, which alone justified his death in Himmler's eyes.

As for me, Himmler had the same loathing for me as he had for Uncle Wilhelm, each of us in his view an aristocratic Jew lover. He was hoping he could put an end to both of us with one shot, so to speak, that by murdering Einstein I would be discovered and my cover blown, either by local police or the FBI. If, somehow, I managed to return to Berlin, he would use implied threats against me as leverage against my uncle, just as he was now using implied threats against my uncle to force me to kill Einstein. Or he might just kill us both. All my fine plans were incomplete now, blown to hell by a new axiom.

It was noon before I returned from Trenton. I hadn't slept at all. I knew I had to get some sleep before tonight's meeting with Einstein, that I needed a rested mind to consider this new world. I did not want to take any sleeping pills, but was forced to do so when I couldn't get to sleep naturally. I had a flawless internal alarm, but I set my alarm clock for 4:00 p.m. as a precaution. Surely five hours would be enough time to come up with a new plan. They weren't.

I parked a half-mile away and walked slowly to the Mercer Street house. I assumed that part or all of my Abwehr team had now been diverted to watching me, but I did not see them, either on my drive down or on my walk. It was a cloudy moonless night, very dark. The air was still, a little cooler than usual for late October. The lingering lemony scent of the still flowering verbena filled my nostrils, cut with the smell of wood being burned in happy family fireplaces.

Einstein answered the door, dressed in a heavy white sweater. He looked at once deeply worried and deeply hopeful, as he often did.

"Shall we meet here on the front porch?" he asked rhetorically.

"Sure, though as it gets cooler we may wish to move inside."

He didn't bother with any preliminaries. "Well, Herr General Seifert, what shall we do?" he asked in a quiet voice. "I have considered all the non-trivial possibilities, and I believe I have several solutions depending on decisions you must make."

By talking softly and not passing notes, Einstein was showing that he discounted the possibility that some of the spies following us might have listening devices and could hear us. I had hoped he would be more careful. Of course, his experience was with the FBI, not with my much more talented Abwehr agents.

I held up my hand, hoping he understood that all plans must stop in light of a new development. I started talking about the weather and casually dropped him the note that I had prepared on my way down. It said: *Everything has changed. We need to go inside.*

I feigned a shiver and asked him if he could retrieve a sweater for me, and followed him inside. Once inside I whispered for him to follow me to the tool shed in the backyard. I knew at least one of my Abwehr agents would almost certainly be covering the rear of the house, probably from the house on the lot adjoining to the rear, but luckily all of the backyard was covered by a wall of thick vegetation. The L itself would block us from what I was sure were other agents covering the front of the house. I was 75% sure we would be undetected going to the tool shed.

Even so, I knew we would have only a few minutes before they figured out where we were, because they had bugged the house and the absence of any sounds would alert them. I was also hoping that the presence of the FBI would prevent my Abwehr team from moving too quickly.

As soon as we shut the front door I whispered to Einstein that he should announce in a normal voice that he needed to go to the bathroom. That would give us some time.

"Sorry, Charlie, but I must visit the little physicist's room. I'll get you a sweater shortly. Just wait here in the foyer." The foyer was the one first floor area without giant windows. We walked quickly and quietly out the back and into the shed, keeping close to the edge of the stairwell to avoid being seen through the dining room's front windows.

"So what is all of this about, General Seifert?" Einstein asked after I closed the door of the shed and all went black. As a disembodied voice Einstein sounded very old and very ordinary.

"I have been ordered to kill you immediately, and I suspect that if I do not my Abwehr team will kill both of us, probably tonight. Himmler has taken control. I am related to Admiral Canaris, he is my friend in high places, and Himmler has had him arrested." I pulled out my gun, which we could both see now that our eyes had begun to adjust to the lack of light.

"So, my dear student, you will kill your teacher?" Einstein's hurricane had sadly becalmed. Of course, I couldn't kill him, could I? He had become my teacher and my friend. But Himmler will kill Uncle Wilhelm if I don't, and my team will kill Einstein anyway. I saw no other way out. I grabbed the gun and placed its barrel in my mouth.

"No, Charlie, this is not the solution," he said gently, reaching out and pulling the gun down with one hand, cupping my face with the other.

"You could pretend to kill me."

"We could never fool my team. Besides, you are the most famous civilian in America. Such a ruse would give us only a few days."

Einstein thought for a few seconds. "Do you believe the FBI team can defeat your Abwehr team?"

"No, not without some other advantage."

"Can you identify your team members? Are they outside now?

"They are so good they are invisible. Even I've never seen them, not once, while they've been following you. But I am sure they are here, waiting to confirm that I've killed you, and to kill both of us if I haven't."

"Can you get the attention of one of the FBI team members?"

"Yes, remember our agreement about that?" He apparently had not remembered.

"Before I tell you my new plan, I need to know your intentions," he said. Will you defect?"

"I will not betray Germany."

"I do not mean become a triple agent. It is too late for that anyway, courtesy of Herr Himmler. I mean leave Germany behind, at least until this war is over, and live here in America honestly, just as you have done for years dishonestly.

"They will kill Uncle Wilhelm."

"They will kill him anyway, just as they will kill you and me."

"Alright, I suppose I could live here until the war is over."

"There is no time for supposition."

"OK, yes." Then I reminded him of our earlier agreement with our FBI team about getting their attention.

We walked quickly back through the house, talking as normally as we could will ourselves to do. Einstein retrieved one of his cardigan sweaters from a closet and I put it on. We opened the front door, sat back down on the front porch, and continued our feigned discussions, which were now about the progress of the war.

I knew the FBI team was not taping us, but was unsure of my Abwehr team. After about 15 minutes of this fake conversation, Einstein gave what we had agreed, after Nelböck's attempt, would be the signal to the FBI team if ever Einstein and I were together and I needed to talk to them. The signal, which I thought was pretty clever, was that Einstein would stretch, look at his pocket watch, and yawn. It was clever because I never saw Einstein yawn. He was incapable of yawning. Life was too interesting and he too energetic.

After his yawn, I announced that now I needed to use the little G-man's room, and went inside. Our plan depended entirely on whether the FBI agent in charge would detect the signal, which I was confident he would, and whether he would figure out that he needed to go around to the back of the house and meet me there, about which I was much less certain.

Einstein remained on the porch, as agreed, hoping to emphasize the point that the agent needed to go to the back to meet with me. Of course, there was no chance my Abwehr team would miss the FBI agent going to the back, but I also knew the team would not act impulsively, and that would give us some time. Though these were assumptions about my team, not Himmler's team.

As I was opening the door to go in, I heard a stirring in the thick hedges off to my left, and caught a glimpse of someone running off to the side. Thank God! The FBI agents had gotten the signal and understood they were to go to the back. It wouldn't have been one of my agents making such a racket, and none of them would ever have allowed himself to be seen. After meeting for seconds with the FBI leader at the back door, I returned to the porch.

I nodded to Einstein and surreptitiously handed him another note: *We are ready. Go inside when I nod next. Quickly but calmly.* I had told the FBI agents to call for help, then follow us in as soon as we started to go in, and barricade us all in until the help arrived.

I knew there were five FBI agents. There were probably only three Abwehr agents, unless Himmler had ordered reinforcements in such a short time. Still, I doubted the FBI's advantage in numbers would outweigh my team's skill. My team was the best of the best, charged with protecting the most important double agent in America, and soon charged with killing him. Our one hope was the FBI radio that had already been used to call for help. We had a telephone, but surely my team will have cut the line.

Before settling on this plan of barricading, I had a short debate with myself about whether Einstein and I should just remain on the front porch until the cavalry arrived, but rejected the idea quickly. We were sitting ducks out here, and there was a reasonable chance Himmler had decided simply to eliminate both of us immediately. After just a few moments back in the chair—time for the FBI team to get ready—I signaled to Einstein and we both got up and walked through the front door.

The instant we were across the threshold two FBI agents were behind us closing the door and directing Einstein to lie on the floor in the back hallway. I heard the back door and several windows throughout the house slam, and locks lock. The house instantly went dark—either my Abwehr team had cut the power or the FBI had done so. It was raven black.

I could hear Terry, the agent in charge and who I knew to be of above average competence, trying the telephone, but my Abwehr team had already cut the lines. Terry was on the radio, confirming the situation, and of course my team was hearing all of this through the bugs we had placed in the house, and I was hoping that would be enough for them to retreat.

I heard Terry moving toward a front window, presumably to see if he could make out any of my agents' positions. We heard a tinkling of glass and Terry cried out that he'd been hit. But we had heard no shots. My team must have used a silenced rifle, probably an MP44 with a snap-on suppressor, and they must also have the night-vision goggles we'd been developing. Within minutes, maybe seconds, they would be inside and would kill us all.

Terry must have moved just as they pulled the trigger, because he had only a minor through-and-through on the soft under part of his right arm, which he expertly bandaged himself, tearing pieces of his shirt sleeve with his teeth while still holding the radio in his right hand. The rest of us were all crouched down, watching every window.

Terry whispered to me that when he had first radioed for help, the Bureau said their team was 15 minutes out and that the police would be there in 10 minutes. I knew we would all be dead by then. I whispered to Terry the only plan I could come up with. He nodded his assent.

Then he said in a soft voice but loud enough for the bugs to pick up, "OK, stay calm everyone, stay down and away from any windows. I've just been told we have a 10-man OSS special ops team one minute out."

There was no such team, of course. OSS had special ops teams, and they were highly respected by us. But they had nothing like the kind of quick response capability of minutes, especially in a town like Princeton, miles from any big city. I knew that because I was an FBI agent. But I was fairly sure my Abwehr team would not be as conversant with OSS logistics.

We waited, and hoped the Abwehr agents would just go away. I was pretty sure my team would have retreated after calculating the odds, but wasn't quite as sure about Himmler's team.

CHAPTER 29

BUT THEY DID GO away, and without a trace. The police ordered a perimeter, but I knew they would never catch them. Had it not been for the cut power and telephone lines, the shattered window, and Terry's flesh wound, they might have all been ghosts of our imaginations.

Right after surviving this ordeal, it was necessary for me to steel myself for yet another, perhaps just as dangerous—the debriefing. I had been careful not to tell any of the FBI agents anything too detailed about my team. Just that I saw suspicious people following us, wearing weird goggles. When the debriefers asked why I thought Terry's ruse would work, I just said that I thought the Germans might have someone right up on the porch, or might even be using powerful remote listening devises like the one I used in Operation Felix and Rolf.

The CYA team covered everything up, which was a little more difficult with the police involvement, but not impossible in wartime and with Einstein's connections.

Inside the Bureau, once again, I was a hero. I had now saved Albert Einstein's life twice. They asked me to head up the whole Benson House operation. I didn't know what to do. I was a man without a family and now without a country, and had deceived everyone. Everyone but Einstein. I asked him for advice, and was surprised to hear him tell me he was about to turn me in.

"We cannot risk the lives of our agents here and in Europe. We cannot have you at the center of our counterintelligence operations." His use of "we" and "our" was very concerning.

"What have you told them about me?" I asked.

"Nothing, yet. Not a soul. But it is only a matter of time before the FBI discovers your treachery. The circumstances at my house were suspicious. They will certainly do a deep background check on you before they let you take over any aspect of counterintelligence, even if they are not suspicious. During that deep check they will learn you are not the real Charlie Richards. And then we will both be facing dire consequences. We must do something before then."

"What?"

"I have a solution, but your life will change dramatically."

"As long as the change does not involve a prison cell or a hangman's noose," I said, and Einstein smiled.

"You must immediately quit the FBI on some pretext. Then we must hide you from your old Abwehr friends, at least until the war is over."

"And who could hide me, you?"

"No, of course not. OSS. Wild Bill will give you a new identity, but you will have to move away and start a new life. Do you have a family, Herr General Seifert? I always assumed you were too young, but now I realize that even your age was a lie."

"My parents and sister died in 1916 when the English sunk the ship on which they were traveling."

"I am so sorry."

"Admiral Canaris is not really my uncle, he is my mother's second cousin, my second cousin once removed. My only real uncle is old, and I'm not even sure he is still alive. I haven't seen him for 15 years. I have no other family left."

"Let me ask you a very important question, the most important of all. What would you do if Germany surrendered tomorrow?"

"You mean assuming the Americans have not already executed me or put me in prison?"

"Of course. Let us assume my friends in high places took care of all of that."

"Then I would probably go back to school, maybe become a teacher. I have enough money for several years of schooling, though it is in Munich, if the Nazis have not confiscated it."

"You are not a Jew. They would not take it from you."

"Don't be so sure."

"But would you stay here, or return to Germany?"

This was an easy question for me. "I would stay here. I haven't lived in Germany for 15 years. I became an adult, at least a kind of fictitious adult, in England and here in America. There is nothing in Germany for me but the memories of youth. I would probably want to go back to visit, to see Munich and the other places of my childhood. But Germany is now just a word to me, devoid of people."

"I feel exactly the same way. I have not been away as long as you have been, and I was already in my 50s when I emigrated. But the people I love are now either dead or here. Germany is full of ghosts, a shadow place and now a shameful place."

Now it was Einstein's turn to save my life. He and I both agreed that my Abwehr team was the most immediate threat. It made perfect sense that Himmler would expend resources to prevent me from defecting with all my Abwehr secrets, if he thought I had ignored his orders to kill Einstein. But the assassination attempt at Mercer Street could also mean I had been arrested by the FBI. I was very careful not to say anything compromising and loud enough to be picked up by the Abwehr bugs. But I couldn't be sure. Himmler would almost certainly continue his efforts to kill Einstein, and might hunt for me too.

The FBI doubled its security around Einstein, and OSS began to try to hunt down my old Abwehr team and any new ones Himmler had sent. OSS knew, as I did, that this would be unlikely to succeed, even with my help, and that the best way to save our lives would be to relocate us. Einstein, of course, was unrelocatable, and in any event he refused. But he insisted that I go.

The FBI would not be happy. They wanted me to lead operations at The House, and would never let any foreign threats change their plans. After all, Hoover himself had been the target of several assassination plots, and the best response to such threats was impeccable security, not operational surrender. So I needed to come up with a reason to quit the Bureau. I came up with a doozy: at my request Einstein arranged for one of his doctors to diagnose me with terminal cancer.

The FBI gave me a tearful goodbye party at the Manhattan office, which Hoover himself attended briefly. He thanked me, in front of the assembled group of CI agents, for my "extraordinary service in predicting two separate Nazi attempts on the life of Professor Albert Einstein, and then foiling both of them." He put the FBI Medal of Valor around my neck. He said it was God's hand that brought me to the Bureau, and God's hand that paused cancer's grip until my mission was finished. He wished me the best of luck.

As he was leaving and shaking hands, he leaned over and whispered to me, "Son, I also want to let you know I transferred that idiot supervisor of yours to the Minneapolis, Minnesota office. His screw ups there will freeze before they can do any damage. Chris Conner is taking his place. God's speed."

Chris hugged me tearfully, and handed me an envelope. Inside was the recipe for Carlo's meatballs.

"I got this from Carlo himself, and it wasn't easy. He protects this like a national secret. I had to promise him that you are not going to open a restaurant anywhere in the world, and that you would not give this recipe to anyone else. He asked why I don't just give you a lifetime coupon for free meatball sandwiches—he even started bargaining about the price for such a coupon—and I told him you were, you were moving away." There were tears in Chris's eyes.

I felt terrible about all the people at the party who thought I was dying, for filling them with unnecessary pain, and especially bad about Chris, who had been so good to me and whom I had deceived so deeply on so many levels. But there was no other way.

OSS gave me a new identity, which I think they relished hiding from the FBI even more than from the Nazis. I became George Duncan, a graduate student in philosophy at the University of Florida at Gainesville. OSS drafted a very nice obituary of Charles Richards, published only as a CI memo. It said I died peacefully at my parents' home in Grand Island, Nebraska.

I assumed, given my undergraduate grades at Princeton, that OSS used some strong-arm tactics to get me admitted into the graduate philosophy program at the University of Florida. But then I discovered that Gödel had recommended me, so no OSS strong arms were necessary. I assumed Gödel wheedled my new identity out of Einstein, and that Einstein wheedled it out of OSS.

I didn't ask either of them for recommendations, of course. That would violate all the protocols of the relocation. In fact, part of me was surprised that the Abwehr had not already discovered the recommendation and assassinated me. Perhaps Himmler had replaced my competent agents with party nincompoops. That was the usual Nazi procedure when higher-ups took day-to-day control.

I would never have known about Gödel's recommendation except that the dean of graduate studies asked me, within the first week of classes, how it was that I took training from Kurt Gödel. When I asked him what he meant, he said, "His letter of recommendation says he trained you informally." I told him as generally as I could that yes, I was taught by Gödel, but that I had no idea about the letter, and asked to see it.

Dear Dr. Kristoffersen:

My name is Kurt Gödel. I am a philosopher of mathematics. Although I am not a teaching professor, I am associated with the Institute of Advanced Study in Princeton, New Jersey. It was in that capacity that I was introduced to Mr. George Duncan through a mutual friend. Because Mr. Duncan expressed interest in my work, our mutual friend and I taught him informally on Cantor's set theory and on my incompleteness theorems.

Despite not being trained in mathematics, Mr. Duncan was perceptive and probing. He has an excellent mind. I do not know whether his interests will turn toward the philosophy of mathematics, but even if they do not, I believe Mr. Duncan will one day be a fine philosopher. More than that, he is a fine young man. Please do not hesitate to contact me if you would like to discuss further Mr. Duncan's qualifications for your graduate program.

Very truly yours,

Kurt Gödel
Institute for Advanced Study
Fuld Hall
Princeton, New Jersey

"Just as the letter says, we had a mutual friend at Princeton, and we fell into this discussion group that ended up with Professor Gödel and this friend teaching us about set theory and his incompleteness theorems."

"Nice friend," the dean responded.

You have no idea, I thought. "Did you ever telephone him about me?"

"Are you kidding? Of course I did. I am a philosopher myself, and in fact was head of this department before I went to the dark side of administration. What philosopher would not take the opportunity to speak with Kurt Gödel? Besides, I have to admit I thought this might be a forgery. He was very complimentary about you. A little abrupt, but he must be a very busy man."

"He's shy, especially in English."

You may wonder whether I was risking exposure just by taking up philosophy, whether the Nazis could find me simply by trolling philosophy departments. It was a bit of a risk, but I doubt they thought I was really interested in any aspects of philosophy. That was just my undergraduate cover. Besides, I was still hoping that once things went dark, they would assume I was captured, or killed. OSS did what it could to give them that impression. Even if they thought I was alive and had defected, they would assume I would relocate into an occupation as far away from student as possible. They never did find me, despite Gödel's recommendation, and neither did the FBI, and by the time I graduated the war had been over for a full year.

Our graduation ceremony was a small affair conducted in an auditorium not far from the philosophy building. There were only ten of us receiving graduate degrees. Seven masters and three of us getting doctorates. As our names were called, parents and spouses clapped politely. I knew my girlfriend, Ann, might not even do that. She was very shy. But just knowing she was out there in the audience settled me down. It was hard to get through this without breaking down, thinking of Mama and Papa and Caroline.

I was very surprised that when the dean of graduate studies called my name and read the title of my dissertation, the announcement was met with whoops and hollers from the audience. It was Einstein, sitting in the back. He could not be controlled, even by his pale thin friend sitting politely next to him.

CHAPTER 30

"You know Einstein, too? Who the hell are you, George?" the dean asked me after the ceremony.

All of this created a certain aura around me, and no doubt helped me in my philosophy career, because, to be brutally honest, I was just an average to below average philosopher. I did not specialize in the philosophy of mathematics, much to the surprise and disappointment of my initial advisor. I knew my math background was simply too shaky. I wrote my dissertation on David Hume, and became a small-sized fish in the medium-sized pond of Hume scholars.

I took an entry level teaching job at Ohio University, in Athens, Ohio. Einstein, Gödel, and I kept in sporadic contact for the next few years, and then I managed to get an associate professorship at Rutgers, in New Brunswick. I called Einstein with the good news, and he invited me to dinner.

"May I bring my family?"

"Family? Did you marry that sweet girl I met at your graduation, Charlie? Why did you not tell us? Of course you may bring her. But I will have to get used to calling you George. Oy, what a terrible name you picked."

"No, I went back to Charlie, though of course I had to keep my new fake last name. G. Charles Duncan. You can call me Charlie," He laughed. "And may we bring our little one?"

We parked in front of my old apartment building down on Brunswick Pike, and walked the same path up through town and over to Mercer Street that I had so often walked during Operations Felix, Rolf, and HW. As we walked up the stairs to the porch, I could smell something delicious, something strong enough to overpower the summer jasmine. The house was freshly painted and looked wonderful. They'd changed the color of the shutters to dark green, perfectly matching the well-trimmed landscape. Even the tired old boxwood hedge seemed to have perked up.

I knocked on the door and Einstein answered, holding a small dog, it's shock of white hair matching Einstein's perfectly. They came out on the porch and Eistein closed the front door behind them. He put his free arm around me and said, in German, "It is so good to see you again, Charlie. Forgive me, but I selfishly wanted to meet your family before all the others." Then in English, "My dear Ann, it is so nice to see you again. It has been too long. And who is this beautiful young lady?"

I said, in English, holding out the baby, "Professor Einstein, this is our daughter, Caroline. Caroline, this is my friend and teacher, Albert Einstein." Caroline was seven months old at the time, just starting to babble words, so she didn't say anything, but she did let out a small fart.

"Aha," Einstein said laughing, "so you would like to come in to meet Herr Professor Gödel?"

As he turned to open the door, the dog yapped a few times. "You are quite right, Chico, I have forgotten my manners. Charlie, Ann, and Caroline, this is Chico Marx. Chico, this is Charlie Duncan, his wife Ann, and their daughter Caroline. Like you, Charlie, Chico saved my life, though everyone thinks I saved his by rescuing him from the dog pound."

Chico, a white wire fox terrier with splashes of brown round his neck and legs, was squirming to be let down. Einstein finally let go of him, opened the door, and Chico ran inside. I'd read that Einstein had also acquired a house cat, but we saw no signs of it that night.

As he was ushering us in, Einstein whispered to me in German, "How much does she know?"

"Everything," I said.

"I am very glad to hear this, Charlie, now come say hello to everyone."

The whole crew was there. Maja, beautiful as ever, Margot, dark and mysterious, Helen, always on duty, Adele, who wrapped me in her arms before any introductions, and Herr Professor Gödel. He looked worse than I had ever seen him, but he smiled warmly as soon as we entered. Everyone spoke English in deference to Ann. After all the introductions, I was surprised that Gödel was the first to say anything formally.

"Herr Professor Duncan," he began, bowing, "before we have drinks, Herr Professor Einstein and I would like to extend to you a standing invitation to join us on our daily walks, which I am happy to say we have resumed. We realize you would have to drive here—we have timed it and it took us about 30 minutes at Adele speed, which you should know is only a bit slower than the speed of light—but we hope you will be able to manage it sometime." Everyone laughed.

"We decided," Einstein said, "to extend this formal invitation to you in front of all of these wonderful people so that you will be intimidated into accepting it."

So my extraordinary lessons continued. I tried every day to make the morning walks. My department head was all too happy to accommodate my class schedule to avoid all morning classes.

Unlike before, if either Einstein or Gödel was out of town, the other almost always walked, with me. And in these years, after the war, it was seldom the case that each of them was unavailable. Einstein's schedule was much less hectic, and Gödel seldom missed a walk due to illness. We continued these glorious walks for more than ten years, the sheer happiness interrupted temporarily only when Einstein's sister Maja died in 1951.

One blustery evening in April 1955, Helen Dukas telephoned me, frantic. Einstein had collapsed at Mercer Street and was at Princeton Hospital. He'd been diagnosed with an abdominal hemorrhage, and was in terrible pain from the internal bleeding. He was on morphine, had refused surgery, and without it would die in a matter of days.

I asked her if he was seeing visitors, and she said yes, a few at a time. Then I asked her if I could bring Gödel, and she said she was conflicted. She said Einstein would want to see him, but would worry about the effects of the visit on the frail philosopher. I told her I'd visit Gödel and assess the situation. She said she'd put both our names on the visitors list for the following morning.

She asked me to try to talk Einstein into the life-saving surgery, but only half-heartedly, because she knew better than anyone that the stubbornness of this man would never allow him to move off this point.

By the time I got to Gödel's house, he'd heard the news. All the world had heard the news. I asked him if he'd like to visit his old friend with me, and he said he would very much like to do so, though I could see him already shuddering at the finality.

Tight security at the hospital was checking the throngs of would-be visitors against the tiny approved list. Throngs more were gathered outside at the hospital entrance, just to be near the history that was passing. When we got up to the flower-filled room, no one was there except a nurse, Helen, and Margot. Einstein was, according to Helen, having a respite from his pain.

His eyes were closed, and I realized at that moment how important those eyes were to his whole countenance. Open, they lit a path which so few understood but so many appreciated. Closed, they belonged to just another old man waiting for the end. None of us spoke. Gödel and I wept quietly, but apparently not quietly enough for Einstein not to notice. With his eyes still closed he said only one thing to us before he apparently went back to sleep and we were ushered out by Helen:

"Stop being so hysterical, all of you. I have to pass sometime, and it does not really matter when."

He died the next day. Helen, according to Einstein's wishes, arranged for a small cremation ceremony in Trenton. The funeral parlor was only a few blocks from my old safe house. There were only six of us there: Einstein's only living child Hans Albert, Helen, Margot and her new husband, me, and Otto Nathan, whom Einstein named as the executor of his estate. I'd asked Gödel if he would like to attend—he was on the very short guest list—but he declined.

"I need not witness the final meaningless steps of corporal nothingness," he said with tears in his eyes, "to remember this man's extraordinary soul."

Otto was the only person who spoke. He read this passage from Goethe's poem *Wanderer's Nightsong*:

> O'er all the hilltops
> Is quiet now,
> In all the treetops
> Hearest thou
> Hardly a breath;
> The birds are asleep in the trees:
> Wait, soon like these
> Thou too shalt rest.

According to his wishes, they cast Einstein's ashes on the Delaware River. The wind was blowing hard from the southwest, and I'm pretty sure some of the ashes must have found their way to the canal and maybe even all the way up to Lake Carnegie.

CHAPTER 31

Gödel's mental health deteriorated significantly after Einstein's death, very much in the manner it did when he learned of my second treason. He recovered slowly, but by the spring of 1956 the two of us resumed our walks. We both imagined what our missing friend would have said during our conversations, sometimes even taking his role. Gödel was surprisingly good at imitating Einstein's accent and especially his mannerisms.

Alas, the recovery was short-lived, a little over 18 months. In December 1958, shortly before Christmas, Adele telephoned me in tears. She said that Kurt would not be walking with me tomorrow or ever again, that he affirmed never to leave the house, for fear of assassins. She did not ask me to try to help, and I saw no prospect for being helpful.

I saw her occasionally over the next few months, out and about town, when errands took me to Princeton, but then his madness walled her in. They paid a young man to shop for them, and I never saw either of them again.

But what a magnificent 18 months they were! Gödel taught me all about his half-successful efforts to prove the independence of the continuum hypothesis and the axiom of choice. In 1963, a mathematician at the University of Chicago named Paul Cohen, who was not even trained as a set theorist, completed the missing halves of Gödel's proofs to show that the continuum hypothesis and the axiom of choice are both independent of the axioms of ZF. How I would have loved to discuss these developments with Gödel, and with Einstein.

Even though Gödel was in his darkest throes, and had not left his Linden Lane house for years, I learned from Cohen that Gödel graciously reviewed his proofs before their publication, made a few suggestions, and congratulated him on them.

That both the continuum hypothesis and the axiom of choice were independent of ZF was no surprise, at least that they would share either dependence or independence. That's because in 1947, while Einstein was still alive, a Polish mathematician named Wacław Sierpiński proved that the general continuum hypothesis implies the axiom of choice. This really excited Einstein.

"Can you imagine?," he said on one of our walks, "These two axioms, which on their face have nothing at all to do with one another—one about the mysteries of the infinite and the superdensity of the irrationals, and another a trivial set-theory rule we needed just to prove the reals are well-ordered—are not only connected, they seem to be the same or nearly the same axiom! These surprising mathematical connections especially delight realists like us, for they show there is some beautiful thing there, a real thing."

Gödel just smiled his usual inscrutable smile, but I was sure he was just as surprised at this surprising result. I have to admit that I could not follow the Cohen or Sierpiński proofs.

I learned on my walks, both before and after Einstein died, that Gödel was still thinking and working on the nature of the continuum hypothesis, and in particular trying to prove it false in some axiomatic extensions beyond ZF. He lost interest in the axiom of choice once Sierpiński showed it is just an echo of the general continuum hypothesis.

While Einstein was still alive the two of them regularly discussed his star-crossed efforts to construct a unified field theory—a theory that would describe gravity and electromagnetism as manifestations of a single phenomenon. Einstein refused to pay attention to quantum mechanics, which doomed his efforts.

Ironically, his stubborn obsession with unification—which the quantum theorists largely ignored in the beginning—played a big role in preserving unification as a worthy subject once the quantumists finally turned their attention back to it, armed with all four forces in a quantum world. After all, if this subject was interesting enough for Albert Einstein, maybe it was worthy of re-examination. It was as if unification had been frozen in the Einstein Refrigerator until quantum physics was ready to defrost it.

To this day, long after the deaths of both my extraordinary friends, and as my own death looms, my thoughts of them return most frequently to a single incident. Not our first "meeting," when I was just recording them, not when Einstein outted me, twice, not when we saved each other's lives, and not when their bodies left us. Rather, I can't help stop thinking about Einstein's 70th birthday party.

On the Sunday before he turned 70, we gathered for a party at the Mercer Street house. Einstein steadfastly refused to celebrate his own birthday—"It is a known fact that I was born, and that is all that is necessary," he once told a reporter. He told me that the wrong people celebrate birthdays. "Birthdays are for mothers, and I suppose also a little for fathers. Mine are dead. The only other living person in the whole universe we know for certain had nothing at all to do with any birth is the child being born."

But this time he relented, because a man named William Rosenwald, who was the president of a Jewish children's refugee organization, asked him if he could bring some of the refugee children down to Princeton to help celebrate the great man's birthday, and in this way help publicize the organization's fund-raising efforts. So, in addition to Rosenwald and a photographer he brought with him, we celebrated Einstein's 70th birthday with eight Jewish refugee children.

They all took turns getting their photographs taken sitting on Einstein's lap with Chico Marx. Before the children arrived, Rosenwald circulated sheets of paper containing brief sketches of each child's life. We read them silently. I broke down in tears. Not just tears, I was sobbing uncontrollably.

"Yes, these are quite moving tales," Rosenwald said. Gödel put his arm around me, I believe the first, and only, time we ever had physical contact other than his dead fish handshake.

Later that evening, after everyone else left, Einstein, Gödel, Adele, Maja, Margot and her husband, and Ann and I lounged in the large parlor nursing glasses of port. We prevailed upon Einstein to entertain us on his violin. He played one movement of a Mozart concerto, and I was quite surprised at how good he was, especially at his age.

"My speed and a little accuracy have left me, but I try to cover that up with more feeling. This is what old age does. Replaces competence with emotion." When he botched a difficult passage, he looked up from the sheet of music and announced, "Mozart wrote such nonsense here."

Chico Marx sat quietly on Cleopatra's couch. When the concerto was over, we applauded and Chico let out one bark.

"An encore, you say, Chico? Well, I suppose I could be talked into doing one more thing."

He played and sang Blue Melody by Hank Penny and his Radio Cowboys. His voice was gravelly and his violin more classical than the fiddle he was shooting for:

Blue melody,
With a broken heart came to me
Got me singing in a minor key
Blue melody.

I had it bad
Thought I'd lost the best friend I had
Every moment I'd hear a sad
Blue melody.

It haunted me, taunted me, all the day
'Til a miracle came my way.

Love walked out the door
Hurt my heart 'til it sure was sore
But love came back
And they'll be no more
Blue melody.

When he finished, he said, "I am still working on sliding into the notes. I have been thinking of buying a steel guitar. Listen, here is how it is supposed to sound." He reached behind the phonograph and pulled a 45 off the bookshelf. Hank Penny and his Radio Cowboys were good, but not anything like Albert Einstein and his classical fiddle.

When the show was over, I handed Einstein my small birthday gift, which he unwrapped greedily. A pair of real sunglasses.

"Charlie, these are perfect," he said as he put them on. "But are you sure," he asked, smiling, "that they will fit Ed?" He kept them on the rest of the night. I should have given them to him before his concert. Now I would just have to imagine him in his new shades singing Blue Melody.

Then Gödel stood and announced, "I have a gift for you, Albert, and also a gift for you, Charlie."

"But it's not my birthday."

"When is your birthday, Charlie, your real birthday, Herr General Seifert's birthday?" Einstein asked.

"May 1, 1905."

"You are older than I?" Gödel asked with much surprise. "I had no idea."

"The baby face that never shaves," Einstein said.

"You knew this, Albert? Well, in any event, let us begin with my gift to Herr Professor Einstein," and Gödel, bowing. He handed Einstein a shoe box wrapped in children's birthday paper—balloons and bright teddy bears. Einstein tore into the box immediately and pulled from it a roll of papers tied together with a dark blue ribbon, like a diploma. He slipped off the ribbon, unrolled the scroll, and shuffled through the papers, lifting his new sunglasses to get a better look.

"The general field equations! You have solved them!"

"Happy Birthday, Albert. This may seem like a selfish gift, but in fact it is quite thoughtful. I have saved you many more years of enduring my complaints about your failure to solve them." Einstein erupted in laughter, then got very serious.

"This means the world to me, my dear colleague. That you would take the time away from your work to do this for me," Einstein said, embracing the logician and wiping tears from his eyes. "I must be getting old, I am crying like a schoolgirl."

"These are tears of joy because you are realizing that you need not ever wrestle with these non-linear bears again."

"I never intended to wrestle with them, but my joy is that you have relieved me of years of future guilt over that fact," Einstein replied, wiping his eyes under his sunglasses. I could see he was fighting against the temptation to open the papers again and study their contents. He fidgeted with the scroll all night.

"Herr Professor Einstein's comment about guilt," Gödel said, now turning to me and handing me an envelope, "is apropos of my gift to you, my friend. It is also mere paper. I will call it now an early birthday present for you, as we will be out of the country on May 1.

"Happy Birthday, Charlie. I am sorry I did not wrap it more gaily. It is a letter. You may read it to yourself now or later, or read it aloud to this special group. I wrote it in German because some of the matters I discuss are difficult for me to express in English. My apologies to you, Ann."

I opened the envelope and read the letter to the assembled group, because it was clear to me Gödel wished me to read it. I read one sentence in German and then translated it into English for Ann, before moving on to the next. Gödel typed it, which was a good thing because, as I've already mentioned, his handwriting, in its perfect but microscopic size, was impossible for me to read on a blackboard let alone on a sheet of paper.

My dear Charlie,

I write this letter to give you two gifts. Please accept them, although I know your own humility and humanity will make acceptance difficult. My gifts to you are forgiveness and absolution. Forgiveness for deceiving me, and absolution for your work with the Nazis. These are different things, one personal to me and the other personal to you.

When Albert told me of your deception, I hated you. I was surprised that it was you whom the Nazis had sent, but of course was not surprised they sent someone. They are still after me, the hundreds who are in exile. And now the Russians, too.

But this hatred of you was surprising to me. I did not hate Nelböck in the same way, and he actually tried to kill me. But I had trusted you. I had befriended you. You reminded me of my brother Rudolph, though younger. [Here Gödel looked up and said with a bit of a scowl, "I *thought* you were younger."] You betrayed all of that. Truth is too important to treat so shabbily, even in war. But there was something else. You shared our wonder. Wonder is a wonderful thing, if you will allow me to be self-referential. You shared our wonder and then stole it from us.

Even so, I knew my hatred of you was irrational. Inconsistent with sets of beliefs to which I thought I adhered. I was becoming another casualty of war. You were such an exemplary student! How could someone so interested in truth live such lies? Then Albert told me about your family, how you lost them all. I am so sorry, Charlie.

I began to analyze things more clearly. I hated you because I had come to love you. You re-awakened in me the wonder of my work. You saved my life twice, Charlie, once from Nelböck's bullet and again from my own complacency. You do not have to take my word for this. When we left for Maine, I was in shambles from the fear. But I did my best work in a decade. Albert can confirm it. This I owe to you, and I forgive you for the path you took to achieve it.

But this is all selfish. Who cares if some crazy logician forgives some double agent? My second gift is absolution. We are all guilty, because this evil of the Nazis lies in all of us. It is what we do about this original sin that matters, even after it has gripped us. Especially after. It was no sin for you to fight for your sinful country. Millions fought who were not Nazis.

What was a sin was letting this happen, not trying to stop it as it was happening. You bear responsibility for that. But so do we. We ran away from the sin. Are we any less responsible?

All of us have this blood on our hands. What matters now is that we fight against the monster in us, and that despite this stain we never stop our search for truth. By this standard, you are absolved. You have faced your treacheries, have said no to the monster, and are seeking truth. Never forget your own responsibility for this evil, Herr General Seifert. But forgive yourself, Charlie, so that you may continue on the moral path you are now walking.

I was not a victim of the Nazis, and therefore have no right to forgive you for the part you played in this terror. Only the victims have the right to forgive. My absolution is for you. I beg you to forgive yourself. You have now earned it. It is the true thing to do, even if you cannot prove it to yourself.

And if you or others ask, "Who is this man who dares think he can declare that Helmut Seifert may absolve himself of his war sins?" just answer that I am Kurt Gödel, the new Aristotle, and Herr Seifert's friend.

Yours truly,

Kurt

Epilogue

When his wife Adele was hospitalized late in 1977, Gödel refused to eat. He died of malnutrition in the Princeton Medical Center on January 14, 1978. He weighed 65 pounds.

In 1970, mathematicians discovered the first of what would be several kinds of "ordinary" conjectures about the natural numbers that were true but unprovable in ZFC. Gödel had been right all along. All of mathematics, not just the quirky corner of obvious self-reference, was riddled with the problem of incompleteness. The gap between truth and proof was everywhere.

Acknowledgments

MY SET THEORY PROFESSOR from so many years ago, J. Donald Monk, planted the seeds of my interest in Gödel's incompleteness theorem, and I thank him for sowing such an exciting and mysterious crop. Those seeds remained largely dormant as I turned my attention to law, but sprouted decades later when I read Douglas Hofstadter's *Gödel, Escher, Bach: An Eternal Golden Braid.* I have borrowed shamelessly from that book's description of Gödel's first incompleteness theorem, and also from similar descriptions in Hofstadter's equally engaging *I am a Strange Loop.* Any mistakes in trying to present the core of Gödel's idea without the benefit of his formal mathematics are mine. Don't blame Professor Monk; he did his best with me.

I also want to thank my best friend, Larry Wood, to whom I have dedicated this book. In junior and senior high schools, Larry and I took long walks home together, perhaps not quite as historic as the walks of Gödel and Einstein; then again, history looms larger as its frame gets smaller. In our small world, these walks were gigantic, especially now, looking back at them.

Although the main topics were girls and sex, we managed to squeeze in a few discussions about what the heck an electron was. We were, of course, not really talking about girls or sex or electrons, but rather our places in the universe, and riveting those places to each other. What could be more historic?

Fifty-five years and a career in medicine later, Dr. Wood was kind enough to read an early draft of this novel, and his probing questions about set theory and incompleteness have sharpened the discussions of them. More than that, they echoed our unshakable friendship.

I also thank my dear wife Kate, who patiently read this manuscript, as she has read all of my scribblings, this time despite what she claims to be her own math phobia. I think this claim is overblown, akin to her claims about not remembering the rules of card games right before she reels all of us in. She is my truth that needs no proving.

Readers steeped in mathematics may be disappointed, and others curious, that when it came to the magical moment of truth, so to speak, in my description of the first incompleteness theorem—Gödel's remarkable diagonalization lemma—I retreated to the world of linguistic analogy, first a Hofstadter analogy he in turn borrowed from the American philosopher William Quine, and then an analogy I borrowed from Raymond Smullyan. Concessions to the spy story drove this approach. In addition to these two linguistic analogies, I highly recommend a wonderful non-technical but less metaphorical treatment of the diagonalization lemma by Natalie Wolchover, published in the Abstractions Blog of Quanta Magazine on July 14, 2020.

I am grateful to the biographers who have given second life to the lives of Einstein and Gödel, including Walter Isaacson (*Einstein: His Life and Universe*), Albrecht Fölsing (*Albert Einstein: A Biography*), John Dawson (*Logical Dilemmas: The Life and Work of Kurt Gödel*), Rebecca Goldstein (*Incompleteness: The Proof and Paradox of Kurt Gödel*), and Stephan Budiansky (*Journey to the Edge of Reason: The Life of Kurt Gödel*). I tried to keep my fictional slices of lives within the contours of these larger known realities, and apologize if my efforts sometimes went astray.

Of course, the great fun of writing historical fiction is that we are free to depart from the historical record, as long as we don't go too far. With any other subject, I'd feel no need to clarify the boundary between fact and fiction; indeed, the fuzziness of that boundary is all part of the fun. But it seems to me that a book about the proposition that truth is larger than proof should spend at least some time distinguishing historical fact from fiction, at least on a few points about which readers unfamiliar with Einstein and especially Gödel might be curious.

Einstein and Gödel did walk together to and from their offices at IAS from late 1940 until Einstein's death in 1955, but there was no "young philosopher from Rutgers" who accompanied them. As far as I know, the FBI did not ever tape record their conversations, though it is true that the U.S. Army refused to clear Einstein for the Manhattan Project, and forbade all who were cleared for it from discussing any aspect of it with him.

Einstein and Gödel did not, to my knowledge, number their walking routes and starting points or decide those points and routes by playing the rock, paper, scissors game. I have no reason to believe anyone tried to assassinate either of them in Princeton, though there was an assassination attempt on Einstein in Berlin in 1925, before he emigrated, which was foiled by his wife Elsa.

I made up Gödel's uncontrollable flatulence, though with his strange diet this fiction is not entirely implausible. There is no evidence Einstein ever tried to wrangle information from the FBI or OSS to help his friend's mental illness. But that mental illness was quite real, and resulted in at least two Austrian hospitalizations before his emigration, in Gödel's delusion that he would be poisoned, in his increasingly self-restricted diet, and, eventually, in his death in 1978 from starvation, when Adele herself was hospitalized and could no longer cook for him and taste his food.

Although Gödel believed he would be assassinated, there is nothing I know to suggest that he was afraid of Johann Nelböck in particular. Nelböck was a real student of the real Moritz Schlick, and really did shoot and kill Schlick on June 22, 1936, as Schlick was walking to the lecture hall at the University of Vienna. Nelböck really did believe that his trial testimony would destroy the logical positivism of the Vienna Circle, was convicted of the murder, and was sentenced to prison for ten years. He became a cause célèbre of the Austro-fascists, who, after the Anschluss, ordered him paroled after just two years of incarceration.

In the truth-is-stranger-than-fiction category, Nelböck and Gödel were treated at the same psychiatric hospital in Vienna, though at different times. Nelböck did not travel to the United States and did not try to kill Gödel. He worked in a department of the Austrian oil ministry after his release from prison. Once the war was over, he toiled in the ministry's Main Measurement Office. He died in Vienna in 1951.

Einstein did have a white wire fox terrier he named Chico Marx, though he did not get it from the dog pound. An acquaintance gave it to him, whom he pretended never to forgive. Chico occasionally bit the mailman, which Einstein wryly attributed to Chico's anger at how much mail was being delivered to his besieged master. In the years during and shortly after the war, Einstein also owned a cat, which I mentioned in absentia, and a parrot named Bibo, who, according to Isaacson, "required an unjustifiable amount of medical care." I didn't mention Bibo because I felt that one profound hypochondriac in this story was more than enough.

Einstein often wore crumpled clothing, but my explanation that he insisted on folding his clothes himself was fiction. Indeed, it seems Einstein did almost nothing by way of domestic chores, relying entirely on his wife Elsa and, after she died, on his sister Maja, his stepdaughter Margot, and especially his devoted secretary/housekeeper Helen Dukas.

He really did love sailing, sailed as often as he could in and around Princeton, and did at about this time own a crummy sailboat he dubbed Tinnef (junk). There is no evidence that the reclusive Gödel ever joined him on board. Einstein was a terrible sailor, and grounded, de-masted, and even capsized several boats over his lifetime. He really could not swim, and never wore a life jacket.

He was a serviceable violinist, owned many violins, and named them all Lina. There is no evidence he loved cowboy music or that he tried to play the violin as a fiddle. The song "Blue Melody" is a real song, recorded by the real Hank Penny and His Radio Cowboys for Vocalion Records in June 1939. The song and lyrics were written by Hank Penny's tenor banjo player, Louis Dumont.

Einstein had a real aversion to celebrating his own birthday (which he deemed part of the dreaded "Einstein cult of personality"), but he was persuaded by William Rosenwald, the president of the National Refugee Service, to host eight Jewish refugee children on the Sunday before his 70th birthday at a party at Mercer Street, at which short biographies of the children were distributed. All the children gathered round Einstein for photographs, Chico Marx in the foreground on the floor and the youngest child on Einstein's lap. As a birthday present, Gödel gave Einstein an elegant solution to the field equations of general relativity. That solution was so novel that it stimulated entirely new notions of time.

Benson House was a real center of U.S. counterintelligence during the war, started in early 1942 when an Argentinian spy named Jorge Mosquera defected. Donworth Johnson, his wife Betty Ann, their daughter Vicki Jean, and their German Shephard Clifford lived there as a cover, but my claims that Betty Ann's cooking was terrible and that Clifford was mean were flights of imagination. Well, at least the part about Betty Ann's cooking. Johnson acquired Clifford specifically to help protect the house from intruders, and by all accounts he did a fine job. The transmitting antenna was not in the attic; it was probably outside, hidden in nearby woods, though the records are not clear on this point. And it was not called Benson House then; that name attached after the war when Margaret Benson bought the property.

In 1947, the Polish mathematician Wacław Sierpiński really did prove that the general continuum hypothesis implies the axiom of choice. Gödel really did half-prove that the continuum hypothesis and the axiom of choice were independent of ZF, and Paul Cohen really did complete those proofs in 1963. And beginning in the 1970s, mathematicians really did start to discover that several ordinary propositions of number theory (including the solubility of some Diophantine equations—equations involving only sums, products, and powers in which all the constants are integers and the only solutions of interest are integers) are true but unprovable in ZFC. Alas, the Goldbach Conjecture (all even numbers greater than two can be written as the sum of two prime numbers) remains open.

Einstein really did say that the only reason he was still at IAS was for the privilege of walking with Gödel, but he made this comment to the economist Oskar Morgenstern, one of von Neumann's collaborators, and not to von Neumann himself.

Einstein collapsed at Mercer Street on April 15, 1955, and died three days later at the Princeton Hospital, from a ruptured abdominal aortic aneurysm. He really did refuse what would have been life-saving surgery. The words I have him speaking to Gödel and Charlie—*Stop being so hysterical, all of you. I have to pass sometime, and it does not really matter when*—he actually said to a distraught Helen Dukas.

At his request, his body was cremated. Also at his request, the "ceremony," which was held at the crematorium of the Ewing Cemetery in West Trenton, was no ceremony at all. Otto Nathan read a poem by Goethe (I am not sure it was really *Wanderer's Nightsong*), and that was it. The cremation was attended only by a handful of close friends and relatives, fewer than a dozen. His ashes were in fact spread on the Delaware River, though I have no idea if any managed to blow all the way north to the canal.

In the year of Einstein's 70th birthday, the Rosa Strauss Memorial Fund created the Albert Einstein Award. Its winners have included such well-known physicists as Richard Feynman, Edward Teller, and Stephen Hawking. Its inaugural winner, in 1951, was Kurt Gödel.

Almost 17 years after Einstein's death, Gödel died at the same hospital, renamed the Princeton Medical Center. He is buried in the Princeton Cemetery alongside Adele, who survived him by just three years.

www.ingramcontent.com/pod-product-compliance
Lightning Source LLC
LaVergne TN
LVHW050629100826
845148LV00011B/1802